VOICE in the
NIGHT

OTHER BOOKS AND AUDIO BOOKS
BY C. PAUL ANDERSEN:

Final Act

VOICE in the NIGHT

a novel

C. PAUL ANDERSEN

Covenant Communications, Inc.

Published by Covenant Communications, Inc.
American Fork, Utah

Printed in Canada
First Printing: February 2006

11 10 09 08 07 06   10 9 8 7 6 5 4 3 2 1

ISBN 1-59156-891-9

To my granddaughter Lesley,
who shares my love of literature, and
to all my grandchildren, who bring me joy

Special thanks to my editors,
Peter Jasinski and Kirk Shaw

PROLOGUE

Rosa was well inside the old, abandoned hotel. Her next obstacle was climbing the rickety stairway to the second floor where her brothers had escaped from the pursuing police. She looked furtively behind her. No one had followed. She placed one foot on the bottom stair to begin her perilous climb.

Suddenly there was a roaring wail from the second floor landing, and she looked up to see her brothers rolling toward the stairs in a locked, wrestling embrace. She yelled, "No, Johnny. He's your brother. Don't hurt him."

It was too late. Johnny sat astride his brother and smashed his fist down hard on his brother's nose. Manuel reached up, grasping for Johnny's eyes, trying to push him away.

"Stop, both of you. You'll kill each other," she cried.

The brothers, standing now, but still locked in heated battle, fell against the balcony railing, and the aged wood gave way. They fell thirty feet. Rosa ran to their huddled heap on the floor. It was over.

She heard the wailing sirens in the distance, and the lights faded to black.

"It's a wrap!" the director shouted, and every actor and technician on the downtown L.A. set cheered simultaneously.

CHAPTER 1

"It's a wrap!" Three little words with bittersweet connotations. The shooting schedule for Lesley's television movie was at an end, and the conflicting emotions that accompanied so many closings were a part of this experience, too. She felt joy in having completed something and a gladness that days mixed with high excitement and boring tedium were over, but there was a sadness that came with the end of a journey—an awareness that the friends made and the acquaintances and phonies encountered would soon be only memories. Finally, her exhilaration at the thought of leaving the sleazy downtown Los Angeles film location was balanced by the sobering realization that the security of employment was only fleeting and that another acting job was not guaranteed.

Johnny and Manuel—not their real names but what she'd come to call them through the course of the filming—picked themselves up from the spot where they had moved to replace their stunt doubles for the final close-up of their deaths. They walked toward Lesley, smiling and swaggering. "Coming to the party later, Rosa?" they asked.

"No, I don't think so. I'm leaving town tomorrow and need some rest tonight."

"Well, you don't know what you're missing," Johnny said tauntingly.

"Yeah, we could show you a real good time, *sister*," Manuel teased.

"Well, thanks, but no thanks," Lesley said, then added, "I'll miss you guys. Keep in touch—let me know what you're doing."

"Sure, sure," Johnny said. "You won't even remember us in a few days."

"I will. I'll never forget you. It was a pleasure working with you, and you'll always be my little brothers."

"We love you too," Manuel said, and hugged her good-bye. Johnny kissed her cheek, and they parted.

The wrap parties that so many looked forward to were one final experience that Lesley had always skipped. Her Santa Monica studio apartment was subleased, her car and furniture were stored, and her bags were packed. In the morning, she would be leaving the city canyons of downtown Los Angeles for the mountain canyons of her native Utah. She had reservations for a flight to Salt Lake City and then for a rental car to drive to Park City, Utah, to the Sundance Film Festival. Then she planned to stick around to experience firsthand some of the 2002 Winter Olympics events. She thought, *I can't wait.* She wanted a change and felt a longing to get back to her roots.

Fortunately, the contract for her major role in the TV movie had paid her enough to live on for a while.

Next morning, she took a cab to L.A. International, arriving two hours before her flight time, as required by check-in regulations since 9-11. When she finally got to the ticket counter, she presented her first-class ticket. "Ms. Lesley Kern? We need a picture ID please," the balding, harassed agent said. She found her driver's license and presented it. "Going to Utah, huh?" he asked without real interest.

"Yes, I'm going home," Lesley volunteered, wondering why she'd said it.

He finished his business, checked in her bags, and said, "Have a nice flight."

She went through one last checkpoint, didn't sound any alarms, and looked forward to the nice flight that he'd perfunctorily wished her. The ninety-minute flight would give her time to relax and look ahead to her holiday.

First class is a spoiler, she reflected, thinking of the few times she'd been able to enjoy it. Buckled in, she opened her purse and removed and reviewed the travel packet sent by her travel agent. She'd be staying at the Silver Princess Hotel in Park City. She had an invitation to the Sundance Festival opening night at Abravanel Hall in Salt Lake City, where Robert Redford would speak, and tickets for several films to be exhibited in Park City and Salt Lake City. She'd stay at the Inn at Temple Square when in Salt Lake. Then she turned to the 2002 Olympics package, reveling in the thought, *I'll see the opening ceremony, all the figure skating—solo and pairs—and the skiing and other events scheduled at Park City. Fun!*

Her daydreaming was interrupted by the arrival of the passenger who would sit beside her in the window seat. A very nice male voice said, "Pardon me. That's my seat, I believe," nodding toward the window.

She looked up to see the handsome, smiling face of a tall man who appeared to be about ten years older than she—in his late thirties or early forties, she guessed. Good teeth, a tan complexion, laugh wrinkles at the eyes, and a full head of brown hair created an interesting first impression. And she couldn't help thinking, *No wedding ring.*

She also thought, *He looks very familiar,* but didn't want to say that to him, since it might sound like the trite flirting line.

Instead she said, "Of course," and drew her legs back a bit so that he could enter easily.

The helpful blonde flight attendant asked, "Is everything all right? Do you need anything?"

"Do you have a newspaper?" he requested.

"Yes, of course. Los Angeles or Salt Lake City?" she asked.

"Salt Lake—the *Tribune* if you have it," he answered.

"Yes, we have it. Anything for you, Ms. Kern?" Lesley shook her head to indicate, "No," and the attendant left to retrieve the gentleman's paper.

"You're from Utah, then?" Lesley asked, noting that he knew the Salt Lake City newspapers.

"Well, not actually from Utah—not a native—but I've lived there for about ten years. I'm in food services and . . ."

"Food services?" she asked, thinking, *He doesn't look like a waiter or a cook.*

"Yes, I own a restaurant—in Park City. Do you know Park City?"

The returning flight attendant interrupted Lesley's reply. "Anything else?" she asked.

They both responded in the negative, so she said, "We'll be departing in about five minutes. Enjoy your flight, and buzz if you need anything."

Lesley realized that she hadn't answered his question and debated giving him the short or long answer. Finally she said, "Yes, I know Park City. I was born nearby in Silver Forks, but I haven't lived there since I was a baby."

"You were born in Silver Forks?" he asked incredulously. "I love that area—one of the few truly peaceful places left. Just the old houses, a country store, the thermal health spa and pools—much the way it was in the nineteenth century. I'd love to live there." His enthusiasm seemed genuine because he babbled on. "In fact, there's an old, two-story, cream-colored Victorian house isolated on the road up Silver Forks Mountain that I'd like to buy and restore. It's the only house on Silver Forks Mountain Road. I've even thought of making it a bed and breakfast for those who want to stay away from the Park City crowds."

"I know just the house you mean," she said, smiling and thinking, *Should I tell him more?* She took the plunge. "In fact, I own it—but it's *not* for sale."

"You're kidding," he said, wide-eyed and open-mouthed.

"No, I'm not kidding. As you said, it's the only house on Silver Forks Mountain Road."

The engines roared, and the plane started to creep toward the runway. "You'd better fasten your seat belt," Lesley urged.

"Yes, I'd better," he said, moving to the task. "I can't believe the coincidence—you actually own my dream house."

"Well, I'm afraid you'll have to dream on. It's been in my family for four generations. My great-grandfather built it," she explained.

"Of course. The flight attendant called you Ms. Kern. Your great-grandfather was Lewis Kern, one of the silver kings?" His eyes and mouth opened even wider.

She had to laugh. "Yes, but don't get too excited. The silver king's fortune is long gone, I'm afraid. He lost much of it in the Depression when silver prices fell."

He paused for a moment then said, "I wasn't thinking of that, I assure you. I'm just totally interested in the history of that place. In fact, it's my hobby—what I do when I'm not running my business. I've scouted all over those hills and mountains, where the mining took place, looking for . . . artifacts and other bits of history. I've even used some of my finds to add atmosphere to my restaurant."

The plane was roaring down the runway, and though she was a much-experienced traveler, having flown across the country for various acting jobs, Lesley still had to close her eyes and clench her teeth until the plane was safely in the air. She hated the feeling of flinging down the runway. Their conversation stopped while she gripped the armrests and said a silent prayer.

When she could sense that they were floating instead of climbing, she unclenched her hands and jaw and opened her eyes to see him watching her with a look of genuine concern.

He paused for a moment, while Lesley caught her breath, then asked, "Are you all right? You must not be used to flying."

"Oh, I am," she answered, laughing nervously. "But I'll never get used to takeoffs and landings. Now that we're in the air, I'm okay."

"I know your name, Ms. Kern, but I haven't introduced myself," he said.

"No, you haven't, and I usually try to avoid extended conversations with fellow passengers on short trips," she answered. "But . . ."

"But . . . ?" he asked.

"But since you live in Park City—and that's where I'm headed—go on, tell me your name," she ventured.

"I'm Gareth Sanders," he said. "My restaurant is called the Silver Fork."

"How clever," she remarked, with some amusement.

"Corny, you mean. I can see what you're thinking," he said.

"No, I mean it. It's a clever name—for a restaurant so near to Silver Forks—the town, I mean." Lesley wanted to reassure him that she wasn't poking fun at something that obviously meant a lot to him.

"Well, it's a nice place, with great food—if I do say so myself."

"You've been there for ten years? I guess it really has been about that long since I've been back to the area. Time flies—when you're having fun," she added.

"Fun? What do you do, then? And what's your first name? I didn't hear that," he said.

"You mean you don't recognize the *great* Lesley Kern?" she asked, laughing at her exaggeration. "I'm an actress—mostly for TV. I guess you don't watch much television."

"Actually, I thought you looked familiar—the dark hair and brown eyes. But I think I remember your hair being longer," he said, looking closely at her.

She smiled in response to his attention. "Yes, I had to cut it for the role I just finished—tough chick in a downtown L.A. gang." She laughed and caught herself almost batting her eyelashes like a silly school girl. "Well, not actually *in* the gang. I played the older sister of two gang members."

"Tough chick? Talk about miscasting," he said.

"Well, I *am* an actress. When I say 'tough,' I mean that she's been toughened by her life. But I do have to take most roles that are offered me. I haven't moved to the point where I can pick and choose," she said more defensively than she'd intended.

"No, I'm just saying that you must be pretty good, because the tough chick label hardly suits you," he said, obviously trying to smooth over his earlier remark.

"Oh, you didn't say anything wrong. But I do have to take some roles I really don't want to play. I don't do anything really offensive, of course. It's in my contracts that I won't do certain things—no nudity, no profanity, no overt sex scenes, no drugs, no smoking. I *have* resorted to violence in a few roles, but nothing really bloody or gory." *I've offered more explanation than necessary,* she realized, getting on her acquired defensive soapbox again. She thought, *I get so tired of explaining my situation to Mormon and non-Mormon friends or even acquaintances. They're usually fascinated to learn I'm an actress, but I sometimes sense a hint of suspicion that I must be a wayward soul.*

She was lost in her thoughts, almost forgetting she was sitting by someone she found rather attractive. She looked at him then, realizing that he was watching her carefully. "I'm sorry," she said. "Most actors tend to talk too much about themselves, and I guess I get defensive about my work. It's a habit I've gotten into."

"Defensive? I didn't think that. I just worried that I'd said something to offend you," he said.

"No, it's just that some seem to think that a good Mormon girl is not supposed to end up in such a worldly profession. It is difficult, of course, to remember my standards in the face of a lot of temptation. Oh, I don't know why I'm telling you these things," she said. "I apologize. Let's change the subject."

"No, tell me more. I'm fascinated. I guessed that you were from Mormon roots. After all, the Kern family is known to have Utah pioneer roots. And you don't have to be defensive about that either. I have a genuine respect for most Mormons I've met—socially and in business," he said. "Though I must admit, in my business, I find Utah's liquor laws quite confusing. But we live with it."

"Well, if you've lived where I've lived, you realize that Utah is very unique, and it's partly because of those laws you're talking about." She was definitely on the defensive by this point.

"Oh, I know what you're saying. And I'm not one of those who's attracted to the special nature of Utah and then moves there to change that. That doesn't make much sense either," he explained.

"Well, I agree with you. I love L.A. and I love New York City, but coming back to Utah seems like a real escape right now. I'm looking forward to a couple of months in a different environment."

The flight attendant arrived at that moment to offer them a drink.

"Just some orange juice for me," Lesley said.

"That sounds good to me too," Gareth said. "Are you serving breakfast?"

"No, sir. The flight is too short, and—I shouldn't say this— the airline is cutting costs wherever they can. The times, you know," she explained.

"Well, that's fine. Just the orange juice, then—for both of us," he said, suggesting a cozy relationship between them, which really had not developed.

"You said that you're on vacation," he continued. "Where will you be staying, then? With relatives? In Salt Lake City?"

He's really pumping me for information, she thought. *Do I really want to answer that question?* she wondered. *Well, what could it hurt? I won't be seeing him again.* "No, I have no close living relatives. I'm staying in Park City for the Sundance Film Festival—and then for the Olympics. I've also made reservations in Salt Lake—for the nights I'll be there."

"I should have guessed you'd be going to the festival. This is a great time for us—for my business. The whole area is booked up through the end of the Olympics in February. Lots of hungry people, I hope," he said. Lesley's general answer about her vacation location didn't seem enough for him. "Which Park City hotel are you staying in?" he asked.

She thought, *Should I or shouldn't I? I guess if he calls or comes by, I can always decide not to talk to him or see him.* She answered, "I'm staying at the Silver Princess—the entire stay, except when I'm in Salt Lake, of course."

"Why aren't you staying at your house in Silver Forks?" he inquired.

"Oh, if you've been by there, you have to be aware that it's probably uninhabitable. No one has cared for it for years. My mother even refused to live there after I was born. I never knew why, but she insisted on moving to Salt Lake City. I grew up there," Lesley explained.

"But it hasn't been uninhabited for that long," he insisted.

"No, my parents rented it to various parties until their deaths and hired a caretaker to watch over the place while it was rented. But it's been closed up for several years—since I moved to California," she said. "I check on it periodically when I'm in the area, which isn't often."

"Your folks are gone, then? They must have died rather young," he said.

"Yes, as I explained, I have no living relatives in the area. I was an only child. Mother wanted it that way, I guess. Anyway, my parents, grandparents, and great-grandparents all died early of natural causes. In fact, each of them had only one child— my great-grandfather and grandfather were only children, and so was my father. I'm the last of the family, and, of course, a girl doesn't usually pass on her maiden name if she marries. The only way the Kern name will live on is as my professional name."

Why have I told him all this? she wondered. *I guess it's his tie to Park City and his interest in my house. Anyway, I've just responded to his natural curiosity,* she reasoned.

The flight attendant brought their juice, interrupting their discussion, so she used that excuse to try to cut the conversation short. She realized that she'd probably already revealed too much personal information. *Actors* do *tend to talk too much about themselves,* she thought. Anyway, Gareth—Mr. Sanders—

appeared, for the moment, to be preoccupied with his own thoughts, so Lesley fished a softcover copy of the book from her purse and turned to Moroni, where she had left off reading.

"The Book of Mormon, eh?" Gareth said.

She automatically answered, "Yes, have you read it?"

"Parts of it, yes, but I wanted to see if you would ask me your 'golden question.' You passed the test," he said, smiling.

"Oh, was I being tested?"

"No, not exactly. I was surprised when you brought out the book and couldn't resist seeing if you were one of those member missionaries I've heard about," he explained.

"Well, now you know—I am. I always bring a copy. Frankly, it sometimes discourages unwanted conversation, but sometimes I pass the book to someone who's curious about it."

"Which am I—unwanted or curious?" he asked, smiling.

Lesley answered by turning to Moroni 10:4–5, and showed him the underlined verses. "I show this promise when I give someone a copy. Would you like this?" she asked, extending the book toward him.

"Oh, I already have one. Your missionaries have knocked on my door several times over the years," he said.

"Good. Did you invite them in?"

"Only once, but I'm seldom home—that is, I'm seldom *in* my home. I live above my restaurant, and I'm a workaholic. Maybe it's too convenient to go downstairs to work," he said.

"Maybe it is," she agreed. "I'm just the opposite. I work hard when I'm working, but when I'm away, I'm *really* away—I escape. I do what I can't do when I'm working—I go out to eat a lot, I sleep a lot, and I have fun. I really go on vacation."

"That's a healthy approach to life, I guess. I've made work my play, too," he said, seeming somewhat regretful.

"All work and no play . . ."

"Yes, I know, makes *Gareth* a dull boy," he said, laughing.

"Oh, I didn't really mean that," she said apologetically.

"I know you didn't, but maybe it's true. And what kind of play brings you to Park City, since you don't have family there?" he asked.

"I told you, I'm going to the Sundance Film Festival," she answered.

"Of course, and you don't realize that's a busman's holiday? Don't tell me about mixing work and play—that's exactly what you're planning," he said, with a teasing smile.

"I suppose you're right," she admitted. "I hadn't thought of it that way. I did come here partly hoping I'd make some good contacts for future work. It's all part of the game, so you've caught me mixing work and pleasure." She finished her orange juice and put the cup in a holder on her tray then added, "But I am staying for the Olympics—that's not work."

"Hey, that's great. Then you'll be around for a while. Maybe we could get together for . . . ?" She knew that he was about to say, "a drink," but he hurriedly changed it to ". . . lunch or dinner."

"We'll see," she said. "I'm going to be very busy, and I'm totally exhausted after doing the film. I really do need a lot of time to catch up on rest."

"But I know where you're staying, and it's close to my place, so don't be surprised if you hear from me," he warned.

"Well, okay, but I reserve the right to say no, without hurting your feelings. Our meeting has been pleasant, but I may feel differently when it's just a memory."

This is true, she thought. *I've made so many acquaintances in my travels and work, but they seldom become more than that—acquaintances. And I have to avoid getting too involved with men who aren't LDS. Past experience with that created real conflicts for me.*

He seemed content with the possibility of their getting together because he said no more and turned to read his newspaper.

Lesley went back to her reading but found herself dozing. She was awakened by the intercom announcement, "Please fasten your seat belts. We will land in Salt Lake City in approximately fifteen minutes. The ground temperature is forty-one degrees. The sun is shining, but there's snow on the ground."

The short trip was over, and Lesley's attention turned to thoughts of getting her luggage and finding the car rental office.

"Well, I guess we're here," Gareth said. "It's nice to have met you, Lesley."

Apparently we've moved to a first name basis, she thought. "Nice to have met you too, Gareth. Good luck."

"And good luck to you. What's the name of that TV movie you've just finished? I'd like to watch for it," he said, seeming sincerely interested.

"The working title is *Casa Grande*—the big house. I played a Latina whose family is in trouble—brothers headed for the big house," she explained.

"Latina? Why did they cast you instead of an actual Latina?" he asked.

"My black hair, dark eyes, and olive skin, I suppose, and I know some Spanish. But I really *can* act," she said, again feeling on the defensive.

"I'm sure you can. I wasn't implying otherwise. I was just surprised. Well, okay, I'll be watching for the 'Big House,'" he promised.

She braced for the landing—another dreaded part of flying. But all went smoothly, and she lost track of Gareth Sanders when they disembarked. Then she noticed that she didn't have her Book of Mormon. She thought, *Maybe I left it with him after all, and maybe this time he might read it.* Then she reflected, *I know I've seen him someplace before.*

CHAPTER 2

After passing through various checkouts, Lesley found a luggage carrier and headed for the baggage pickup area. Fortunately, her luggage popped up just as she was arriving, and she retrieved it without much difficulty and placed it on her cart. She showed the required documents to the baggage checkout guards, and despite the added security because of the Olympics, she was able to move along in good time and find the car rental office nearby. If things continued to go this well, she'd be in the city by lunchtime and in Park City by early afternoon.

She had rented a big four-wheel-drive SUV, a Lincoln Navigator, anticipating the snowy roads. She wished she'd carried on her winter coat rather than packing it. But the car heater warmed up in a hurry, and she was on her way to the freeway leading from Salt Lake International Airport to downtown. The roads were clear, and the sun was shining, so she enjoyed the vista of the snow in the valley and on the Wasatch Mountains, east of the city. It had been quite a while since she'd experienced a real winter and since she'd seen those mountains. They were majestic, and their familiarity welcomed her.

The freeway led to a downtown Salt Lake turnoff, and she decided to drive into the city and then along South Temple Street to see the Salt Lake LDS Temple and the changes in the city. Those changes were numerous, she discovered, as she almost collided with a Trax train. The temple was still the same impressive building, but it had been dwarfed by skyscrapers, including the LDS Church Office Building and the new Conference Center, which were visible above the temple. She'd heard that the Christmas lighting of the temple grounds had been left in place till the end of the Olympics. She looked forward to seeing the lights at night.

It was at that point that she became aware of the big black passenger car that seemed to be following at a distance. *Is it my imagination, or did it follow me from the freeway?* she wondered. She laughed at herself, thinking, *I've been in too many movies.*

She passed the beautiful old mansions along the east end of South Temple Street, some of which were built with mining fortunes. Many had been converted to office space. Then she drove to Thirteenth East to take a look at the University of Utah, where she'd studied acting and later performed at Pioneer Memorial Theater, the resident professional theater company.

Next she headed toward Foothill Boulevard, which would take her to Parley's Canyon and from there to Park City. The black car that she'd suspected was following her had disappeared, so her silly paranoia was replaced with a sense of nostalgia upon returning to these areas where she'd lived throughout her young life. *There have been many changes,* she thought, *but there's still a familiarity in the old landmarks. They make me feel that I've come home.* Then she thought of her parents. *I still miss them— especially Mother.*

Her stomach rumbled, reminding her that she was hungry. Breakfast seemed a better choice than lunch, so she found an IHOP. Pulling into a parking space, she remembered to lock the car, and went inside.

A pleasant middle-aged hostess led her to a booth near the front window and gave her a menu. When the college-age, ponytailed waitress arrived, she ordered big. She hadn't eaten much since the previous day, so ham, scrambled eggs, hash browns, and toast sounded delicious. *I'll eat a light dinner,* she promised herself.

Absently looking out the big window at the blue, snow-covered mountains, she thought that she saw the same black car that had followed her earlier. It was pulling into the far side of the parking lot. The car windows were tinted, so she couldn't see a driver or passengers but made a mental note of the Utah license plate number—an unforgettable vanity plate—FORTUNE.

Her nervous imaginings were interrupted by the intrusion of two older ladies, who were leaving the restaurant and thought they recognized her. "Oh, look, Lucille, isn't she that young girl who played the daughter on *A Brighter Time?*" She pointed in Lesley's direction. "I'm sure it's *her.* There are so many actors in town for the Sundance Festival, you know." Then she crossed to Lesley's table. "Miss, aren't you an actress? Didn't you play Celia on *A Brighter Time?*" She leaned in, looking over her glasses as if her bifocals weren't adequate to see Lesley closely. At that range, the fan's big-toothed smile was almost overwhelming.

"Yes, I did," Lesley admitted, drawing back a little.

"See, I told you, Lucille. Oh, that's my favorite soap. I was so sorry when you died," she said sincerely.

"Well, as you see, I didn't actually die. I'm still here." Lesley smiled.

"Oh, of course not—you know what I mean," she said, patting Lesley's shoulder. "Well, you've just made my day. I can't wait to tell everybody that I saw Celia—I mean, what's your real name?" she asked, revealing that Lesley's professional—"real"—name had not become a household word.

"Well, thank you," Lesley answered. "My *real* name is Lesley Kern."

"Oh, we're so glad to have met you," she said, grabbing her wide-eyed, gum-chewing friend by the arm and dragging her unwillingly toward the cashier.

Well, at least I'm becoming a familiar face, Lesley thought, *even if she doesn't know my name.* She turned toward the window—the black car was gone. *How ridiculous to have imagined someone was stalking me,* she realized.

She finished her brunch in peace, got her check, left a tip, and headed for the Navigator. Park City was less than an hour away if she remembered right. However, she wasn't prepared for the traffic hurtling up Parley's Canyon like stock cars racing in three packed lanes. There was little opportunity to enjoy the scenery, so she was relieved to escape the mountain-climbing freeway at a Park City turnoff.

Again, she was amazed at the changes in the area. The buildings at Kimball Junction just off the freeway resembled a California strip mall, except that some rather rustic designs had been used in some of the exteriors. There were homes everywhere, almost like any American suburb, and driving into Park City proper, she spotted a chain grocery store, a multiplex movie theater, and some big chain hotels. *So much for escape to the country,* she thought. She had noticed several Olympics sites on the way.

While climbing the road into the narrow, winding streets of Old Park City, she became excited at the nineteenth-century ambiance that it still retained. She thought, *This is what I'd hoped for—a step backward to a simpler time. Or, at least, it seems as if things were simpler. I have to remember that Park City also had a sometimes violent and lurid past,* she reminded herself.

She found the Silver Princess, one of the older hotels high up in the old part of town. It had been rebuilt after the destructive fire in the 1930s but was still small and personal, which Lesley preferred to the newer, larger hotels. She parked in a spot reserved for check-ins, got her purse, and locked the car. There was more snow in Park City than in Salt Lake, but the boardwalk was covered by a roof overhang, and the streets had been cleared.

Heavy wooden doors with beveled glass inserts announced in gilded lettering, THE SILVER PRINCESS—WELCOME. Lesley stepped inside and felt as if she'd entered an inviting, nineteenth-century parlor. Victorian decor abounded in the velvet and fringed draperies at the windows and arches. Brass cuspidors now served as potted palm planters. Tiffany glass chandeliers hung from high ceilings, and antique Victorian sofas and chairs were upholstered in gold, wine, and green velveteen. The front desk, which ran the width of the room, resembled the counter of an old-style bank, with glassed-in booths and metal grates at the windows. The atmosphere was further enhanced by music from a player piano quietly playing nineteenth-century tunes.

She stepped to one of the windows and announced, "I'm Lesley Kern. I have a reservation."

In keeping with the decor, the desk clerk sported a handlebar mustache, sideburns, and a part in the middle of his gray-black hair. He wore a vest, a starched collar, a string tie, armbands, and striped pants.

Lesley thought, *If my room is as appealing as the reception area, I've chosen well.*

"I hope you'll enjoy your long stay with us, Miss Kern. We're honored that an actress of your reputation has chosen the Silver Princess," the clerk said too effusively. "Barnaby will get your bags and then will show you to your room." He patted a sweet-sounding bell with his palm, and a college-age, tall, and sinewy bellhop in knee breeches, knee socks, and a vest appeared, removing his cap and bowing awkwardly at the waist. The desk clerk instructed, "Please give Barnaby your car keys and have a seat, Miss Kern, to await his return." She did as instructed and sat in a high-backed Victorian chair decorated with carved wood rosettes.

Barnaby returned with her luggage, indicating that after showing her to her room, he would move her car to their garage if she desired.

Lesley responded, "Yes, I'd appreciate that," and followed him to a gilded birdcage elevator which jerkily lifted them to a mezzanine balcony and her second-floor room.

The room was delightful, continuing the nineteenth-century atmosphere of the lobby: a high, antique brass bed, a window seat, marble-topped tables, a chaise lounge, and a comfortable chair, all promising a relaxing stay at the Silver Princess. She kneeled on the cushioned window seat and could see through the bay window the city and the entire valley spreading before her.

She thanked Barnaby and tipped him well. He indicated, "Thank you, Ms. Kern. Your car keys can be picked up from the front desk when you need your car. The desk clerk will give you directions to the garage. Anything else, Ms. Kern?"

"No, thank you, Barnaby. Oh, unless you can recommend a nice place for dinner," she said.

He seemed pleased that she had asked. "You'll find good restaurants all along Main Street, but I like the Silver Fork, and it's in walking distance," he suggested.

"Well, how coincidental," Lesley said.

"Coincidental?" he asked, seeming rather surprised.

"Yes, a man who sat by me on the plane said that he owned the Silver Fork."

"Oh—uh—Mr. Sanders? Yes, I—uh—know him," he offered.

At that point, Lesley began to smell something fishy. "Just how well do you know him?" she asked suspiciously.

"Well, uh—" Barnaby struggled with his answer, casting his seemingly innocent brown eyes to the floor.

"The truth."

"Well, the truth is . . ."

"Yes?"

"The truth is he called this afternoon and asked that I suggest his place if you asked for recommendations for a place to eat," he said sheepishly. "I'm sorry, but it *is* a nice place, so I thought, why not?"

"And I suppose he offered you something in return. Right? Or do you give this kind of special attention to all your guests—and their would-be callers?" she asked accusingly.

"Well, no—but he is a nice guy," he added, his face turning beet red with guilt.

"We'll see about that, Barnaby, but in the future, let me arrange my own get-togethers. Okay?"

"I'm really sorry, Ms. Kern, if I've offended you," he said sincerely.

"Oh, no harm done, I suppose." She laughed, trying to alleviate his embarrassment.

"Well, thank you," he said. "But let me—us—know, if there's anything we can do for you—in the future."

"I will—but wait until I let you know. Okay?"

"I promise, Ms. Kern," he said, and left in a hurry, pocketing his tip and anticipating, she suspected, another from a Mr. Sanders.

She thought, *I don't know whether to be irritated or amused at the meddling of Gareth Sanders. I suppose I should be flattered that he's gone to that much trouble to see me again.*

She hefted a suitcase onto the window seat and began to hang and place her clothes in a massive, cedar-lined antique armoire with mirrors in the doors and a built-in set of drawers. The easy-rolling drawers and the cedar smell created an air of luxury. Then she moved to the bath where she found a large tub on tiger-claw feet. The towels and soaps were plentiful and sweet smelling. *I'm really going to enjoy my vacation here,* she decided.

She lay on the bed just to test its comfort but, fatigued from her work and travel, fell asleep instead.

CHAPTER 3

When she awakened, Lesley was disoriented by the darkness in the room and by the unfamiliar surroundings. Finally realizing where she was, she reached for a bedside lamp and thought, *Glad I'm not back in the days of no electricity.* She checked her watch—it was seven o'clock.

She was hungry but took time to freshen up and to reapply some makeup. She retrieved her winter coat from the armoire and was glad she'd brought it. She found her lined leather gloves in a coat pocket and picked up the heavy hotel key from the bedside table where Barnaby had left it. *No plastic computerized keys here,* she reflected.

When she opened the door she realized that she'd fallen asleep without sliding the dead bolt. *I'm travel savvy enough to know better than that. Come to think of it, was I wise to turn over my key ring, with all my personal keys, to a hotel bellboy? I won't do that again. I'm too trusting,* she reminded herself.

Locking her room, she took the stairs down one flight to the lobby, responding again to the magic of the decor and a crackling log in the ornate hearth fireplace. A different desk clerk, costumed like the previous one, was on duty and seemed to know exactly where to find Lesley's keys.

"Have a pleasant evening, Ms. Kern. Do you need directions to the garage?" he asked.

"Well, I think I'll just walk to a restaurant tonight, but I do need to know for another time," she said.

He pointed to a hall behind the elevator. "You go down that rear hall to a stairway, or you can use the elevator, which will take you downstairs to our garage behind the hotel," he explained. "It's locked after ten PM, however, so you'll need a card key to open the garage door. I'll process one for you, and you can pick it up here when you return to the hotel this evening. Any other way we can help you?"

"No, thanks. That will be fine. I'll stop by when I come back from dinner." She thought, *So much for no plastic keys, but I'm glad the garage is secure. I guess I'll be eating at the Silver Fork.* She stepped out into the brisk winter night, glad for her coat and gloves. There was no wind, however, and the stillness of the snow-blanketed environs was comforting. The few cars that passed drove slowly and carefully, and there were more people walking than driving. Again, Lesley felt pleasure at that slower-paced existence.

Lit shop windows were varied and appealing. Antique stores, boutiques, candy shops, a barber-beauty shop, and a real estate office were mixed with the several small restaurants, bars, and hostelries along the block leading to the Silver Fork Restaurant.

Am I doing the right thing going to Gareth Sanders's place? she wondered. But by the time she finished musing on the situation she was there—at the entrance to the Silver Fork, and it did look nice. She checked the menu posted by the doorway. The prices ranged from very nominal to moderately expensive, and the menu varied from soups and salads to steaks and seafood. *And it smells so good,* she thought. The enticing aroma of char-broiling drew her inside, without her having made a conscious decision to go in.

The restaurant was busy but large enough to accommodate a crowd, so she didn't have to wait for a table. The youthful host, dressed in western attire, led her to a seat by the window, where she could look out at passersby on the sidewalk and at the snow-painted street.

The decor in the restaurant combined early American and western influences, correlating with the western attire of the employees. Windsor chairs, pedestal tables, silver-plated chandeliers, and country-western music added to the atmosphere. Also, the items that Gareth Sanders had collected—some of them from her property perhaps—were hung artistically on the walls, along with sepia-toned photographs of various Park City sites, buildings, and old-timers. Linen tablecloths and napkins and heavy silverware lent an upscale quality to the dining room. The only discordant theme for Lesley was the taxidermy—more than a dozen buck deer heads displaying huge racks of antlers hung alternately with the artifacts and photos. A song lyric from Disney's *Beauty and the Beast* popped into her head: "I use antlers in all of my decorating . . ."

A bearded young waiter brought the menu and addressed her by name. "Miss Kern, Mr. Sanders expresses his welcome and his pleasure that you chose to dine at the Silver Fork this evening."

"Well, tell Mr. Sanders thanks and that I felt very *persuaded* to come," she responded.

"I will, ma'am. The specials of the evening are included in the menu," he said, presenting Lesley with a large, impressive copy. "Would you like a drink?" he asked.

"Just ice water, please."

"I'll return in a moment for your order," he said, bowing slightly.

She browsed through the large menu, remembering her resolve to eat a light dinner. But she was very hungry and

reasoned, *I've eaten only once today, even if it was a big meal.
Anyway, I'm not working. I'll lose weight.* She decided on the
mesquite-broiled chicken breast with seasoned wild rice and
southwestern spiced vegetables.

The grinning waiter took her order and said that she was
the guest of Mr. Sanders this evening. Lesley looked around to
try to see Gareth but was unsuccessful.

"Well, that isn't necessary, but thank Mr. Sanders for me,"
she said.

"Yes, ma'am. Your food should be ready in about ten
minutes."

She sipped the mountain water and looked out into the
narrow street lit by replicas of nineteenth-century streetlights.
The bundled-up people strolling by and a softly falling snow
suggested an old-fashioned holiday picture postcard. She
relaxed and enjoyed the moment—that is, until she saw the
long, black car drive slowly by. She turned to check the license
plate. *Sure enough,* she thought, *there's that unmistakable vanity
plate—FORTUNE. Is it just another coincidence, or is someone
really stalking me?* Anyway, she was unnerved at the incident.
*Maybe I should ask to see Gareth and tell him. Or should I tell the
hotel manager and ask him to call the police?*

It seemed so silly, though, and she certainly had nothing to
charge against anyone. *No one has tried to approach me,* she
thought. *It's probable that the driver of that car simply left the
airport at the same time and followed the same routes as me. After
all, lots of people are coming to Park City. It's all a coincidence,* she
tried to reason, but couldn't completely put it to rest.

The arrival of the waiter with her dinner stole her attention
for the time being.

She savored the smell of the spicy southwestern flavors of
the chicken and vegetables. The waiter had brought a small loaf

of just-baked bread with garlic butter. She thought, *Gareth's right—his food is good,* so she concentrated entirely on her excellent dinner and on the warm, cozy surroundings.

When she finished, somewhat embarrassed at having licked her plate clean, she sat back and listened to the music, which she realized was live—a small group playing from a raised dais at the back of the restaurant. A very good female vocalist sang the old Tammy Wynette country-western hit, "Stand by Your Man," and Lesley thought, *I don't have one to stand by.* Then, at that moment, she noticed standing by her none other than Gareth Sanders, her host for the evening.

"You came," he said. "I'm pleased."

"Well, I could hardly resist Barnaby's *subtle* suggestion," she said, laughing.

"You can't blame a fella for trying," he said. "Anyway, I'm glad it worked. Did you enjoy your dinner?"

"I did—too much," she said, nodding toward her empty plate.

"Well, I'm glad you liked it. How about dessert? We specialize in our own home-baked pies and pastries."

"Oh, no, thank you. Maybe another time. I'm very full," she said, looking out the window to see huge snowflakes coming down. "In fact, it looks like I'd better start back to the hotel before I can't get through the snow." She started to rise.

"Do you want me to arrange for a ride?" he asked in his consistent gentlemanly manner.

"Oh, no, thanks. I'll enjoy the walk in the snow. I haven't experienced a real winter for a long time. It's enchanting," she mused.

"Well, if you say so, but you'll come back again some time—for dessert?" he asked.

"Yes—I will—for dessert," she said. "I'll be eating out *every* day so I'm sure you'll see me again."

"I hope so," he said, looking into Lesley's eyes and then helping her put on her coat.

"Well, thank you. You really do have a very nice place. I'm glad that you—and Barnaby—recommended it," she teased.

"I hope you won't hold that against me—or Barnaby. After all, he makes his living through tips," he said, smiling at her.

"Yes, I understand," she said. "Well, thanks again." She started to leave a tip for the waiter.

"I'll take care of that, too," Gareth said. "You're my guest, after all."

"My goodness. Such hospitality."

"Only the best for a famous actress."

"Yes, so famous that you didn't even recognize me on the plane."

"Well, I'm sure your day will come," he offered. "I can't wait to see *Casa Grande*."

"I'm sure you're holding your breath."

"No, I mean it. I really will be watching for it."

"Well, thanks. I'll be off, then."

"Let me walk you to the door," he said, and showed her the way. She couldn't help feeling rather important, ushered by the owner of the place. She left him at the door, and he watched as she stepped gingerly though the deepening snow. *What a pleasant evening*, she thought. At that moment she was very happy at her decision to come to Park City.

Her walk up the hill to the Silver Princess presented challenges. She found she'd forgotten how to walk on packed or powdered snow, either slipping like a clown on ice or trudging like a polar bear in the drifts. Somehow she made it to the covered porch of the hotel.

It was still rather early in the evening, but the thought of cozying up in her room was appealing. She stopped at the desk for her garage pass, and the clerk said, "I believe you have a message, Ms. Kern." He turned to a row of boxes behind him and withdrew an envelope. "Yes, here it is." He handed the small, white envelope to Lesley, and she noted it was simply addressed to *Ms. Lesley Kern.* "Anything else, Ms. Kern?"

"Yes, do you have a magazine shop?"

"There's a gift shop at the far side of the lobby." He pointed past the elevator. "They carry magazines, newspapers, paperbacks, and snack food," he explained.

"Thank you," she said and headed in the direction he'd indicated. She hadn't opened the envelope, thinking she'd read the message in her room. Then she thought, *It might be a message from my agent—a job offer,* so she stopped and ripped it open. The message on a plain white sheet of paper was brief and inadequate—*Please call,* then an 801 area code number. No name and no other details.

She purchased a newspaper, a mystery novel, and a Milky Way from the genial silver-haired lady in the gift shop, then returned to the desk clerk for more information about the message.

The clerk turned from his work when she approached. "Yes, ma'am?"

"Do you know if this message for me came by telephone, or was it delivered?" she asked, holding up the note.

"Oh, it must have been delivered. That's not our stationery. It's just as it was when Barnaby gave it to me," he said.

"Oh, then you didn't see who delivered it?"

"No, ma'am. Someone gave it to Barnaby at the door, and he gave it to me. He's off duty now, or we could ask him about it. I'm sorry," he said.

"Oh, it's all right. It just seems unusual that the message isn't signed. Anyway, thank you." She turned toward the elevator.

"Good night, Ms. Kern," he said.

"Yes, good night."

She felt strangely relieved when her door was locked and bolted behind her. Somehow the unidentified message was disconcerting. She checked the number on the bedside telephone and saw that the area code was the same as that on the message—a Utah telephone number, as she'd guessed. She wondered, *Could Gareth have sent the note? Not likely, since he just saw me in person.*

After brushing the melted snow from her coat, she hung it to dry on a freestanding Victorian coat rack and kicked off her wet shoes. Her socks were wet, too, and she realized, *I'll need to buy some snow boots.*

A warm terry robe, furnished by the hotel, was folded on the linen shelf, and she found her furry slippers still zipped in a pocket of one of her bags.

The room was warm and snug, so she curled up on the chaise with her newspaper, novel, and Milky Way. She decided, *I'll play Scarlett O'Hara for tonight and worry about the message tomorrow.*

She read for a while then retired early, fatigued from the previous week's rush and from the travels of the day. She kneeled on the thick rug and prayed, thanking the Lord for the material security which her work had provided, for her safe trip, and for the general serenity she felt in returning to her Utah home. She prayed for friends she'd left behind and, as she always did, for those in the troubled world who were hurting, grieving, or denied their basic freedoms.

The bed was so comfortable, and leaving the cares of the day behind, Lesley fell asleep immediately.

CHAPTER 4

Lesley awakened late, feeling rested and glad to be alive. *Several months without the stresses of work will be so pleasant,* she thought. She kneeled in morning prayer and thanked her Heavenly Father for her many blessings and asked for His daily watchful care.

Reluctant to leave the comfy cocoon of her room, she found the hotel food services menu beside the phone and ordered a room service breakfast of French toast, fresh fruit, and juice. She lounged about in the terry robe, waiting for her food to arrive.

Then she remembered the unidentified message. *Should I make the call or should I ignore it?* she wondered. *Oh, why not call. I can always hang up if it's someone I don't want to deal with.* She dialed the number, and it rang four times. She was about to hang up when a man answered, "Hullo." *This must not be a professional office,* she thought, but said, "This is Lesley Kern. I received a written request to call this number."

"Yeah, wull—let me see if I can find anything out about it," he said, and dropped the phone on a hard surface, hurting her ear. Again, she almost hung up, but he returned. "Someone wants to talk to ya."

A female voice took over, sounding much more communicative. "Missus Kern," she said, obviously unacquainted with Lesley's single marital status. "This is Silver Forks Realty

Company, and I'm Connie Evans. I've been authorized to make you an offer on your Silver Forks Mountain property."

Lesley interrupted her. "But that property isn't for sale."

"Oh, we know you haven't put it on the market, but the party who wants to buy it said that we should make you an offer you can't refuse," she clarified, and giggled. "We thought that . . ."

Lesley interrupted her again. "I'm not interested in considering offers, thank you. The property isn't for sale, as I explained."

"But don't you even want to hear the offer? It may change your mind," she insisted, then yelled, "Rudy, turn down that radio, will ya?" Returning her attention to the phone, she said, "Sorry about that. Well, what do ya think? Could we get together and discuss it anyway?"

"No, I'm sorry. I don't wish to be rude, but I'm not planning to sell the property. Thank you, anyway—by the way, how did you know I was in town?"

That thought made Lesley want to hang up, but Connie was persistent. "I'm not at liberty to say, and I'm really not *supposed* to do this—but could I just tell you the offer over the phone? That way you can think about it."

She paused while Lesley gritted her teeth to help control her feelings. "Well, go ahead, but it won't make any difference. I'm *not* interested in selling the property."

"Well, would an offer of—one million dollars change your mind?" she asked, obviously enjoying the drama of the moment.

One million dollars, Lesley thought. *That property can't be worth that much.*

Lesley was slow with her response, which seemed to encourage Connie. "There now. I knew that would blow your socks off," she said. "Can we meet and talk now?"

Lesley was almost tempted to agree to meet her—just to talk—but something moved her to stand her ground. "No, I'm still not interested."

"Oh, gonna hold out for more, huh? Well, you may be sorry, but I'll tell the interested party what you said. Maybe I can get them to jack their offer up a little higher. Whaddayasay?" she asked.

"Connie, is it? I don't know how to make it more clear. You have my answer. Thank you. Good-bye." She gently replaced the receiver on the cradle of the late nineteenth-century phone, resisting the urge to slam it down. She thought, *Silver Forks Realty, huh. I don't remember a real estate office in Silver Forks or anyone named Evans. Things have changed. And just how did she know I was here?*

A knock at her door interrupted her thoughts and announced the arrival of her breakfast. She looked through the door peephole to see none other than Barnaby delivering her food. *Apparently his duties are varied in this small hotel,* she thought. She opened the door to his greeting, "Good morning, Ms. Kern. Your breakfast."

"Just put the tray on that little table by the chaise, will you?" she asked, pointing.

"Sure thing, Ms. Kern." He removed the tray from his cart then said, "Anything else, Ms. Kern?"

"No, thank you, but I'm grateful that you asked this time," she said, smiling.

"Oh, yeah, by the way, was your—dinner good?" he asked expectantly.

"Yes, it was, thank you."

He paused for a moment, seeming to wait for her to reveal more, but she disappointed him. "Well, then, I'll be on my way," he said, grinning and not moving.

"Oh, let me get my purse." She found some bills and tipped him again.

He left seeming happy, so she went to the chaise and her breakfast. The food was excellent, and she congratulated herself again on her choice of hotels.

After eating every bite, she showered and thought about her day. She had two days and two nights to enjoy before the Sundance Film Festival was to begin on Thursday. *Guess I'll get in the Navigator and explore the area,* she thought. *Maybe I ought to drive up to the old house and see what condition it's in— if the roads aren't too bad.*

Wearing her winter coat, a little knit cap, and her gloves, she set out for the garage, taking the stairs all the way down. The hotel lobby was bustling that morning, undoubtedly with festival participants. She found her SUV and backed carefully out of the narrow parking stall, then drove up a cement ramp where a folding metal door rolled up automatically at her approach.

Outside there was snow on the ground, but the sun was shining. She rolled down the window and breathed in the crisp, clean winter air. It was invigorating but soon became too cold. She drove out of Park City and back onto the freeway heading south toward Silver Forks Junction and other hamlets dotted across the mountainside.

She found the turnoff and then followed the arrow directing her to the Silver Forks business district. *It's hardly a district,* she thought. The same old buildings were there that existed in the late nineteenth century were there, but instead of retaining their charm of yesteryear, they had become nondescript after attempts had been made to modernize them. Aluminum storefronts and tacky signs had robbed the buildings of their originality. She thought, *Gareth was wrong about that—the downtown, if it could be called that, has changed—and for the worse.*

There was still the Silver Forks Bank, the barbershop, and the general store, but she noted the addition of a gas station and, of course, the Silver Forks Realty, a lean-to beside the bank. She thought, *Connie must be in there wheeling and dealing away,* so she drove past in a hurry, looking for the winding road up the mountain to her property. She passed the entrance to Silver Fork Health Spa, as it was now called. A sign indicated "Open Year Round. Greatest Little Health Spa on Earth. Come on in!"

About a half mile from the spa, she crossed a bridge over Silver Forks Creek and turned onto a dirt road that she remembered well. However, it had been improved with a layer of some kind of ground-up material—not gravel. Anyway, her concerns about muddy roads were unnecessary—the road was much better than the last time she'd driven it. The Navigator climbed and wound for about two miles through increasingly abundant fir and pine trees masking the remnants of the mining that had occurred there. Then, turning a bend, she saw the house on a flat of about ten acres—all hers.

The creek that she'd crossed near town also ran through her property, and evergreen trees dotted the entire acreage, creating a very picturesque setting even in winter. She remembered that in warmer weather, the varied foliage of Rocky Mountain maple, aspen, pine, fir, and scrub oak were mixed in nature's perfect landscaping, and outcroppings of rock provided contrast to the softness of the foliage. *But the winter landscape is beautiful—it's a beautiful place to live.* She thought, *I own a little piece of heaven on earth. Why didn't my mother, or for that matter my grandmother and great-grandmother, want to live here?*

She turned into the lane leading to a utility gate, which had always been locked with a padlock. She had brought the key, having placed it on her key ring before she left California.

Climbing out of the SUV to open the gate, she was startled to find the padlock unlocked and hanging on a wire. The gate was shut, but obviously someone had entered the property—a set of tire ruts in the frozen mud and snow along the lane evidenced the entry. She was curious, then angry. *I'll have to hire someone to watch over this place,* she thought. *I've been too trusting and naïve.*

She pushed the gate open, returned to the car, started it, and then drove along the rutty, frozen tracks toward the house. *I'm glad the mud's frozen, or even this four-wheeler might get stuck.* She stopped about twenty feet from the steps of the big, wooden wraparound porch to get an overview of the house. At first sight the house appeared just as she'd remembered it. The Queen Anne design included many typically Victorian elements—a turret at each end of the roof, decorative finials, scalloped cedar shingles, and the welcoming porch with turned newel posts and columns. She thought, *All those little window panes may be charming, but I remember how hard they are to clean. But it is a beautiful old house.*

Lesley pulled up to the weathered front steps, turned off the engine, and climbed out to take a closer look at how the house had withstood her neglect. The house had been repainted before she left the area, and the stain had held up rather well in most places. However, the ten-year period of the guarantee was over, and the cedar-shingle siding needed a new coat, especially on the north side of the house. She had to walk through about two inches of snow to get up the stairs but made it, even without boots, to the covered porch landing.

The heavy wooden front door was locked—she was relieved to find—and the draped windows appeared intact. She walked around one end of the porch, still examining the general condition of the exterior. When she rounded the corner, a distressing sight greeted her. *It looks as if someone has been shooting bullets at the house,* she thought. Then she examined the small round holes more closely and realized, *A woodpecker has been finding his dinner under the siding of my house. It's drilled a hundred holes in those cedar shingles.* Involuntarily, she began to search the eaves and under the porch roof for the bird. *Or is there more than one?* she wondered, *Aren't woodpeckers fair-weather birds? Maybe this happened in the summer or fall.* Annoyed at the pesky pest, she continued her examination of the house, walking around the porch and looking at the front part of the exterior. Then she stepped off into the snow and made her way carefully around to the back, where she found another surprise. The metal door that covered an unused coal chute was open, and pawprints revealed that some creature or creatures had been using it as an entrance to the basement furnace room. *Well, that settles it,* she thought, *I'm not stepping inside this house until I can get someone to check it out.* She had no experience with animals, tame or wild, and she certainly didn't want to meet up with one in the house.

She slipped and slid her way back to the car, started it, and rounded the circular drive in front of the house taking her back to the rutty lane. She felt uneasy upon leaving the house, which contrasted with her joy in coming there. *Who has been here before me?* she wondered. *Who knew I would be in town? Who would want to contact me about buying the property? And what am I going to do about the pests damaging the house?* These questions dominated her thinking on her drive back to Park City, and she forgot to enjoy the scenery.

CHAPTER 5

It took about thirty minutes to return to her hotel in Park City. Rather than going into the garage, she parked out front, congratulating herself on finding a parking place. The town was literally packed with people.

She locked the car, noting the one-hour parking limit announced on a utility pole sign. That would give her time to scan the phone book to try to find an exterminator.

I'll call, then I'll get some lunch, she decided.

There were lines of prospective guests waiting at the front desk, so she didn't stop for messages and took the stairs rather than waiting for the elevator. Somehow the crowds had diminished the charm of the place, replacing the ambiance of quiet dignity with loud, chattering hustle. She was glad to escape to her room.

She lay her coat across a chair, kicked off her wet shoes, and removed the tight little cap from her head. She had returned to find a phone directory and located it in the bedside table drawer. She settled into the chaise to peruse the yellow pages and found "Exterminators" and directions to "See Pest Control." When she found that subject heading, she was amazed to find only two listings in the local area—the others were all in Salt Lake City. She found the only Park City listing and walked to the bedside phone, sat on the bed, and dialed the number for "Wild Animal Specialist—Live Animal Trapping and Removal." *I've just got to find some help before the festival begins,* she thought.

The phone rang for a long time before a male voice answered, "Yeah, what can I do for you?"

Informality's the rule around here, she decided, and said, "This is Lesley Kern. I own a house on Silver Forks Mountain, and I think a woodpecker has been drilling holes in the siding. Also, some kind of animal has been getting into the basement through a coal chute. I need someone to go there and advise me what to do."

"Hold on a minute," the voice replied. "You're rattling on so fast, I'm not sure I got all that. Where's your place?" he asked.

"On Silver Forks Mountain Road. It's the only house up there," she answered.

"Oh, yeah—that old abandoned place up there," he said. "I know it."

"It isn't abandoned—maybe not used—but not abandoned," she said rather defensively.

"Well, I'm a one-man operation here, and I'm busy," he said.

"Who am I speaking to?" Lesley asked.

"Oh, I'm Jim—Jim Shepherd," he said. "Sorry, I can't help ya, ma'am."

She stood and became insistent. "But, Jim—Mr. Shepherd—I've got to have some help, and you're the only 'wild animal specialist' listed in Park City. I'm only here for a few weeks and I *have* to get rid of those—pests," she said persuasively. "You just have to help me."

"No, ma'am. I don't *have* to do anything," he said, and laughed.

Oh, why does everyone have to be so stubborn here? she thought. "I'm sorry. I didn't mean to say it that way. I just mean that I have to have some help. I don't dare go in my house knowing something's in there, and the woodpecker is going to peck my house away," she exaggerated, sounding almost hysterical. "You're the only one who can help me."

He laughed another warm, rumbling laugh, and she liked that sound. "A damsel in distress, eh? Well, that's hard to resist," he said, and laughed again.

"Please," she begged. "I'll make it worth your while. Won't you come help me?"

"I know you'll make it worth my while. One hundred dollars up front, plus mileage," he offered. "Then we'll see what I have to do and how long it takes."

"I'll pay it," she said, desperate for his assistance. "When can you go there?"

"Well, might as well get it over with," he said. "I have to grab some lunch, then—how about this afternoon?"

"Oh, that would be wonderful. I'll get lunch too and meet you up there at . . . ?" She waited for him to suggest a time.

"Well, there's no sense driving two cars up there. Why don't you ride up there with me in my truck? Then we'll be sure not to miss each other. I don't want to waste time waiting for you or trying to find you. In fact, I'll pick you up in fifteen minutes, and we can get some lunch together," he suggested.

Is he some kind of fast mover or is he really going to do the job? she wondered. *But I like his voice and laugh. After all, I called him. There can't be anything wrong in going along with him,* she decided.

"Well, okay. It's a little unusual, but then, so are my problems. Where should I meet you?" she asked.

"As I said, I can pick you up, if you want me to," he offered, sounding much more congenial than he had when he first answered the phone.

"No, why don't I meet you where we're going for lunch. You tell me where," she requested.

"Well, there's a burger place about one mile from the entrance to the freeway. It's called Burger Barn. It's on the east side of the road. Ya can't miss it," he said.

"That sounds fine, Mr. Shepherd, and thank you," she said, sincerely grateful.

"Oh, call me Jim," he said. "I'll meet ya there in about fifteen minutes, then. Oh, how will I know you, and what's your name, again?" he asked.

"Well, I don't have a red rose to carry, so just look for a brunette, short hair, dark eyes. I'm about five seven, and I'll be wearing a tan overcoat and a brown knit cap. My name is Lesley Kern," she explained. "And how will I know you?"

"Oh, I look just like everybody else around here, so I'll find you—Lesley. Okay?" he said, and hung up the phone, not waiting for her answer.

She put on her winter things again, got her purse, and went out, locking the door behind her. She hurried down the stairs, made her way through the crowd in the lobby, and went to the Navigator. It took less than ten minutes to get to the Burger Barn, which was, indeed, like a barn with its gambrel barn roof, red siding, and hitching rail fences defining the parking area. It looked fun, much better than the fast food chains.

She went inside, hoping that Jim would come as he'd promised. *I want to get the house taken care of before the film festival begins,* she thought again.

The cashier-hostess greeted her, "How many in your party, please?"

"Oh, there will be two of us, but I don't think he's arrived yet—so I'll just wait here if that's okay," Lesley said.

"Yes, that's fine. There's a bench over there if you'd like to sit down," she offered, pointing toward a waiting area.

"Thanks, but I think I'll just wait here. He should be here soon."

And Lesley was right. She saw his arrival through the window. He pulled up in a muddy old pickup, and she could just see through the mud a painted sign on the truck door reading, "Wild Animal Specialist" and the phone number. *Business must not be too good,* she thought. Then he climbed out and slammed the truck door.

Lesley was prepared for a scruffy, trapper type and was shocked to see, instead, one of the most appealing men in her experience. He was at least six feet tall, lean, and rugged looking. Beneath his baseball cap she could see blond hair. And his skin was blond, too, and sunburn-tanned even in winter. He came through the door, saw her, and smiled, revealing the whitest and straightest teeth anyone could wish for. Lesley thought, *You ought to be in movies,* then laughed inwardly at her version of the cliché.

"You must be Lesley," he said.

"And you must be Jim," she said, trying to hide her open-mouth response. "Thanks for—for arranging to come."

"Oh, now that I'm here—anyway, it's no trouble," he said. "Shall we eat? I could eat a horse."

I'll bet you could, she thought, but said, "I'm hungry too." She wasn't really hungry after her big breakfast. *But I'm going to enjoy this meal,* she decided.

The smiling hostess knew him. "Hi, Jim," she said. "Who's your friend?"

"Oh, she's—a client," he explained, sounding more professional than she'd have thought he could. "This is Lesley—Kern. She owns that big old house on the road to Silver Forks Mountain—in Silver Forks. Lesley, this is Clara." Lesley looked at Clara more closely then and noted a pleasantly plump, middle-aged lady with a square jaw and thick dark hair piled high on her head.

He had given out more information than Lesley wanted him to, but she thought, *I guess this is still a small town in some ways, where everyone knows everybody and everything about them.*

The hostess, Clara, said, "Glad to meetcha," and Lesley responded with, "I'm glad to meet you too." Clara led them to a booth by the front window, where they could see the mountains and the sky, and gave each of them a menu. "Karen's your waitress. She'll be right with ya." She smiled a knowing grin, winked at Jim, and left them.

Jim helped Lesley off with her coat, waited for her to sit, removed his cap, and then sat across from her. *A gentleman, anyway,* she thought, admiring his short-cropped, thick hair.

"Well," he said, "when did you find those critters you told me about on the phone?"

"I just got into town yesterday and I drove up this morning. That's when I found the damage done by the woodpecker and the tracks leading in and out of the coal chute."

"Have any idea what kind of animal it is?" he asked.

"No, the prints were quite small. But I really didn't take much time to examine them. I just wanted to get out of there," she admitted. "Anyway, I wouldn't know one track from another. That's why I called you."

He looked at the menu. "Well, let's order. The service is pretty good here, so we can get on our way in a hurry. I recommend the Burger Barn Special."

"Well, if it isn't too big."

"Oh, you women," he said good-naturedly. "Always worrying about your looks."

"It's more than that with me—my looks are my living," she said.

"Oh, yeah?" He smiled. "I'm almost afraid to ask what you do."

"Well, it's not what you're thinking," she said. "I'm an actress."

"You're kiddin' me," he said. "You mean I'm having lunch with a genuine actress?" He faked a wide-eyed look of surprise.

"Yes, you are. That's what I do, as you put it," she said.

"Where do you act?" he asked, sounding genuinely interested.

"Mostly in television," she explained. "But I do some live theater, too, when I get a chance. And, of course, I wouldn't mind doing a major movie, either, if the right script were offered me."

"The right script? What would that have to be?" he asked.

"Something where I could play someone who makes a difference. Someone admirable," she said. "I like films that leave the audience better prepared to face life than they were when they came into the theater."

"I like that idea," he said. "But there aren't many films like that nowadays, are there?"

"There are, but most of the good scripts are for men, I'm afraid." *I'm impressed that he's interested in my work. He's shown more interest than most of the men I know well,* she thought.

Their discussion was interrupted by the waitress, who looked like she could be Clara's daughter.

"Well, how about the Burger Barn Special for me," Jim said. "How about you?" he asked, looking at Lesley with raised, questioning eyebrows.

"Oh, I'm sorry. I was so busy talking about myself that I didn't look at the menu. Just get me a Barn Burger Special too. What the heck!" she said, laughing. She reflected, *I feel very comfortable with him.*

"No, that's Burger Barn—not Barn Burger. Anyway, you could use a little fattening up," he said, looking at her.

"Not in my business. The TV camera adds ten pounds, you know," she said.

"Well, you look great to me," he said, with what seemed genuine admiration rather than the usual old line.

I like this guy, she thought. *He seems for real—not like so many phonies I meet.*

He seemed to see her thoughts in her eyes and face. He smiled. "I'm glad you called me," he said very openly.

"Well—I am too," she said, then hurriedly added, "because I really need your help."

The service was good. The waitress brought their food almost immediately. "Smells good," Lesley said, suddenly finding herself with an appetite.

"It looks good, too," he added. "And, most important, it tastes good—always does." He took a giant bite with his beautiful teeth, and she thought, *I like a man who likes to eat.* Then she checked her thoughts. *What am I doing? I'm thinking like a boy-crazy high school junior. Get a grip, girl.*

They both ate the delicious burgers without much conversation—a tribute to the food. Then, Lesley said, "We've talked about my work. Tell me more about yours."

"Not much to tell, really. Pest control doesn't sound like a very exciting job title compared to actress, does it?" he asked, teasing.

"I don't know. At least you have the satisfaction of knowing that you're really needed when someone calls you," she said.

"Well, that's true, I suppose," he said, appearing rather deep in thought.

"I guess that I meant—how did you decide to do what you do?" she asked, trying to draw him out further.

"I just fell into it. I love animals. You see, I don't really go after them to kill them—I do what I can to save them," he explained. "That's my real work—protecting wild animals."

"I would never have thought of it that way," she admitted. "Somehow the words *pest control* make me think of someone with a spray gun, killing bugs."

"Yeah, that's what most people think. But I really don't do that. Apparently you saw my yellow pages ad—"Wild Animal Specialist"—and you may have noted the words *trapping and removal?* There's nothing there about killing," he emphasized. "As I said, I love animals. I really wanted to be a veterinarian," he said quietly.

She looked into his blue eyes and at his big weathered hands. *He's one of the nicest men I've ever met,* she thought. Then she mentally slapped her face. *Stop right now. You don't really know a thing about this guy.*

"Well, that was good. But you're not finished," he observed.

"I'll hurry," she said. "Have you always lived in Park City?"

"Yes, but not right in the city. My folks moved to the area before I was born. Dad did the same thing as I do. He was a trapper—but he did it for furs. Quite a different goal from mine. But I guess he had to do what he had to do—to put bread on our table," he said.

"That's true, I'm sure," she said. "My forefathers were in mining, and they took advantage of nature too, I suppose you could say."

"Yes, you could say that. The environment really has never recovered from those old mining operations around here," he agreed.

Somehow she wanted in the worst way to ask him about his church background but couldn't think of how to broach the subject. So she just blurted it out. "Are you Mormon?"

"Yes," he said, and smiled. "Does that matter to you?"

"Well, yes, I guess it does—in some instances. I'm sorry if I'm being too nosy. It's a fault I have—I'm used to studying people, you see, in my work." *Does that sound like a good enough excuse for prying?* she wondered.

"Well, 'I am a Mormon boy,'" he sang, and she recognized that tune from Primary, a hymn that she'd read was so loved by President Benson. *This really is a nice man,* she thought. *And he has a sense of humor.*

Lesley laughed. "I didn't mean that you had to sing to prove it," she said.

"Well, it might be more accurate to sing, 'I *was born* a Mormon boy.' I'm afraid I haven't been much of a Mormon since . . ." He stopped, looking very serious and pensive. "There aren't many real Mormons around here—just gentiles and Jack Mormons, I'm afraid."

"I'm sorry. I've been prying too much. And we've only just met," she said apologetically.

"No, it's okay. Somehow I feel like talking—to you." He looked at her plate, "Well, you're finished. Better be on our way," he said, standing.

"Yes, but I think maybe I'll—follow you in my car," she suggested.

"Why, are you afraid of the big, bad wolf?"

"No—not really—but I don't usually—take rides with strangers," she said, somewhat embarrassed at her excuse.

He sat down again and pulled a cell phone out of his denim jacket pocket. He pressed one button—a preset number—and waited a moment. "Hello, Mom," he said. "I'm sitting here with a very pretty, young girl, and she's afraid to trust me. Will you tell her I'm okay?" he requested, and laughed, thrusting the phone at her.

Lesley didn't know how to react, so she just said, "Hello?"

On the other end she heard a sweet older voice. "Hello, dear. I suggest you slap that boy of mine across the face and tell him not to be so fresh. He's harmless—but relentless. Don't you fall for his pretty face or big line," she advised, laughing happily.

"Do you think I'd be safe riding with him to Silver Forks Mountain?" Lesley asked, trying to match her mood but also seriously wanting her opinion.

"The thing you'd have to worry about wouldn't be Jim's behavior—he's a smart aleck, but he's a gentleman—you'd have to worry about that old truck breaking down. That's my advice," she said. "Hope I can meet you in person sometime, dear."

"Me too," she said without reservation. *I like his mother,* she thought. "Thank you."

"Of course, dear. He really is a good boy," she added. "Could I talk with him just a minute?"

"Yes. Thanks, and good-bye." She handed the phone back to Jim. He talked with his mother, and Lesley watched him and listened to his kind way with her. *Someone said that you can tell what a man is by how he treats his mother. If that's true, this is a good man,* she thought.

He pressed the "end" button and asked, "Well, do you trust me now?"

"A mother's recommendation is about as good as you can get, I guess. Yes, I trust you. But she did warn me about your truck."

"That truck's in great shape; it doesn't look so good because I work it to death, but mechanically it's sound. A great old Chevy truck—can't beat 'em."

"Well, I'm still not sure that I shouldn't take my car."

"Oh, you need another reference, I suppose. Clara, come here," he said as they were passing the cashier's station.

"Yeah, what now? Ready to pay your bill?" she asked.

"Just put it on my tab, will ya?" he asked. "No, what I really need is—will you tell Lesley whether you think she's safe with me?"

Clara looked at Lesley seriously. "Honey, he's so safe I'd even let my daughter Karen go with him," she said, nodding her head toward the waitress who had served them.

"Oh, she's your daughter?" Lesley asked.

"Yeah, she's a sweetheart, and I wouldn't let her loose with just anyone. Jim may come on strong, but he's really just a teddy bear," she said, smiling and returning to her work.

"Well, okay. Two positive recommendations have to be taken seriously, I suppose. Where should I leave my car?" she asked.

"Why don't you pull it into a parking spot around back. That way you won't take up one of their prime parking places. I'll pull around back and pick you up—in my pickup," he said, laughing at his lame joke.

She did as he suggested then climbed into the dusty interior of his old Chevy truck, happy to be on her way to solve her pest problems—and to be with Jim, she admitted to herself. *What an unusual morning this has been,* she thought.

CHAPTER 6

The trip back to Silver Forks seemed short since the conversation was so interesting. Lesley asked Jim how he would handle the woodpecker problem, and his response demonstrated the truth of his philosophy regarding wild animals.

"Well, we should probably find out what species the woodpecker is, if that's really what's causing the damage to your house. There are eleven species common to Utah. It's probably a northern flicker or a yellow-bellied sapsucker. But it's likely a flicker, because sapsuckers tend to look for insects in trees—they suck sap," he suggested, and laughed.

"My goodness. I wouldn't have thought it would be so complicated," she said. "Do you think it's still there—the woodpecker—the flicker—at the house?"

"Well, they tend not to migrate out of Utah, unless they can't find food. When bugs aren't so available, they eat berries or seeds to keep alive. We'll just have to see if he's still around. We can probably tell from the holes he made when he was pecking at your house—recently or in the past."

"Well, you seem to know all about woodpeckers. Are you that knowledgeable about all wild creatures?"

"Aw, shucks, Lesley, ya shouldn't talk me up like that," he mimicked, and laughed loudly.

"Well, I mean it. I'm glad to find I contacted the right person. But how will you get rid of him—or them?"

"Oh, it's probably a him. If it was spring, he might have paired with a female. Then we'd have to look for eggs—in a cavity in a tree or some other suitable place. He'd be helping her take care of the eggs or feed their young."

"Sounds so sweet," she said, meaning it. "He sounds like such a nice little creature when you talk of him that way. How can we get rid of him without hurting him?"

"I'm glad you agree. You're a girl after muh own heart," he said, again mocking his own cliché. Then he became serious. "I have real trouble hurting wildlife. As I said, I try to find other ways than killing them," he reiterated. "Oh, I'm not against legitimate hunting, of course, so long as the hunters really need the meat—the food—and really use it for their families. But the deer herd is shrinking—fawn production is down. Still deer hunters will keep hunting whether they need the meat or not."

I like him, she thought. *He's not one of those guys who'd shoot Bambi just for the fun of it. And he can laugh at himself—a rare quality.*

"What can we do then—about the woodpecker?" she asked.

"Well, it would have been better and cheaper if you could have prevented the damage, but now that it's done, we'll have to look at the siding and see if there are still insects or their nests under the wood. Then you could try to scare the woodpecker away," he suggested.

She laughed. "What do you mean—stand outside and shoo him every time he comes? That won't work since I don't actually live there."

"No, that wouldn't work. There are all sorts of things you could hang around the exterior of the house to try to frighten him away. Sometimes we hang strips of aluminum foil or tape or cloth or plastic. Or we could hang tin can lids, pie tins, or almost anything that would move in the wind and reflect the sun. That movement and reflecting sunlight tend to discourage the woodpecker from returning to the site," he said, confidently displaying his knowledge and experience.

I sure got the right guy, she thought. *Jim really knows what he's talking about.* She returned to the reality of their trip when Jim turned off the freeway toward Silver Forks. "We're there already," she said. "I've been so interested in woodpecker-scaring that the miles flew."

"Yeah, just get me talking and it's hard to get me to shut up," he said, seeming somewhat embarrassed.

"Well, it really is interesting. Most of us don't even think about these things—until we find woodpecker holes in the walls of our house," she said.

"Well, there's more. You can also hang fake birds of prey—like hawks or owls—but I think they aren't really as effective. They tend to hang more motionless, and the woodpecker gets used to them being there. Oh, you can also use sound to frighten them. Just any device—like a radio—can help. Some people bang pans or shoot off cap pistols, but for that you have to be on site."

"Sounds fun, but it wouldn't work for me, I'm afraid."

They were entering the so-called Silver Forks business district, and Jim looked at the Chevy's dash and said, "Maybe I'd better get some gas here. I didn't take time to fill up after you telephoned—just rushed right over at your beck and call," he said, and looked at her with those heart-melting eyes and big smile.

"Well, I'm glad you did," she said.

He pulled into the town's only gas station and only gas pump, turned off the ignition, and got out. "Do you want to stretch your legs?" he asked.

"Well, maybe I'd better find the little room," she said. "The plumbing isn't working at my house, of course."

"Yeah, what do you do about keeping everything intact up there? How do you keep the pipes from freezing if there's no heat?"

"Well, I don't know that they haven't frozen. I haven't been in there for so long. But before I left, I had a man go there to drain all of the pipes. Then he put antifreeze in the traps under the sinks and other critical spots and turned off the water. I hope it worked."

"I hope so too, but that may not be legal," he said, then began filling the Chevy's tank at the slow-running pump.

Not legal? What does he mean? she wondered. "I'll just go inside then," she said, starting in the direction of the station.

"There's only one restroom for men and women, and I'm afraid they don't keep it up like they should," he warned.

"Okay, I'll close my eyes," she said, preparing for the worst. There was no one inside the office, but she saw the sign reading RESTROOM and found the door unlocked. It was as bad as Jim had suggested, so she hurried, glad for the bar of soap but not so sure about the dirty, rolling cloth towel. It wouldn't roll. She tugged but nothing happened. So she wiped her hands on her shirt and accepted the fact that she was in the country.

She heard metal on metal banging in the garage, so someone was about. She went outside, where Jim was hanging up the gas hose. "I'll take a turn, I guess, and try to find someone I can pay for the gas," he said.

He went inside, and Lesley walked around the truck to the passenger side. It was then that she saw it—the big, black sedan that she'd seen on the way from the airport and while she was eating both lunch and dinner. She could see that same vanity plate—FORTUNE. The car had come from the direction of the road leading from Silver Forks Mountain—the road from her house. It turned slowly into the entrance of the Silver Forks Health Spa, then disappeared among the evergreen trees lining the entry road. *Stranger and stranger,* she thought.

Just then Jim returned, taking her attention from the car. "You look like you've seen a ghost," he said, crossing to her side of the truck and opening the door for her. "What's the matter?"

"Oh, it's nothing—just being silly, I guess," she said, dismissing his concern.

"Well, if something's worrying you, tell me about it. Maybe I can help," he said, boosting her up into the truck.

"No, it's just my paranoia," she explained as he got into the truck and started it.

Why not tell him? she decided. "I keep seeing this big black car everywhere I go. It seemed to follow me from the airport. Then I saw it pull into a parking lot where I was eating lunch yesterday, and I saw it again last night in Park City. Just now it came down the mountain road and turned into the health spa."

"Big black car, huh? Well, there are a lot of big cars around Summit County—the wealthy and famous live here, at least part of the time, ya know," he said.

"Well, I know it's the same car that I see each time," she explained, "because it has FORTUNE on its plates."

He smiled. "Oh, yeah, it's not enough that he has a fortune—he has to brag about it. What do they call them— nouveau riche?" he asked.

"Newly rich? Then it's someone you know—someone from around here?" she asked, feeling somewhat relieved.

"Yes. I guess he isn't exactly newly rich—he's the son of the man who owned this whole town—the bank, the store, the spa—and most of the land hereabouts," he said, "and he inherited it. But most people think he's a real jerk," he added.

"Are you included in that group?" she asked.

"Well—let's just say that I wouldn't cross the street to see him, but I might cross the street to avoid him," he said, smiling.

"I'm relieved to know who it is, anyway, and that there's good reason for him to be everywhere. What's his name?" she asked.

Jim drove across the Silver Forks Creek bridge and started up Silver Forks Mountain Road. "Joseph Spencer Jr. is his formal title, but most old-timers call him Sticky Finger Joe," he said, laughing. "Of course, no one calls him that to his face. I guess I shouldn't have told you that."

"Sticky Finger—you mean he's a thief?" she asked, rather alarmed.

"Well, it's not my place to judge, I guess. Let's just say that nickname should serve as a warning to anyone about to have business dealings with him—I won't go beyond that," he said.

"I don't suppose I'll ever have anything to do with him—but I'm glad for the warning." After a pause, she asked, "What do you think he was doing on Silver Forks Mountain?"

"Well, it might not actually be Joe in his Lincoln Town Car. He has a lot of people on his payroll. It might be someone just using his car," he explained.

"Well, let's not talk about Joe anymore. We need to get back to the woodpecker problem."

"Yeah, let's. I was also going to suggest that if the damage to your siding is too bad, it might be well to remove some of it and underlay it with plastic or even metal sheathing. Or sometimes we hang netting close to the color of the building to keep the woodpecker from his pecking. Say, that reminds me of a woodpecker joke my daughter told me."

"Your daughter?" she said, unable to control her shock. "Then—you're married?" she asked, failing to hide her disappointment.

"No—I'm not married," he said quietly.

"Well, I didn't mean to pry again. I was just surprised, somehow, that you had a daughter," she said, attempting to regain her composure.

"It's all right. Most people are surprised," he said, and Lesley's imagination raced to all sorts of explanations for that. "She's my adopted daughter," he explained. "She's my older sister's daughter."

"I see," she said, relieved, but not completely understanding.

"No, you don't—see," he said rather bitterly. "My sister worked in the ski patrol at Park City. She was killed in an avalanche—trying to save someone else."

I've opened a bitter wound with my stupid, self-serving questions, she thought.

"I'm sorry. I didn't mean to bring up difficult memories for you."

He paused before continuing, "No, it's all right—you asked a logical question, I guess. Anyway, no harm done. I might as well tell you the rest of the story. My sister fell in love with a ski bum from Salt Lake City, and he took off for Colorado when she told him she was pregnant. He's never had anything to do with his biological daughter. I'm the only parent Julie has ever known. She was just a baby when my sister, Jenny, was killed—trying to save someone hardly worth saving. And I adopted Julie soon after." He paused, deep in thought. "Of course, my mother actually raises her," he admitted. "I've had a lot to learn about being a dad."

"I'll bet you're a great dad," she said. "I'm sure you're a kind one."

"That's nice of you to say. I try hard, but it's difficult trying to be a single parent. Thank heaven for Mom, but she's getting older and it's hard for her to return to raising a child," he said, concerned.

I want to ask if he's ever married—or why he hasn't married. Do I dare? she wondered.

Seeming to read her thoughts, Jim said, "You're wondering now if I've always been single. Right?" Not waiting for her answer, he continued, "Well, I never married—I came close once, but somehow we Shepherds—my sister and I—seem to scare off the good prospects." They had arrived at the gate to her property, so she didn't get the opportunity to respond to his negative assessment of himself.

"The gate's open," she observed. "I closed it myself when I was up here this morning. I didn't lock it, but I know I closed it."

"Well, the wind could have blown it open if it wasn't locked," he said. Then he saw the tire tracks along the lane. "No, looks like you've had a visitor—or visitors—there are two sets of fresh tire tracks in the snow."

"One of them is mine, of course, but the other is new. This morning all the tracks appeared to be frozen and less recent," she said.

"Maybe our Mr. Sticky Finger Joe did come to your place earlier."

"Why in the world would he come here?" she asked, thinking aloud.

"Like I said before, he owns most of the land around here—that includes most of the land surrounding your place. Maybe he's got his eye on your property too."

"Well, that would answer some of my questions."

"Questions?"

"Yes, last night I got a message asking me to call a phone number. It turned out it was Silver Forks Realty wanting to make an offer for a client on my house."

"So it might just be old Sticky Finger Joe who made the offer. Like I said, be careful," he warned.

"Oh, I told them the place wasn't for sale—that I wasn't interested. I'm not."

"Well that settles it, then. Maybe we'd better check how well your house is secured, while we're here, if Joe's nosing about," he suggested.

"Yes, I was thinking about that—or maybe even hiring someone to watch the place," she ventured.

"That might be a good idea."

He'd driven down the lane and pulled up to the front steps. "Okay, show me where the woodpecker had his fun," he said, climbing out of the truck. "Want to hear that woodpecker joke?" he asked, laughing.

"Do I really have a choice?" she asked, sensing that he was going to tell the joke anyway.

"Well, yes, but my daughter told it to me—she read it in a school *Kid's Club* magazine." He paused for a moment until Lesley came around to his side of the truck.

"Ready?" he asked, smiling.

"I'm ready," she said, preparing to laugh whether or not the joke was funny.

"What do you call a woodpecker with no beak?" he asked.

"I'm not going to guess."

"A headbanger!" he said, and laughed like he'd heard it for the first time.

Lesley laughed too, and she didn't have to pretend. "Tell your daughter I like her joke." *But don't tell her I'm beginning to like her father a bit too much,* she thought.

He went up the front steps, and Lesley followed. "The damage is over here," she said, going to the side of the house where the woodpecker had drilled.

He took one look and said, "This is old damage. He was here probably over a year ago, so I wouldn't worry about trapping him right now. He's probably moved on to better pickings."

"So I should just leave it?"

"You could just leave it, but I think it would be better to repair it. We could fill in those holes and grooves with putty after we make sure there aren't any more bugs hiding under the siding," he explained.

"How do you do that?"

"I have a stiff wire brush that I can run through the core gap," he said, showing her the line of holes forming a groove between the boards. "Then we can plug it, and you shouldn't have any more trouble right here. Of course, a woodpecker could go to work on another part of the house. They love this cedar wood siding, and when the building is this old, bugs are more likely to be under the wood—so he could come back in the spring or fall," he said frankly.

"Well that's the bad news, I guess. The good news is that you can help me fix the present damage, did you say?"

"Yes, I usually do that when I'm called out to trap something—then there's less chance I'll be called back again," he explained.

"You mean you're working yourself out of business? That doesn't seem very smart," she said, smiling.

"Well, no, I'm not a very smart businessman. I have to admit that. I care more about saving the animals than about the money, I'm afraid." He smiled, and Lesley realized she loved that smile and the truth behind it. She must have looked at him too long.

He raised his eyebrows quizzically and brought her back to reality. "Did you say there were some other critters getting into your house?" he asked.

"Oh, yes, around back. Follow me," she said, going down the side steps and treading through the snow where she had made footprints earlier. "Right there," she said, pointing to the open coal chute at the back of the house.

He went over, kneeled, and examined the tracks. "Looks like a cat," he said.

"A cat. You mean a bobcat?" she asked, alarmed at the thought.

Jim laughed again.

"What is it? What's so funny?" she asked, wondering if he was making fun of her fear that wild animals were in her house.

"Well, you don't have to be frightened to go inside," he said. "Looks to me like your visitor is a domestic mother cat and her kittens. She was probably left out here by someone trying to get rid of her, and she found a warm place to have her litter."

Lesley laughed, embarrassed at her unnecessary concern. "I'm relieved, but what should I do? Even if they're just tame cats, I can't leave them in there, can I?" she asked, revealing her lack of experience with animals.

"No, but let's go inside and see where she nested and make sure she's your only visitor. Then we can decide what to do. Maybe I can find a home for them," he suggested, sighing with resignation.

She looked at him. *A sweet man,* she thought. "I can't ask you to do that," she protested lamely. "I've already put you to too much trouble." Secretly, she was hoping he'd insist on finding them a home. *What will I do otherwise?*

"Let's take a look," he said, heading back toward the porch.

She followed dutifully, searching her pocket for the big old key to the front door.

She handed the key to him, and he placed it in the keyhole. The door swung open at his touch. "The door's unlocked," he said, surprised.

"That can't be," she said nervously. "I tried it earlier, and it was locked." It frightened her to think that someone—possibly Mr. Sticky Finger—had tinkered with the lock and had been inside her house. Then she remembered having left all her keys at the hotel front desk. Had someone copied them? *You're paranoid,* she told herself.

"Well, it doesn't take much to pick a lock like this," Jim said, stamping the snow from his feet and stepping inside the big entry hall.

"I'm upset that someone could break in so easily," she said. "I'll have to get some better locks installed."

"That's a good idea," he agreed, "and following through with your plan to have someone check on the place once in a while would be smart."

"Maybe it's foolish to try to hold on to this house when I really can't take care of it," she said, thinking aloud.

"No, it isn't foolish. I'd hold on to it if it were mine. There aren't many old houses like this around anymore," he said, looking up the stairway toward the second floor and then through the arch leading to the big, old front parlor and beyond that to the dining room.

Lesley followed his example, stamping the snow off her shoes and entering the hall.

"Pretty musty," he said, sniffing at the dust. "Achooo!" He pulled out a white handkerchief from his pants pocket. "'Scuse me," he said. "Dust gets to me."

"Me too," she said, looking around. "Oh, I'm ashamed that I've let this place go. It really needs some care and cleaning, doesn't it?"

"Yes, maybe you ought to rent to someone who would care for it," he suggested.

"My parents did that for about ten years, but I'd never thought of it. I wouldn't even begin to know how to be a landlord."

"Well, you have a lot to consider, but let's face the immediate problem first. How do I get downstairs?" he asked.

"The stairs down to the basement are beneath these main stairs," she said, pointing down the hall. "I'll show you." Her shoes actually left footprints in the dust, and she saw others— two sets—ahead of her in the hallway. "Look—two sets of footprints."

"Yes, two men from the size of the prints," he said suspiciously. "I wonder what old Sticky Finger could be up to."

"Do you really think he came here?" she asked.

"Well, if not him, I'll bet he's had someone up here looking over the place. I guess we could play detective and check his tire prints against his tires and his footprints against his shoes," he said, smiling.

"Well, unless we find something's missing or damaged, I won't go that far," she said, "but I do intend to find out why he—or someone—came onto my property and into my house."

"We'll look around after I check on the cats," he said.

They had reached the door to the basement, and she opened it for him. It creaked like a haunted-house door, and she peered into the darkness. "Oh, I forgot . . . it's dark down there; the electricity is off," she said.

"No problem," he announced, drawing a flashlight from his jacket pocket. "I was a Boy Scout."

"Always prepared—I get it. Well, I'm glad. I wouldn't want you to go down without light."

"You wait here. I'm pretty sure the mother cat and her kittens are all that's down there, but just in case—stay here." He descended the rickety wooden stairs.

"Be careful. I don't know how safe those old steps are," she warned.

"I'm always careful. I've done this kind of thing before, you know," he said, and moved out of sight.

She could hear him knocking around in the basement; he must have run into something. She backed away from the stairs, looking behind her into the kitchen and dining room areas. The furniture was in place, protected by dust covers, and the ancient refrigerator with high legs and a compressor on top sat quietly by the big black and white combination coal and electric stove. She remembered having come here several times with her parents while they cleaned the house. Once she'd climbed behind the stove to hide, chopping at her long hair with a pair of mother's scissors. Had she been angry at something? She couldn't remember.

The footprints of the earlier intruders went into the parlor, the dining room, and kitchen, and then back down the hall to the foot of the stairs leading up to the bedrooms. Lesley followed the prints to the bottom of the stairs. She squinted in the dim light and felt drawn into the semidarkness, but there were no footprints ahead of her on the stairs. *Guess their curiosity didn't extend to the second floor,* she thought. She touched the handrail as she ascended and noted that it was free of dust. *Strange, no footprints on the dusty stairs yet no dust on the rail.* She tried to shake off the eerie feeling that intensified as she climbed higher. Then at the top of the stairs, Lesley saw her—a wide-eyed girl staring back at her. She screamed and backed away, almost falling backward down the stairs. She laughed nervously, recovering when she realized she'd probably seen herself in the full-length mirror at the top of the stairs.

She heard Jim running up from the basement. "Lesley, are you all right? You screamed," he said, puffing as he reached her at the top of the second flight of stairs. "You scared me to death," he said, leaning against the handrail.

"I'm sorry. I came upstairs, forgetting about the mirror at the top. I scared myself—looking at myself," she said, embarrassed. Then she looked back toward the mirror and saw them—a child's footprints in the dust, heading along the upstairs hall away from the mirror. She turned back to Jim, "But there are footprints in the . . ." She looked again, pointing to the child's footprints, but they were gone. "I must be going crazy," she said. "I thought I saw footprints up here, too, but—I guess I didn't."

"Hey, maybe coming back here has been kind of a shock to you," he said, trying to reassure her. "These old places can be kinda creepy, but I doubt it's really a haunted house," he said, laughing.

"I'm sure you're right," she said, hesitating. They went back down the stairs to the entry. "I'd never thought of the house as creepy. Of course, I haven't been here that often. I've never really stayed here—lived here—that I can remember."

"Anyway, it doesn't look like anyone went up, so we don't have to worry about that. There's nothing in your basement but old boxes, dust, dirt, and a calico mother cat with five multicolored kittens. I'd say they're about two weeks old," he said, smiling.

"What can we do with them?" she asked, already including him in the plan.

"I'll go back down, find a box, and pack them up if the mother will let me. She's being protective—a good little mother," he said fondly.

"Oh, I can't wait to see them," she said truthfully. She'd never had much to do with animals but had always loved the look of kittens.

"You look around here—see if anything's been disturbed. I'll just be a minute," he said, reassuringly. "Don't look in any more mirrors," he warned, laughing as he went down the stairs.

Ha! Ha! she thought. It hadn't been a funny experience, and she couldn't entirely forget what she thought she'd seen. Had the image in the hallway been dressed in nineteenth-century clothing? Her mind really was playing tricks on her. She wandered into the big parlor. Again, everything was under dust covers and hadn't been disturbed except for the footprints in the dust. Lesley liked the room. The wide bay window looked out toward the big sky, the mountains, and the evergreen-dotted hillsides. Across from the window, a big fireplace with a wooden mantle and a mirror balanced the room. This time when she looked in the mirror, she saw only her reflection. *This room could be made very cozy.* Her thoughts were interrupted by Jim's return.

"Well, here they are," he said. "They're cute, and their mama has decided she can trust me."

He held out the box for Lesley to see the mother and her litter, but the mother wasn't so sure about her. She hissed and hovered around her cute babies. "She's a little wary of me," Lesley said, drawing back.

"Oh, she'll get used to you before we get back to Park City," he said. "Did you find any problems up here?"

"No, in fact no one seems to have disturbed anything, and no one has been upstairs as far as I can tell, so I guess we're done—for now," she said, almost wishing that weren't true.

"I'll put the cats in the truck. I have a little carrier they'll fit in. It's insulated so they'll be warm. We probably ought to stop in Silver Forks and get them some milk and food," he suggested.

"What about the coal chute? Shouldn't we close it so that nothing else can get in?" she asked.

"Yes, I'll see what I can do after I take care of the cats," he said in his helpful way.

He really had helped her—beyond the call of duty. *What would it be like to have someone like Jim to help with my problems all the time?* she wondered. She followed him onto the porch, taking pains to lock the front door securely. Maybe Jim would know a locksmith she could get to replace these old locks. She was becoming very dependent on him, she realized.

He returned from his duties with the cats. "I'll go back and see if I can secure that coal chute so nothing else can get in," he offered.

"Thanks so much. I've been a lot of trouble today, but I'm very grateful," she said.

"It's nice to be needed," he said, smiling that wonderful smile again.

Lesley had never known a man so sweet and cheerful. A lot of the creative types she had worked with were demanding, rude, and complaining. Jim was a very pleasant change. She felt so at ease with him. *What am I thinking?* She suddenly realized she was romanticizing their meeting, when in reality he was just doing his job—but he was doing it in such a nice way.

She jumped when he spoke, startled from her daydreaming. "I closed the chute and wired it shut," he said. "That should do until I come back to fix the woodpecker damage. Then I can secure it more permanently."

"Thanks," she said again.

"Aw, shucks, ma'am, it ain't nothin'," he said, mocking a western gentleman, she supposed.

"Sounds like you've been watching some old westerns," Lesley said, laughing.

"Yup! Ah do like John Wayne," he admitted.

"Well, so do I . . . especially the one with Katharine Hepburn. What's it called?"

"That's one of his later ones—*Rooster Cogburn*—but it's not really vintage John Wayne, ya know," he explained.

"How so?" she asked.

"Well, the plot line is thin—really just a vehicle for including Hepburn, in my opinion. It was kind of like another *African Queen*."

She was amazed at the depth of his evaluation. *This man is full of surprises,* she thought. "Well, you're right. Maybe I responded more to Hepburn than to Wayne."

"Yeah, that's probably it," he agreed. "Guess we'd better get back. I have an appointment in town this afternoon."

They went to the truck, and Lesley peeked at the cat and her kittens in the carrier, which Jim had secured in the truck bed. They appeared very content, and the mother didn't hiss at her this time.

They drove out the lane, and Jim stopped to lock the gate. When he climbed back in, he said, "You probably should replace that old padlock with a better one."

"Okay. Where could I get one?" she asked.

"Oh, we could stop at the general store in Silver Forks if you want. Then I could bring the padlock with me when I come back to finish my job," he suggested, driving the truck downhill toward the town.

"Okay, why not? You can help me pick out a good one," she said. "That reminds me, do you know of a good locksmith who could replace the door locks?"

"Yes, I do," he said.

"Could you help me locate him?"

"Don't have to look far," he said. She was beginning to think he really was like John Wayne, a man of few words.

"Well, where should I look?" she asked, trying to hide her irritation at having to pry for the information.

"Right next door," he said.

"Next door?"

"Yep, right next door—to you," he said, laughing.

"You mean you could change the locks, too?" she asked, not believing her good luck.

"Yep, I can do most household repairs," he said. "I'm a jack-of-all-trades."

"Well, would you have time to do that?" she asked, hoping so, because it would simplify matters so much.

"Yes, I'm really not that busy with my animal rescue business," he explained. "I mostly go out on emergencies. I have to be a handyman, to make a go of it."

"Then you could help me fix up the place?" she asked.

"Well, depends on what you need done, but I'm pretty good with odd jobs—small jobs," he said.

"Oh, it would be so wonderful if you could help me get my house back in shape," she said. "It would be such a relief if I didn't have to go around trying to find help with everything."

"Well, it will cost you," he said.

"I know. I expected to pay for it, but I'd rather pay you than someone else," she admitted. "I can trust you, and I wouldn't have to spend my entire vacation trying to get things done."

"Well, ma'am, after today, I'm at your disposal," he said, smiling and seeming glad at the thought.

They had come to the creek and drove over the bridge into Silver Forks. Lesley looked down the road toward the health spa but couldn't see Sticky Finger Joe's big black car. *I shouldn't judge him without knowing him,* she reminded herself, but somehow she trusted Jim's opinion about him.

He pulled up to the general store and asked, "Do you want to go in, or should I just buy the best lock they have?"

"Oh, I'd like to go in—to see what a general store is like," she said, climbing out of the truck.

They met at the aluminum and glass doors of the old-fashioned general store. "I know it's tacky and modern outside, but it really hasn't changed much inside. Bare, oiled wood floors, sawdust behind the meat counter, pickle barrels, potbellied stove, and bad lighting—just like in the old days—except for the prices. Old Sticky . . ." He stopped himself and rephrased. "Joe takes advantage of the fact that Silver Forks is isolated. He knows if you stop here, you must really need something. But I know the clerk, so maybe I can get her best price," he said with a wink.

Jim had described the store well. The fixtures and almost everything else looked very nineteenth century. It even smelled oily and old. There was a definite ambiance—it didn't look like every chain store of today. Then Lesley saw her—the clerk Jim had mentioned—and she knew why he'd winked. The woman looked more like a casino change girl than a cashier in an old-fashioned general store—big golden loop earrings, turquoise eye shadow, full and very red lips, and bleached straw hair. The tight jeans and sweater and the spike heels completed the image. Lesley smiled, realizing that Jim's wink was a way of preparing her.

"Well, look what the cat dragged in," the cashier said, smiling and striking a pose that Lesley was sure she thought voluptuous.

"Pearlie, you don't know how right you are," Jim said. "I've been trapping some big, mean cats." He laughed and looked at Lesley, sharing the amusement.

Pearlie's big eyes widened. "Really? Up on the mountain?" she asked, alarmed and fascinated.

"Yeah. They'd crawled into this lady's basement," he said, not correcting the misunderstanding.

"Well, I'm glad you told me. I'll warn everybody about it," she said.

"Yeah, I'd let Joe and his cronies know that they might have a bigger cat by the tail than they expected," he said, adding to the exaggeration but also, Lesley realized from his next words, motivating Pearlie to let Joe know that they'd been to the house and found his tracks there. "This lady owns the big house on Silver Forks Mountain Road," he said, nodding in Lesley's direction. "She's had trespassers there—some big cats—or at least they think they are," he said, laughing but also hinting that Pearlie should repeat his words to Joe.

"Well, I'll be sure to tell Joe," she said knowingly, probably figuring that Jim had been putting her on. She changed the subject. "What can I do for ya, love?"

"We need a padlock—a good one—but don't want to pay Joe's full price, of course," he said, and winked at her.

She smiled and winked back. "Okay, I'll see what I can do, but it might cost you down the line," she warned.

"Down the line?" Lesley asked Jim.

"She means that it might cost *me* later," he whispered. "But you'll see—I won't make any promises."

"Where are the locks?" he asked.

"Over on that counter next to the wall," she said, pointing an overlong, painted fingernail.

Lesley cataloged Pearlie along with Clara, the other interesting woman she'd met that day, in her mental storehouse of characters—a collection of observations that she had the habit of making as part of her profession. Who knew when she might get opportunity to draw on those observations in playing a Clara or a Pearlie?

She followed Jim to the far counter, noting that the place did seem to have some of almost everything. She liked a little wicker basket and decided to buy some cleaning supplies for the house—window cleaner, all-purpose cleaner, dust cloths, and a broom, dustpan, bucket, and mop.

"Say, you're really getting prepared for some hard work," Jim observed.

"I don't know how much time I'll have, but my house really does need a cleaning."

"Yes, it does. Maybe I could get you some help for that?" he ventured.

"Oh, could you? That would be wonderful." She realized that everything was coming out as "wonderful," but she really was happy at the turn of events for fixing up the house.

"Here's a good padlock," Jim said, holding it up.

"Looks good to me—sturdy," she said.

"Well, any lock is just designed to discourage a trespasser. If someone really wants to get in, all they have to do is climb your fence and then break a window. But only inexperienced thieves resort to that. Others usually want to hide their break-in. So should we buy this one? I'll try to get my *discount* on all the stuff you're buying," he said, laughing again.

"Yes, I'll buy it and all of these cleaning supplies. But I'll let you negotiate the price. Okay?"

"Okay," he said, picking up a bag of cat food and a quart of milk and helping her carry her purchases to the ancient cash register.

"Find everything you need?" Pearlie asked, still flirting with Jim.

I guess I shouldn't be surprised that other women find him attractive, Lesley thought.

"Yes, everything we need and then some," he answered.

"I'll just ring it up. Cat food, huh?" Pearlie asked, smiling.

"Yes, and when you tally it up, remember my discount," he said.

Lesley began to wonder just how friendly Jim and Pearlie really were but then realized that it was none of her business. *After all, we have a very temporary service arrangement—that's all,* she reminded herself.

She paid for the purchases and carried some of them toward the door.

Pearlie said, "Come again, Jim, when you're not with—when you're not in such a hurry."

"Now, Pearlie, you know I'm always in a hurry when I come this way. It's always just business with me," he reminded her. "If I need something—from the store—I'll be back," he said, and followed Lesley out.

She looked back to see Pearlie's pouting face and was pleased at Jim's having clarified his platonic relationship with Pearlie.

Jim checked on the cats while putting the purchases in the back of the truck.

"They're all cuddled up and keeping each other warm," he said. "Can't say the same for myself. The sun's going down along with the temperature," he said, rubbing his hands together.

They got inside, and he started the truck and turned up the heat. "Glad this old truck has a good heater. It'll warm up in just a minute."

"Oh, I'm okay. My coat's heavy enough to keep even a California girl warm," she said.

"Yeah, guess you're pretty thin blooded, living in all that sunshine."

"Sunshine and smog, you mean. California can get pretty damp and cold sometimes. You've heard that Sinatra song, haven't you?"

"Sure—'Hates California, it's cold and it's damp, that's why the lady is a—'"

He stopped just in time to avoid saying "tramp."

"Yes, go on," she teased.

"No, believe me, that's not what I think of you," he said, looking at her with what she hoped were admiring eyes. "I know California can be cold for short periods, but if we had a real winter, you'd know what snow and cold are," he said. "We haven't had a real winter for years. In fact, we're lucky that it's snowed as much as it has for the Olympics. If we hadn't had enough snow, it would have been pretty embarrassing."

They had a pleasant drive back to Park City in Jim's old but cozy truck. The western skyline was glowing yellow, predicting a beautiful sunset later in the evening.

Jim drove to Lesley's car where she'd left it at the Burger Barn and asked, "Care for another burger?"

"No thanks," she said, opening the door. "It was good, but I think I'll eat lighter tonight." She realized that her purchases were still in his truck. "Oh, what am I going to do with all the cleaning stuff?" she thought aloud.

"Oh, I'll take care of it—and the cats," he said, smiling.

"Oh, I'm so sorry. I've made so much work for you. But I can't take all of it, all of them, back to my hotel."

"No, you can't. And you haven't been so much trouble," he reassured her. "I've had a great day." He looked at her again with those heart-melting eyes, and she admitted, "I have too. Thanks for everything."

"Now, how about tomorrow? Do you want to go back with me?" he asked. "Otherwise, I'll need your keys."

"Well, I have a couple of days before the Sundance Festival begins. Why not? I'd like to go back," she said, hoping that she wasn't getting in over her head.

"I think maybe I'll bring my mom along," he said, "if you don't mind. She'll help you clean the place."

After hearing that, Lesley felt foolish at having worried about his intentions. *He's bringing his mother along.* "I'd love to have your mother come. I'd like to meet her," she answered sincerely. "Should we take my car?" she asked. "We'd have more room for everything."

"Oh, the truck's fine. Mom doesn't take much room, and she'll be our chaperone," he said, laughing loudly.

"I didn't really think we needed one," she said, actually relieved that his mother would be coming. She didn't want to rush into anything, and she wasn't sure she could trust her heart where this man was concerned. *He's really one of the nicest guys I've ever met,* she thought. "But I'm glad she's coming too."

"We'll pick you up at your hotel. Now which hotel did you say you're staying in?" he asked.

"I didn't. I'm at the Silver Princess."

"Okay, then let's go early and get some breakfast at McDonald's on the way. How about eight?"

"Sounds good to me. I'll be waiting in the hotel lobby, where I can see you out the window." She looked directly at him. "Thanks again for your help today—and tomorrow. I really am grateful."

He assumed his John Wayne impersonation again, "Being 'round ya pleases me," he said, and she recognized the line from the end of *Rooster Cogburn.* So she answered appropriately with what she remembered of Katharine Hepburn's response. "That's about the nicest thing anyone's ever said to me."

"You do know John Wayne movies," he said, and smiled his pleasure. "See ya in the mornin', ma'am," he added, and drove away, leaving her smiling too.

When she returned to the Silver Princess, the noisy crowd had completely taken over the lobby, so she fled to her room. On the floor just inside the door was an envelope. Stooping to pick it up, she glanced at the bedside table. A beautiful arrangement of lilies, daisies, mums, and small carnations in shades and tints of pink had been placed there.

There was no card attached, so she wondered, *A nice gesture from the hotel?*

She sat on the bed and absently opened the envelope and read:

Good morning! Hope your first day at Park City is a pleasant one.
Best wishes, Gareth.

P.S. Enjoy the flowers. Remember, you promised to come by for dessert.

Well, he's very determined, she thought. *And I have had a nice day.*

She decided not to go out that evening. Instead she'd order soup and toast from room service, read the scriptures and her novel, say her prayers, and go to bed early. She needed energy for tomorrow's work.

CHAPTER 7

Jim and his mother arrived promptly on Wednesday morning to pick up Lesley. She saw his truck through the lobby window and rushed out as Jim opened his door. "I'm ready for the big day," she said, pleased to see him again.

He walked around the truck with her and opened the passenger door. "Mom, this is Lesley. Lesley, this is my mother," he said.

"I'm so pleased to meet you, dear," the tanned and wiry little woman said. Lesley could see where Jim got his smile and blue eyes. "Call me Carol. Let me slide out so you can sit in the middle."

"Oh, no, you're fine, Carol. Don't move," Lesley urged.

"Nonsense, you need to sit by my boy." Then she leaned in to whisper, "Besides, I have orders. He told me he wanted it that way." She laughed a hearty laugh, which made Lesley like her even more.

"Okay," she whispered back. "We'd better obey orders. Thanks."

"What are you two whispering about?" Jim asked.

"Never you mind," his mother said. "We don't need to tell you men everything."

As directed, Lesley climbed in the middle, and Jim helped his mother get back into the truck, even though she didn't really need his assistance. Then he slid in beside Lesley and, very cozy in the narrow cab, they were off to McDonald's for breakfast.

Carol said, "I don't really like eating fast food, but Jim thought it would save time. I wanted to have you over for breakfast."

"Well, that would have been nice, but I do have a lot to do at my house," she said. "Thanks for the thought, though." *I really enjoy these warm, friendly people,* she thought.

"Well, I'll be there to help you," Carol reassured her. "I can still wield a mean broom and mop," she added, laughing, and Lesley didn't doubt her word. "By the way, I brought some cleaning rags, an extra broom, and another mop and bucket."

"Good, I'll be grateful for your help. Oh, I didn't think about the need for water," she realized aloud.

"I told you I was a Boy Scout," Jim bragged. "I brought a big insulated barrel of water. Also, I remembered the need for some heat—I brought a portable kerosene heater. How's that?"

"That's wonderful," she said. "Thanks. I would have gone off half-cocked, as my father used to say. I can't believe how helpful you've been. It's a real blessing that I called you."

"Well, we aim tuh please, ma'am," Jim said. "We'll work for two days and have that house cleaned and secured so that you won't have to worry about it anymore."

"Thanks so much," she said. "I've been thinking, too— could you help me find someone to check on the place once in a while—when I'm gone?"

"When you're gone?" Carol asked. "You're leaving? I thought you'd be planning to move into your place." She sounded disappointed.

"Well, I'd like to stay for a while. But it all depends on my work," Lesley explained. "I have to go where the acting jobs are, I'm afraid."

"We're planning to make you like it here so much that you won't want to leave," Jim said, smiling.

"It would be nice to have a place to call home, but I have to make a living," she said. "And I love my work. I'm not sure I could give it up."

"Oh, I didn't mean you should do that," Jim clarified. "Just suggesting that you could make your house a home base."

"I'd have to think about it. But I'd be worried all the time about the house, when I was away from it."

"Do you worry about it now?" Carol asked.

"No, not really," she admitted. "That's why I've neglected it, I guess."

"I can't see why it would be more of a worry if it's kept up than if it isn't," Jim said, logically. "At least you'd be protecting your assets."

"That makes sense. I'll think about it," she repeated. "But in the meantime, how about recommending someone to be a periodic watchman up there? Do you know anyone who lives near Silver Forks who might be interested?"

"Well, it seems Sticky Finger Joe is interested in your place. Maybe we could ask him," Jim said, laughing.

"Thanks a lot," she said, joining in the joke.

"Sticky Finger Joe?" Carol asked. "Jim, have you been spreading gossip about Joe Spencer?" Leaning past Lesley to look directly at her son, she said, "You look guilty. Shame on you."

"Mom, all I did was warn Lesley not to get involved in any business deals with him."

"I should think not. Don't you dare let Sticky—I mean, don't let Joe Spencer offer you anything without looking at what he's holding behind his back," she emphasized. "Oh, dear, I'm judging him too. I'm sorry."

"Well, don't be sorry. I'd rather be forewarned than end up in some kind of bad financial deal. Thanks for the warning," she said.

"Well, now I sound nosy, but what's he trying to get you to do?" Carol asked.

"I'm not sure, but I think he's trying to buy my Silver Forks house and property," she said.

"Oh, oh. Well, I won't say more—but remember what we've talked about," she urged.

Jim said, "Sorry I sidetracked your question, Lesley. I do know someone who would watch over your place."

"You do? Who?"

"He's right next door," he said, repeating the word game he'd used the day before.

"I'm not going to bite on that again, Mr. Joker," she said. "Are you saying that I could hire you to watch my place?"

"Don't know why not. I'm the most dependable fella I know," he said, laughing but serious at the same time.

"You don't know what a relief that would be to me. Thanks, Jim—for everything."

"As Ah said, we aim tuh please. Well, here we are at the golden arches. I'm hungry," he said, pulling into a parking spot.

Jim ate the Big Breakfast, his mother had an Egg McMuffin, and Lesley had fruit and yogurt and a plain toasted bagel.

"That won't be enough to get you through the day," Jim said.

"Oh, I hadn't thought of that. What will we do for lunch?" she asked.

Carol laughed. "He's pullin' your leg. I packed a lunch—at his request," she explained.

"I guess I should have known—he was a Boy Scout, after all." She smiled at Jim, grateful again for his resourceful ways. It was very nice to have someone else taking care of things, she had to admit.

Jim had gassed up the truck already, so they drove directly to Lesley's house on Silver Forks Mountain, where they found the gate still locked. She gave Jim the keys to the padlock and the front door. He unlocked the gate, then replaced the old padlock with the new one they had bought. "I'll hold onto one key. Here's the other for you," he said, handing her a key.

They stopped at the front porch stairs to unload the cleaning supplies, tools, water barrel, heater, and lunch from the truck bed. Carol, dressed in jeans much like Lesley's, pitched right in, working like someone Lesley's age instead of a woman in her sixties. She looked quite youthful, except for the gray streaks in her long, dark hair, which she'd pulled back in a ponytail. Lesley asked her, "Why don't you let us take this stuff inside?"

"Many hands make light work," was her only reply. Carol obviously was a woman accustomed to hard work, and Lesley admired her inner and outer strength. She said a silent prayer, thanking the Lord for bringing these hearty people into her life when she really needed them.

Once the supplies and equipment had been placed inside, Carol said, "Well, time's a wastin'—let's get to work. I'll start at the back of the house and you start at the front, Lesley, and we'll meet in the middle," she suggested after looking over the interior.

"Okay, I guess sweeping and mopping come first. Or should I shake out those dust covers?" Lesley asked.

"That might be a good idea. Otherwise, you'll get it all cleaned up and then have to do it all over again. You shake them outside on the front porch, and I'll start to sweep. This is really a beautiful old house," Carol said, heading back toward the kitchen and dining room.

Jim set up the water barrel in the entry and the heater in the parlor, then said, "I'm going to work on the woodpecker damage. Then I'll install the lock in the front door."

"That sounds good, Jim—and thanks for bringing your mother. She's a great lady," Lesley said, thinking that she'd also place Carol in her mental file of interesting women characters she might play someday.

"She is great, isn't she?" Jim said, and Lesley liked him for his sincere expression of love for his mother.

"Oh, by the way, how do you want to be paid? By the day? Or when the job's finished?" she asked.

"Well, you paid me the one hundred dollars up front, so why don't we wait until the job's finished to your satisfaction. Okay?"

"Okay, and I want to pay your mother for her service," she said.

"She could use it." He paused. "But you'll have to talk to her about that—she just wanted to help out—and supervise a little," he said, laughing.

"Well, thank heaven for both of you. I really didn't plan for this clean-up job, but I'm glad we're doing it." *And I'm also having fun being with you,* she thought.

"I'll head outdoors," he said, going out the front door.

Lesley began to gather the very dusty covers from all the downstairs furniture. She threw them in a pile on the front porch and went about the sneezy, dirty job of shaking them. Covered with dust afterward, she folded the covers and left them stacked outside.

Inside, she looked at the antique furniture, which was worn but still beautiful and usable. Nineteenth-century Victorian style abounded here, as it did in her hotel, and she felt momentarily transported back to another time. She swept the dust carefully out into the hall, where she met Carol doing the same from the kitchen and dining room.

Then they washed the woodwork, fireplace, counters, and cupboards. They didn't have a ladder, so they decided to leave the drapes, windows, mirrors, and chandeliers for the next day. Then, streaked with dirt, they sat down in the parlor to rest.

"It's almost lunchtime," Carol said, checking her rather mannish watch. "I'm hungry."

"I'll go check with Jim and see if he's ready for lunch. You rest for a while," Lesley said, going out the front door. She found Jim at the side of the house just finishing his job filling the woodpecker holes with putty.

"That should do the trick," he said as he saw her. "At least until he decides to try looking for bugs in another place. Maybe I should string some netting around the outside. What do you think?"

"Well, you know best. But if there's no more damage, maybe we could see if what you've done will take care of the problem," she suggested.

"You're probably right. I don't think he'd come back until spring anyway, so in the meantime I could watch for any signs of his visits. I'll just hang a few foil pie pans around. They might scare him off if he comes back," he offered.

"Your mother says it's time for lunch."

He held the door for her, and they went in together. Carol joined them in washing their hands with water from the barrel and then opened the picnic basket she'd placed on the dining room table.

They sat around the circular pedestal table, enjoying the good tiredness that comes from hard work. Carol had packed fried chicken, rolls with honey, coleslaw, and sodas—KFC menu but home cooked instead. The mountain air and the hard work combined to make that meal one of the best Lesley had ever tasted. She told Carol so. "Carol, you're a wonderful cook. This is delicious."

"Well, I've always enjoyed cooking—for people who like good food," she added. "I can't stand to cook for picky eaters."

Lesley placed that bit of advice in her memory bank. If she were to eat with the Shepherds in the future, she'd better come hungry.

After lunch Carol and Lesley packed away the leftovers and began mopping the floors. Jim went back to the truck for the replacement locks and some tools.

Lesley worked in the living room and entry while Carol returned to mopping the kitchen and dining room floors. They finished at about the same time. Carol was showing her first signs of fatigue that day, and Lesley offered to empty the mop buckets outside while Carol sat down.

"I'll take you up on that. 'The old gray mare, she ain't what she used to be,'" she said, laughing.

"Are you kidding? I couldn't keep up with you today," she said.

"Oh, I can still do most things, but I tucker out faster than I used to," she said, sighing and leaning back on the sofa.

Lesley started toward the front door with one of the buckets, but Carol stopped her with a question. "Why do you want to keep running all over the country? You oughtta settle down and make this place a home for yourself."

She set the bucket down before answering, giving her time to think about Carol's question. "Well, I really do love to act.

It's been my life since I was in high school. But I would like to settle in one place for a while. Unfortunately, theater and film in the United States are centralized on the East and West Coasts—live theater in New York and movies and television in Los Angeles. So I've had to make a temporary home in L.A.," she explained.

"Oh, I understand what you're saying, but don't you ever think about marriage and a family?" she asked pointedly.

"Of course—that's in my plans or at least my dreams—someday."

"Well, don't wait too long. Marriage and family is really what life is all about, you know, when all is said and done," she advised.

"Well, you may be right—when all is said and done," Lesley repeated. Carol had given her something to think about as she picked up the bucket and went outside.

Jim had hung the pie pans, which appeared rather ludicrous, turning near the eaves, but she trusted that he knew what he was doing. He was about to start replacing the front door lock.

"Where did you get the lock?" she asked.

"Oh, I got one for the front and one for the backdoor last night—in Park City. These are good locks—almost pick proof," he added.

"You really are a handyman," she said with real admiration. "I'm glad I found you." Then she realized that her words could be taken two ways.

"I'm glad you *found* me too," Jim said, smiling with that breathtaking combination of white teeth and blue eyes.

Lesley blushed and was trying to think of something else to say when they heard a yell from Carol inside. They rushed in and saw her standing in the center of the room, staring at the ice-frosted bay window.

"What's the matter, Mom?" Jim asked.

"I—I can't see it now, but I could swear there was a word in that melting frost on the window," she whispered.

"A word?" Lesley asked.

"Yes, I was sitting on the sofa looking toward the bay window. I turned away for a second, and when I looked back, the word *WATER* was printed on the window. I swear I saw it. But it's gone now," she said, finding a chair.

"Mom, you've maybe overdone it today," Jim said, going to her. "Let me get you a drink."

"No—no, I'm all right now. It just startled me," she said. "I'm seeing things, I guess."

"Well, I had a similar experience yesterday," Lesley said, trying to reassure her. "I thought I saw a child—a girl—in the mirror at the top of the stairs, but then decided it must have been my own reflection." *But what about the disappearing footprints?* Then a picture of the young girl appeared in her memory. *It couldn't have been my reflection—she wore a dress, a nineteenth-century dress,* she realized.

"Yeah, Mom. The word would still be there if someone had actually written it," Jim said. "Like I told Lesley yesterday, sometimes these old places can spook you."

"Yes, that's it, I'm sure," she chuckled bravely. "I'm okay now. I guess *WATER* isn't too scary a word anyway."

"No, maybe the house was just saying thank you for bringing some water to clean it," Lesley suggested, laughing and trying unsuccessfully to lighten the mood.

Jim said, "Well, you two sit here where it's warm. I'll just install the new lock in the front door. Then we'll go home, and I'll do the backdoor lock tomorrow."

"Sounds good to me," Lesley said, feeling that the coziness of the parlor had diminished with the memory of the footprints and the old-fashioned girl she thought she'd seen at the top of the stairs, and now with the mysterious writing on the window. She thought, *I have a vivid imagination, but Carol seems to be a real no-nonsense lady. It's hard to believe she'd react so strongly to something she'd imagined.*

Jim finished the lock. Then they loaded the barrel and the picnic basket in the truck and locked the house securely. *Let Sticky Finger try to pick that lock,* Lesley thought, pocketing the key Jim gave her.

Three weary souls returned to Park City, their only stop the restroom at the Silver Forks gas station. Lesley couldn't wait to have a bath and relax for the evening, but Jim had other ideas. "How about dinner tonight, Lesley. Want to join us?" he asked, without consulting his mother.

Carol chimed in, "Yes, come over to our house for dinner and you can meet Julie—Jim's daughter."

"That sounds nice, but I have another idea. You provided breakfast and lunch. Why don't you let me take care of dinner," she suggested.

"But you don't have a kitchen, dear," Carol said seriously.

"Oh, no, I wouldn't cook for you. Even if I did, I wouldn't want you sampling my cooking. Let's go out to dinner—on me. Please, let me do this to thank you," she begged.

"Well, we'd have to go home and get cleaned up first," Carol said. "How about it, Jim? Want a night out on the town?" she asked.

"Sounds fun to me," he said. "What time?"

"I'll come pick you up this time—in my Navigator—if you'll tell me how to get to your place," she said.

"Better than that, we can show you." He drove into the old residential streets near downtown Park City and stopped in front of a quaint nineteenth-century cottage with an inviting front porch.

"This is where we live now. It was a miner's house," Carol said. "We moved into town after my husband died. Thought it would be easier for everybody—for me and Julie especially. I'm not sure that Jim likes it as well as our little acreage farther out of town. But the newcomers are buying up all the land around it and building great big houses. There won't be much country left out there in a few years," she said wistfully.

"Oh, Ah do miss the wide open spaces," Jim agreed, laughing, "but I get more handyman business living here than I would in the old place. People can find me easier here. So it's a toss-up, I guess."

"Well, it's a charming house," Lesley said. "I love it. Kind of a storybook cottage."

"You are a make-believe girl," Jim said, smiling.

"Yes, I guess I am—always have been," she said. "Well, take me to the hotel, and I'll come back to get you at about six thirty. Would that be good?"

"Just right," Carol said. "I may as well get out, as long as we're here. I'll tell Julie our plans so that she can get her homework done before we go." She climbed out of the truck and said, "See ya in a while."

"See you, Carol. And thanks for all your help today," Lesley said.

"You're very welcome."

"Your mother's so sweet," she said as Jim drove up the hill toward her hotel.

"She likes you."

"I like her too."

"I like you too," he said. "I've enjoyed our two days together. Hope you have."

"I can honestly say that I have. We've worked hard but it's been so different . . . it almost feels like a vacation."

When Jim stopped in front of the Silver Princess, Lesley stepped out and repeated, "I like you—too." He smiled. She smiled. What a day it had been, disturbed only by Carol's mysterious experience with the disappearing word on the window. But they still had the evening to look forward to. Lesley was reenergized by the thought.

CHAPTER 8

While taking her bath, Lesley naturally had water on her mind. But Lesley was haunted by Carol's thinking she saw that word etched on the frosted window. Were animals and Sticky Finger the only intruders in her house, or were there things going on there that she really didn't dare think about? Was someone trying to frighten her away from her house? She hadn't thought to check for footprints in the snow below the bay window.

She pulled herself back to reality and realized the town would be bustling with tourists and festival patrons and she should have made a reservation for dinner. After toweling off, she put on the terry robe, went to the yellow pages, and turned to "Restaurants." She began calling those that had advertisements showing their specialties but without success. Every restaurant was booked until nine PM or later. *What should I do?* she thought.

Then she decided to call the front desk. "Do you have a concierge?" she asked the clerk.

"No, we don't, ma'am. We're too small for that. Could I help you with something?" he asked pleasantly.

"Well, this is Lesley Kern. I'm planning to take some guests to dinner and realized I don't have a reservation. I've tried everywhere, but every place is booked until late. Can you think of anywhere I wouldn't need a reservation?"

"Well, Ms. Kern, I do have a thought. It has come to my attention that you'll be welcome at the Silver Fork Restaurant anytime you want to go there," he suggested in a conspiring tone.

"Oh, it has, has it?" She thought a moment, then decided, *I guess there's no choice, and why not?* "Okay, could you call the Silver Fork and tell them I'll be bringing a party of four for dinner at seven?"

"I'll do that, Ms. Kern. I'll call you back if there's a problem, but I don't think there will be. If you don't hear from me, you're all set," he said. "Anything else?"

"No, and—thank you."

"Happy to serve you, ma'am," he said, and hung up.

She dressed up a bit but didn't want to do the Hollywood thing—a simple black pant suit and silver earrings seemed right. Then she grabbed her warm coat and gloves and headed for the hotel garage. The parking spaces were narrow, but she managed to squeeze into the car and back out. Again the garage door opened automatically at her approach.

How grateful she was that the weather had been so beautiful—chilly but sunny—and the roads were clear. She gave silent thanks for the wonderful days she'd had in Park City and for the helpful and interesting people she'd met.

Then she began to wonder if she'd done the right thing in making a reservation at the Silver Fork. Would Gareth Sanders be working? Was she creating a potential problem in taking Jim and his family there? Then she laughed at herself. *You think they're going to fight over you or something?* Anyway, the deed was done, and she had tried without success to get a reservation elsewhere. She was hungry and knew the food would be good. Also, she was looking forward to being with Jim so she dismissed her worries about where they were going.

She found the Shepherds' little house without difficulty and went to the front porch. Raising her hand to knock, she was startled by the opening door. "Come in, please," said a cute, tow-headed ten-year-old with freckles on her nose. She wore a floral print shirt and skirt. The girl looked up at Lesley with wide blue eyes, and Lesley thought, *Your mother must have had the same blue eyes as Jim.*

She smiled and said, "You must be Julie. I'm Lesley."

"I know. Dad says you're a movie star. You're pretty," she said, then ushered Lesley inside.

"Well, thank you, Julie, and so are you—very pretty."

She led Lesley from the narrow entry into a small, nineteenth-century parlor furnished with items that must have been brought from the Shepherds' ranch house: a leather horsehair loveseat, a big matching leather rocking chair, a library case, a corner knickknack shelf, and several tiger-maple side tables. An early twentieth-century table radio and a later innovation—a small television—shared space on a table. Quilted satin and needlepoint-covered pillows were arranged neatly on the love seat. Lace curtains adorned the windows, and a braided, multicolored, oval rug covered the wooden floor. It was a delightful, cozy room.

Julie directed her to sit on the love seat and said, "Dad and Grandma will be ready in a minute." She sat in the big rocker, dwarfed by its size, then stared at Lesley for several moments before asking, "Do you think I could see one of your movies?"

"Well, sure, I think that could be arranged. Do you have a VCR or DVD player?"

"Yeah, we have a video player. Would any of your movies be on video?"

"Yes, a couple in which I have very small roles are on video. I act mostly in television movies, and most of them don't come out in video versions, I'm afraid."

She looked disappointed, so Lesley added, "But my newest movie will be on television soon. I'll try to find out when and let you know."

"Okay, that would be cool," Julie said. Then another shy, quiet moment followed before Jim came in, filling the little room with his size and presence and dressed in an off-white western-cut shirt and brown pants and boots.

"Hi, sorry to keep you waiting. Looks like you two have met," he said, smiling and looking back and forth from Lesley to Julie.

"Yes, we have," Lesley said, standing. "Julie is a very good hostess, and she's so bright and charming."

"Is that the Julie I know?" he asked, teasing. "She must really be using her company manners. The girl I know is quite a little handful." He reached out and gave Julie a hug. And, of course, Lesley was touched at the sight of their mutual love. She thought, *This man is perfect. How come no one has snatched him up?*

Carol's entrance interrupted Lesley's thoughts. "Well, I've done all I can with myself," she said, laughing. In fact, she looked very nice in her unique style—a denim pant suit and Navajo turquoise-and-silver jewelry.

"I love your clothes," Lesley said honestly. "Shall we go?"

They picked up coats from the entry hall rack and went out to the car. Jim opened a rear door for his mother and daughter, then moved around to open Lesley's. She was already halfway in, used to taking care of herself, so he closed her door and then sat beside her up front.

Lesley made a U-turn, and Jim asked, "Where are we going?"

"Oh, I had to make a quick decision when I realized how busy the restaurants would be tonight. I tried everywhere to make a reservation but was unsuccessful. I finally was able to make a reservation at the Silver Fork," she said. "Will that be all right?"

He looked at her quizzically then said sarcastically, "Pretty fancy."

"Well, I ate there once before and the food was good, so I thought it might be all right," she said.

"Oh, the food's great. No problem with *that*," Jim said, suggesting by his emphasis that there might be some other problem.

"Well, I'm looking forward to eating at a nice place," Carol said. "None of that fast food for me."

"Do they have grilled cheese sandwiches?" Julie asked.

Lesley covered a smile. "I don't know for sure, but I think it could be arranged," she answered. "If not, I'm sure they'll have something you like. They have a big menu."

Luckily, a car was pulling out of a parallel parking space about a half block from the restaurant. Lesley grabbed it since parking on Main Street was very limited. "Do you mind a short walk?" she asked.

"No, we're up to it," Jim said, and she sensed a change from his usual genial mood.

She tried to ignore it, but it seemed evident that she'd made a poor choice of restaurants as far as Jim was concerned.

He helped them out of the car onto the narrow, cracked, and uneven sidewalk—part of the charm of the place, Lesley supposed. Jim walked with his mother, and Lesley was left to walk beside Julie, who reached out and took her hand. She was touched by Julie's accepting and friendly gesture. She hoped that Jim's decision to walk ahead with his mother was motivated by his concern for her welfare, rather than by his displeasure at something she'd said or done.

There was a line of people waiting when Lesley gave her name to the host, who said without hesitation, "Yes, Ms. Kern. We're glad to have you back again. Follow me, please." He led the way to a table near a window marked RESERVED. "Will this be all right, Ms. Kern?" he asked deferentially.

"Yes, fine, thank you," she said, and sat as the host held her chair. Jim seated Julie at one side of Lesley and Carol at the other. Then he sat at a distance, across from Lesley, still appearing a bit sullen.

"Seems they know you pretty well here. The big movie star treatment, I guess," he said sulkily.

"No, as I said, I've been here once before, but Gareth—Gareth Sanders, the owner, was seated next to me on my flight from L.A. He told me about his restaurant, and I tried it the first night I was here." She felt somewhat resentful at having to explain why they went there. Besides, wasn't she treating them? She thought, *Maybe this dinner isn't such a good idea after all.*

Julie broke the ice. "I like it."

And Carol added, "Well, I've never been here, but it's nice," she said. "Thanks, Lesley, for bringing us." She glared at her son, and from his reaction, Lesley sensed that Carol might also have kicked his shin under the table.

He looked up from his hands. "I'm sorry, Lesley. Of course it's a nice place. Thanks—for bringing us," he said with half a smile.

Lesley didn't respond but said instead, "Well, the food is good. Anything look interesting to you?" There was a pause, so she suggested, "The charbroiling smells good. How about a steak?"

"Sounds good to me—a small one," Carol said. "How about you, Julie?"

"I'd like a grilled cheese sandwich, but I can't find it on the menu," she answered.

"I'll ask them if they can make one," Lesley offered. "Jim?"

"Yeah, somehow I can't eat a steak in here," he said, looking about at the mounted trophy deer heads on the wall. "I'll take a chef salad."

The waiter came, took their orders for beverages, a grilled cheese sandwich, two steaks, and a chef salad, saying, "Thank you, Ms. Kern," as he left for the kitchen.

"They really do seem to know you here," Carol remarked. "Guess we're with a real celebrity."

That made Lesley a bit uncomfortable, since she'd hardly played the celebrity in her dealings with the Shepherds. "No, as I explained, it's just that I met the owner, and I guess he told the staff to take good care of me if I came here. I don't always get the star treatment, believe me," she said.

"Oh, I didn't mean anything, dear," Carol said, reaching over to pat her hand. "I'm just proud to be with you."

"Thanks, and I'm glad to be with you," she said. "Frankly, I usually eat alone, and that can get old."

"Well, you don't have to eat alone while you're here," Carol said. "You're welcome at our table anytime."

"You're so sweet. Thank you."

Julie leaned across the table to her grandmother and whispered, "I need to use the bathroom."

"Oh, I'll take you, dear," Carol said, rising from her chair. "Will you excuse us for a moment?"

"Of course," Lesley said, "but hurry back. The service is fast here." She wasn't sure she wanted to be left alone with Jim in his present mood.

Carol and Julie headed for the rear of the restaurant, and their absence left Lesley and Jim with an awkward lull in the conversation. Finally, she decided to tackle Jim's attitude head-on. "Is something the matter? You're not acting like the Jim I've known the past two days."

"Oh, nothing's wrong really. I'm not the simple country hick you may think I am. I can be moody—and jealous, I'm afraid," he said, looking down at his hands again.

"Jealous? Of what? Of whom?" she asked incredulously.

"Well, I guess you can tell I don't like this place. Like its owner, it's kind of a monument to exploiting the environment," he explained, gesturing at the mounted animal trophies on the walls.

"Oh, I guess it was thoughtless of me to bring you here, knowing your feelings about wildlife."

"Well, that's part of it—not all," he said, then stopped.

"Go on. I'm listening," she urged, anxious to learn what was going on in his handsome head.

"Well, it's like this. I don't think much of your friend—Mr. Sanders—the owner of this place," he blurted out.

"My friend—but I just met him briefly on the plane. He's hardly a friend. He was very nice, but he's only an acquaintance," she explained, wondering about this newly revealed insecurity in Jim's personality. "All I know about him is that he owns this place and that he's been very cordial to me."

"You're going to think I don't trust anyone around here," he said.

"What do you mean?"

"Well, I warned you against Sticky—Joe Spencer. Now, if I say anything about Gareth Sanders, you'll think I'm paranoid or worse—just jealous."

"No, I appreciated the information about Joe Spencer, especially since he may be the one who wants to buy my property. And I don't really know Gareth Sanders, so I don't feel the need to defend him—or myself."

"Oh, forget I said anything. We—Gareth and I—have had a few run-ins at city council and county commission meetings.

He has money and influence—I don't. So his opinions and wishes often win support. And our thinking on most issues couldn't be further apart," he explained.

"You're on the council and the commission?" she asked.

"No, but would it surprise you if I were? Think I'm too much of a yokel to be involved in politics?" he asked, smiling again at last. "I just attend a lot of council and commission meetings."

"No, no, I didn't mean that you wouldn't be a good council member. You just hadn't mentioned your interest before. I'm pleased, actually, to know someone who cares enough about the future of this place to get involved. Now *I'm* sounding like a politician," she said, embarrassed at delivering a little speech.

"No, you're right. Too many people complain about things but do nothing about them. They don't vote, and they don't attend meetings where decisions are made," he said. "Now who's making speeches?" He laughed.

She was relieved to see him laugh at himself again. "Well, that's one of the things I've liked about you—you really seem to care about your world—your environment. I'm sorry I brought you here. I really had no idea that it would make you so—so uncomfortable, but I honestly did try to find another restaurant."

"Oh, like I said, it's part bitterness and part—jealousy, I guess. Somehow I didn't like the idea that Gareth Sanders knew you before I did—but I have other reasons for not liking him much. I guess I'm still juvenile in some ways," he said, looking out the window.

"Well, I'm flattered if you're just a little jealous, but there's no reason to be," she stressed.

"Okay, I've had my little sulk. Now, let's enjoy the rest of the evening," he said, smiling. "I really am sorry I acted so childish."

"Forget it. We all do that sometimes."

Further conversation was interrupted by the return of Julie and Carol. "Oh, good," Carol said. "They haven't brought the food yet."

When the dinners came, Carol said, "Lesley, I hope you'll join us in a family tradition." Then she reached out to clasp hands with Jim and Lesley. Jim took Julie's hand, so Lesley followed his example, a bit awkwardly, and reached out to Julie. Then, oblivious of other patrons, Carol bowed her head and said a quiet, simple prayer of thanks and blessing. Lesley was surprised but moved by her gesture, and a spirit of peace changed the atmosphere.

They enjoyed their dinners, and Lesley was somewhat relieved that Gareth didn't come to their table. She supposed that Jim and Gareth would have behaved civilly, but then she didn't really know either of them.

When Lesley took them home, Carol said, "We'll bring Julie tomorrow to help. She's out of school on Saturday anyway, so we'll bring her along."

"Yeah, I'm glad you came here, Lesley," Julie said.

"Julie, it will be fun having you along. I'll drive," she offered.

"Oh, I have another truck," Jim said. "It's an extended-cab Chevy. Just as comfortable as a car. Besides we've got to haul a ladder and some other stuff."

"Well, all right. Same time, same place tomorrow?" she asked.

"Yeah, we'll pick you up and stop again for breakfast. Okay?" Jim suggested.

"Okay, that sounds good."

He opened the door for Julie and Carol, and Lesley wished them good night. Julie and her grandma walked hand in hand toward their house. Then Jim came around to the driver's side. Lesley opened the window, and he leaned in. "Forgive me for my behavior earlier?"

"There's nothing to forgive. I was just a little surprised at your reaction. I understand now," she said. "Let's forget it."

"Thanks. It won't happen again," he said, and leaned in further—to kiss her.

She didn't resist. With a simple "good night," he left her and walked toward the house. She didn't move for several minutes, still surprised at what had just happened. Then she drove back to her hotel, not really aware of where she was going.

CHAPTER 9

The next morning's activities were much like those of the previous day, except that Julie joined them for breakfast and for the ride to Silver Forks. She sat in back with Carol and seemed very content to come along.

"This really is a great little truck," Lesley said, when they climbed in following breakfast.

"Yep, it's not a gas guzzler, and it's another good ole Chevy—as American made as they come these days," he replied.

"So your patriotism includes buying American?" she asked, making conversation.

"Yes, it does. Some say it doesn't really matter anymore, because American car companies use foreign-made parts, but it seems logical to me that if you buy foreign cars, the money goes back to companies in those countries. Doesn't make sense to me to do that since one in six American jobs is related to the auto industry. And the trade deficit is huge." He paused and took a breath. "Now I'm on my soapbox again. Gotta be careful about getting me wound up," he said, laughing.

"I've never bought a new car, but I'll think of what you've said if I ever do."

They talked about Jim's work most of the way to Silver Forks. Then as they pulled into town, Jim said, "Guess we better make a pit stop here."

"Jim, use your manners," his mother scolded. "You shouldn't be talking that way to ladies."

"I'm sorry, Mom. I'll repent," he said.

"Well, you'd better—but you've reminded me of something—speaking of repentance. Lesley, will you come to church with us Sunday morning and then come to dinner after?" Carol asked.

"Well, yes, I'd love to." She paused and took a deep breath. "But *only* if Jim agrees to come along," she said, braving his possible negative reaction.

"So you're really making me pay for that kiss," he whispered between his teeth.

"If you want to look at it that way—yes," she said, smiling.

"Well—I'll come—but I may just stay for sacrament meeting," he warned. "Now, you ladies go freshen up while I fill the gas tank."

Lesley felt a warm glow as they walked together toward the gas station. This family feeling was very nice, and the Spirit was telling her that she'd done the right thing inviting Jim to join them at church. *Maybe Carol's right—I could make my house here a home base.*

Then she saw it—the long black car, Joe Spencer's Lincoln—turning in to the entrance of the spa road and disappearing behind some evergreen trees. A cloud crossed over the sun, and she shivered from more than the cold.

As Lesley was returning to the car, Jim saved her from her worried imaginings. "Well, let's go. Still have a lot of work to do," he said.

"Yes," she agreed, "and I have to leave earlier this afternoon so that I can get to the Sundance Festival opening in Salt Lake."

"Oh, I'd managed to forget that's why you came to Park City," he said. "We've been so busy, I was getting to think fixing up your house was your reason for coming here."

"Well, no, I really didn't plan all this work on the house, but I'm so glad that we're doing it—that you're all helping me."

"What time do we need to leave?" he asked.

"About three. Do you think that's enough time to do all the work?"

"We can get the essential stuff done, anyway. Then maybe we can come back next week," he suggested.

"Okay, maybe we can," she said, thinking that would be a good way to continue this developing relationship.

When they reached her property, the gate was padlocked securely, and there were no signs of intruders. *Maybe they've been scared off by Jim's hint to Pearlie that we knew who had invaded my house,* she hoped. She really didn't want to deal with Joe Spencer or his messengers.

Again they carried in the supplies: the ladder, the water barrel, the lunch Carol had prepared, and the other things they needed for cleaning and repairs. Julie helped without complaint, proving herself a product of her grandmother's hard-working example and teaching.

Jim groaned and set down the heavy water barrel, then turned on the kerosene heater. Then he went to the back door to install the new lock. Lesley, Julie, and Carol cleaned the downstairs windows, mirrors, and chandeliers and took down the drapes and curtains to be washed or dry-cleaned later in Park City. Julie was the first to sit down. "I need a break," she said. "This is harder work than at school."

"Sweetheart, I appreciate your help so much," Lesley said. "Let's all take a break."

They joined Julie, sitting in the front parlor, but the moment they sat down, her youthful energy rebounded. She jumped up. "I'm going out to see what Dad's doing," she said, and was gone down the hall toward the back door.

"Oh, how I'd like to have all that pep," Carol said, laughing.

"I think you do pretty well," Lesley said. "And Julie is so much like you. You've done so well—raising her."

"Well, it's been hard—for all of us—but it's also been a blessing. Jim grew up in a hurry when he chose to adopt her. But Julie's kept me young. I've had to keep going—for her," she said. "Overall, it's worked out. Of course we still miss Jenny, Julie's mother, every day and wish the accident had never happened."

"Jim told me a little about it. I'm sure it was so difficult for all of you," she sympathized. "Do you talk about it—with Julie?"

"Oh, we didn't keep anything from her. She knows she has a biological father somewhere, and she knows about her mother's accident. Of course, she's really never known her father and can't remember her mother—so our substituting for them is the only reality she's experienced." She wiped away a tear with the back of her hand.

Lesley went to her, sat beside her, and hugged her. "You're wonderful people—you and Jim. I admire you so much for what you've tried to do for Julie," she said honestly.

"Well thanks, dear. But, of course, I worry about the future. I don't know how well Jim could handle a teenage daughter without me around. Their future happiness is all I care about now. I've achieved most of my other goals in life."

"You seem so healthy and so strong for your age," Lesley said. "You'll be around for a long time, I'm sure."

"Hope so, but Julie really needs a mother—not just a grandmother."

Lesley didn't know how to respond to that, so she repeated, "But you and Jim have made her happy and secure. At least she has a good father—a father who cares about her." She paused. "Jim said that Julie's mother died helping someone in trouble on the ski slopes, but that doesn't seem to give him much comfort," Lesley observed.

"No, it doesn't. In fact, that's been one of the most difficult things for him to bear," Carol said. "I was finally able to forgive and forget, but Jim took it pretty hard—the idea that Jenny was called out with the ski patrol to help—to help a man who was cross-country skiing in a closed area where he shouldn't have been in the first place. They got him out, but Jenny was buried in a small avalanche."

"Oh, how horrible for you." She took Carol's hand.

"Yes, the other ski patrol members went right to work to dig her out, but they couldn't get to her in time." Carol paused, lost in memory. Then she sighed and continued, "My faith in the gospel kept me going—knowing I'd see Jenny again—but it wasn't so easy for Jim to accept—or forgive. Every time Jim sees *him*, the bad feelings come rushing back."

"Then you knew the skier—the man who Jenny went to help?" Lesley asked.

"Yes, we knew—know him. He was a newcomer to the area when the accident happened. I guess that helped me to accept his stupidity in going onto those closed slopes. I told myself that he didn't really understand the danger," she explained.

"You said that Jim sees him—he's still here?"

"Yes, he's still here." She waited a moment, as if trying to decide whether to say more. "You see, that's part of the reason Jim was so upset last night—at dinner," she said, looking away toward the bay window.

"You don't mean . . . ?" Lesley couldn't finish her question.

"Yes, Jim isn't usually that bad tempered. Gareth Sanders was the skier that Jenny went up to save. Somehow, Jim can't accept the fact that Gareth is still alive—thanks to Jenny and her crew—and Jenny's gone."

"He blames Gareth?" she asked.

"Oh, I wouldn't really say that. He doesn't exactly *blame* him. It's just that Sanders seemed to have had so little remorse about it. I think that if he'd even come around to express his sympathy—to say he was sorry—and to express his gratitude for Jenny's sacrifice, we all would have felt better about it. But he didn't. I just told myself that he didn't know us personally and that it was natural that he wouldn't feel he was the cause of Jenny's death." She sighed deeply again. "But it's all water under the bridge. Trying to blame someone for Jenny's death won't bring her back—and resentment can be hurtful. Jim struggles with that. I pray that someday he can just let it go—put it behind him," Carol said.

After learning the details of Jenny's death, Lesley felt terrible about having taken the Shepherds to the Silver Fork the previous night. Of course she didn't know, but she had unwittingly placed them in a painful situation. She thought, *It is hard to forgive and forget. And what's with Gareth being Mr. Insensitive?*

They sat quietly for a moment, then Carol said, "This is a lovely room. Look at those crown moldings and that stained glass at the top of the window. You don't often see that anymore."

"Yes, I've been thinking about what you said yesterday. Maybe I could make this a home when I'm not working else-where," Lesley said, qualifying the possibility.

"Jim said that your parents didn't live here for long—that you grew up in Salt Lake City."

"That's right. I don't really know why, but my mother refused to live here. Maybe she liked city living better," she wondered aloud.

"Oh, I can understand how some don't like the isolation, but the city's not for me, I'm afraid. I'm glad we live close enough to visit, but I'm always happy to come home. It's generally peaceful around Park City, at least if we avoid going into the old town where the crowds are."

Lesley leaned back in the sofa, closing her eyes for a moment, but the quiet was broken by the return of Julie and Jim. They were covered with dust and had dirt smudges on their arms and faces. "Hey, isn't it about time for lunch?" Jim asked.

"Where have you two been?" Lesley asked.

"I finished the lock and went down to the basement to clean and organize things. As I told you, there's not much down there but dust and a few old boxes," he explained.

"We swept up some of the dirt and put it in an empty box," Julie said proudly, then sneezed. "Sorry, I'm allergic to dust."

"Like Jim," Carol said. "Well, let's wash up at the water barrel and have our picnic."

"Sounds good," Jim agreed.

They joined hands around the dining table, and Carol asked Julie to pray. She said, "Dear Heavenly Father, thanks for this good food and for the good time we're having today. Keep us safe when we go home. Bless us, and, oh, and thanks for— for Lesley. Bless her too . . ."

Lesley was touched by Julie's sweet recognition of her. "Thank you, Julie. I feel blessed just to be here with all of you."

Carol had prepared ham and cheese sandwiches with excellent bread and had made a potato salad.

"This is a real picnic," Lesley said. "Did you bake the bread yourself?"

"Yes, I always bake. I don't like that boughten stuff," Carol answered.

"Boughten?"

"Oh, that was my mother's word for baked goods bought at the store. I used to think it was spelled like cotton—botton—

because it tasted that way. Like it was filled with cotton," Carol explained, laughing.

"Well, you're a wonderful baker," Lesley observed. "This is the best bread I've ever tasted."

"Oh, you're just very hungry," Carol said, but she seemed pleased by the compliment.

"Mom is a great cook," Jim agreed. "We're lucky, aren't we, Julie?"

"Yeah, Grandma's the greatest," Julie said, looking with adoring eyes at her grandmother.

"Homemade lemonade, too?" Lesley asked.

"Yep, lemonade made in the shade," Jim said, laughing.

"I'd heard that saying, but now I know what it means," she said.

"Oh, you're gonna turn an old lady's head," Carol said. "But I'm glad you've enjoyed it. It's one o'clock. Are we finished for today, or do you want to start cleaning the upstairs?"

Jim asked, "You said you didn't need to leave until three, right?"

Lesley nodded.

"Well then, let's do some cleaning upstairs for two hours. Might as well, unless you're all too tired," he said.

"I'm not tired," Julie answered.

And Carol said, "I guess I've got another two hours' work in me."

"Well, I suppose I do too," Lesley agreed.

Jim lugged two buckets of water upstairs, and Carol, Julie, and Lesley followed with mops, brooms, cleaning items, and a dustpan. Again Lesley noted there was no dust on the handrail—only on the treads of the stairs.

Jim went downstairs and outside to repair some loose shingles on the back of the house and to permanently secure the coal chute, while they swept the empty bedrooms, cleaned the bath, and mopped the hardwood floors. Each of them worked separately in one of the three bedrooms, and there wasn't as much dust on the second floor as on the first, so the work went faster.

A sudden scream came from the second floor hallway. Lesley ran out and met Carol rushing toward Julie, who was standing at the top of the stairs staring into the mirror.

Jim came running up the stairs to where Julie stood transfixed. "What happened?" he asked.

"What is it, Julie?" Carol asked, reaching out to her granddaughter.

"I—I saw a girl—a girl like me—in the mirror," Julie stammered, pointing at it.

"You mean you saw yourself in the mirror?" Lesley asked, remembering the day before yesterday's experience in seeing her own reflection in the mirror and thinking it was someone else.

"I saw a girl—in an old-fashioned dress. It wasn't me," she said, and started to cry. Jim and Carol embraced her.

"The same thing happened to me a couple days ago. I saw my own reflection and thought it was someone else," Lesley said, forcing a laugh. "It scared me too."

"But it wasn't me," Julie insisted. "She—she said something."

"Said something?" Jim asked, unbelieving.

"Yes, Dad. She said *water*. Then she disappeared."

The adults looked at each other dumbfounded. Lesley was sure they were all thinking of Carol's experience yesterday with *WATER* written on the frosted window.

Julie pleaded hysterically. "I'm not lying. I saw her. I heard her!"

"Well, of course you're not lying, dear," her grandmother said. "We didn't think that. We just thought your own image had scared you—like Lesley's scared her a couple days ago."

"Let's go downstairs," Julie said in nothing more than a terrified whisper as she pulled away from the adults and stepped back toward the stairs.

"We've done enough for today anyway," Lesley said. "Maybe it's time to call it a day and go back to Park City." Somehow she didn't want to stay there any longer, either.

"Okay, I'll empty the buckets. Then let's pack up the other stuff and get out of here," Jim agreed.

They said very little while they loaded the truck, locked up, and headed down the Silver Forks Mountain Road, all of them too stunned and confused to discuss what had happened. Julie stared straight ahead, still shaken by her experience, and the rest of them didn't know what to say to comfort her.

The unusual occurrences of the past few days at Lesley's house seemed too real to have been imagined. Three different people had witnessed someone—or something—trying in earnest to communicate. But what could it all mean? She was glad when Park City came in sight, and she thought a prayer for Julie and gave thanks for their safe return.

Jim drove to her hotel without stopping to drop off Carol and Julie. "Can I walk you in?" he asked, opening her door.

"No thanks. I think Julie needs you right now," she said.

"Well, will you call me when you have a free moment?"

"Yes, yes, I will, Jim. And thanks for all you've done for me this week. I've written you a check," she said, fishing it from her coat pocket.

"Ah shucks, ma'am. Ah hate to take money from yuh," he joked.

"Nonsense. You've all worked very hard for me. Payment up front was part of the bargain," she reminded him.

"Well, I hope it's not the end—of everything," he said, and hugged Lesley tightly.

"I don't want it to be the end, either. Remember—we're going to church Sunday," she said.

"Yeah—I remember. I believe it starts at nine, but if you'll call, I'll tell you for sure," he promised.

"Well, bye for now—and thanks," she said.

"Yeah, bye—for now," he said with a smile and a tip of his cap.

CHAPTER 10

Barnaby was on duty when Lesley stepped into the hotel lobby. The check-in crowds had diminished, so he was occupied in leaning on the front desk. She approached him. "Barnaby, do you know anything about the weather forecast? I've been too busy to check."

"Hello, Ms. Kern," he said, standing straight. "Yeah, there'll be a few snow flurries tonight but nothing threatening. The roads'll be good for your drive to Salt Lake."

"How do you know I'm going to Salt Lake?" she asked, suspicious that he was nosing into her business again.

"Oh, I—uh—just assumed you'd be going to the Sundance Film Festival opening. You are, aren't you?" he asked.

"Why, yes, I am. Thanks, Barnaby," she said, half accepting his explanation.

"Anytime. Anything else, Ms. Kern?"

"No thanks, Barnaby." She used the elevator to her room, too tired to brave the stairs. While riding in the open elevator cage, she saw Barnaby using a phone.

Inside her door, she found an envelope on the floor and opened it. Another message to call Silver Forks Realty. She threw it in the wastebasket.

Then she made a decision—she suddenly decided not to stay in Salt Lake City that night. The opening night ceremony shouldn't run too late, she reasoned, and since the roads weren't bad, she wanted to come back to Park City. She called the front desk and asked the clerk to call the Inn at Temple Square and cancel her reservation for the night.

Then a hot, sudsy bath and a short nap revived her. She wanted to go Hollywood, so she chose a long black silky dress, pearl earrings, and a pearl necklace. Her short hair was easily fixed. She wore her animal-friendly, fake-fur jacket, thinking of Jim, then made sure she had her keys and purse and took the elevator to the garage.

Barnaby looked up as the elevator descended. He gave her the thumbs-up sign. His positive assessment of her appearance was reassuring, so she waved and smiled back.

The traffic going down the canyon from Park City to Salt Lake was pretty heavy since many Sundance Festival patrons were also headed there. On South Temple Street she drove into the public parking section of the Best Western Plaza, across from Abravanel Hall, where the opening event would take place. It was also conveniently close to a restaurant adjacent to the hotel.

The day's work had made her hungry. A chicken salad and roll followed by a piece of cherry pie fortified her for the evening.

Then after paying the check, she stepped into the beautiful Temple Square atmosphere on South Temple Street and through the crosswalk leading the short distance to Abravanel Hall. Named for Maestro Maurice Abravanel, the late conductor of the Utah Symphony, the concert hall was impressive—a dramatic, three-story length of glass and brick enhanced the entry. She'd read that the hall was an acoustical wonder, rivaling the Metropolitan Opera House and the Kennedy Center for sound, and she was excited to go inside.

A large crowd had gathered in the foyer, and she looked for a familiar face in the throng. She wasn't disappointed, seeing exactly the person she'd hoped to see—her agent, Heidi Sigurd—near an entry door. Heidi's full figure adorned in red, along with her gleaming red hair, strands of gold jewelry, and a red-painted smile, made her stand out even in that crowd. Lesley hurried directly toward her, anxious to learn if she'd lined up any work for her.

"Heidi," she said, and her agent turned away from the short, distinguished, silver-haired man she had been talking with and smiled. Lesley hoped the smile wasn't just a put-on but instead suggested good news for her.

"Lesley, I'm so glad I found you."

"Well, actually, I found you," Lesley corrected.

"Oh, I'd misplaced the name of your hotel and have really been trying to contact you." She took Lesley by the arm, completely forgetting the man she was with, and led her to a more private spot.

Lesley thought, *Of course you could have called my cell phone,* but didn't say it. *Best not to alienate my agent.*

"Is something the matter?" Lesley asked, alarmed at Heidi's urgency in pulling her away.

"No, quite the contrary. They want you to do an episode of *Touched by an Angel,* and I thought it was a natural since you're already here. They'll start shooting in a few weeks, right after the Olympics. How about it? They need an answer tomorrow."

"What's the role?" Lesley asked.

"You know I'm always looking out for your career," Heidi said, sounding miffed. "It's a wonderful role. You'll be playing a young blind woman—a potential Emmy role," she effused.

"Well, it does sound promising. But could I read the script before deciding?"

"No, I can't get it for you before they need your decision. Oh, you don't have to worry about the subject matter or anything. You know their reputation. The show is the best-scrubbed series in TV," she emphasized.

"Okay, I trust you, but remember the stipulations of my contracts. I won't . . ."

"I know, I know. I'll make certain they're in the contract. Do I have your okay to go ahead?" she asked, sounding irritated.

"Yes, I need the money, and I do like the series. Try to get me a little more than scale, though, will you?"

"I always try—always. I do."

"Well, I'll write this down. I'm at the Silver Princess in Park City. Don't forget. Call me as soon as you learn more," Lesley insisted, handing Heidi a card with her Silver Princess number. Then she said it, "Or you could call my cell phone."

Heidi ignored that and hurried back to her man of the evening, seemingly trying to soothe his ruffled feelings.

Lesley gazed out the huge windows at the massive Olympic banners that decorated the tall buildings. The well-lit banners portraying individual athletes in their specific sports seemed an integral part of each structure and added to the beauty of the winter evening, an evening made better by the knowledge she might have a job.

The doors to the concert hall opened, and the crowd funneled toward them. Then she spied Gareth Sanders standing by an entry door watching her.

She purposely avoided using the door near Gareth and pretended not to have seen him. She entered the beautiful concert hall—a combination of brass, gold leaf, oak wood, and forest-green carpeting. Six geometric chandeliers with crystal beads lit the interior. The hall looked large enough to hold several thousand people.

Then she took a seat about halfway back and waited for the opening ceremony of the Sundance Film Festival to begin.

Robert Redford would depart from his usual behind-the-scenes activities to address the festival goers, so she was excited to see and hear this film legend. She felt a tap on her left shoulder and turned to see no one behind her. No one. Another tap followed on the opposite shoulder, and she turned again to meet Gareth face-to-face, literally. *So he plays junior high games,* she thought.

"Fancy meeting you here," he said, smiling.

"Yes—what a coincidence," she said sarcastically. Her assessment of Gareth had changed somewhat. Was he stalking her? "Could it be that your messenger, Barnaby, told you I'd be here?" she asked.

"Well, I'm not going to lie to you. Barnaby did call me, but only to tell me that you'd left. I'd already guessed you'd be here for the opening of the festival. Or you might even have told me that. I don't remember."

"But I remember not telling you," she countered, facing front again.

"C'mon, don't be angry. You can't blame a guy for trying. I wanted to get involved with the festival anyway this year. It's good for my business too," he pointed out.

"Of course you have a right to go anywhere you want, but I don't like the feeling that you have Barnaby watching my every move and that you seem to have followed me here," she said frankly.

"Would you rather I move to another seat?" he asked, sounding like a pouting, little boy.

"No, that would be silly. But I do need some space without wondering who's lurking about watching me. That's part of the reason I came to Utah—to unwind and live unencumbered for a few weeks," she said, irritated at having to explain.

"Well, if I've come on too strong, I apologize," Gareth said, still pouting. "I just thought you might like some company—someone who could carry on an intelligent conversation about film."

She wondered if Gareth had seen her with Jim or had gotten a report from Barnaby about their being together. Was Gareth's remark about intelligence a dig at Jim? She said, "I do enjoy that topic, but I want to make my own decisions about being alone or with someone. I don't like those decisions made for me."

"I'll be more careful—I mean—I'll be more thoughtful in the future. I promise," he said. "But we're both here now. Would you mind if I move into that seat next to you?" he asked.

Do I mind? She decided there was nothing to be gained in being rude to Gareth, so she said, reluctantly, "No, it's fine."

No sooner was Gareth seated beside her than the house lights dimmed and Robert Redford appeared onstage to applause and whistles. He talked of the origins of his ideas and objectives for the Sundance Film Festival, stressing that those original goals were still paramount—giving independent filmmakers the opportunity to showcase their work. Lesley found herself admiring this man who was so passionate about so many causes, including protection of the environment. This made her think of Jim, and she was warmed by the thought.

When the opening ceremony ended, participants and audience members were invited to a reception on the second floor. Gareth asked if she was going to the reception, and she answered with a firm no. She'd decided earlier to opt out of that event unless she hadn't found Heidi. Since she already had, she just wanted to return to Park City.

"Well, it's too early to call it a night," Gareth suggested. "There're some great country and folk artists performing in

Park City tonight at the Sundance Music Café on Main Street. It's in the old Elks Lodge. Will you go with me to hear them?" he asked.

"I like your direct invitation better than your coincidental showing up, so let me think about it while I drive back," she said, putting off a response.

"Okay, so can I meet you somewhere or pick you up at the Princess?" he asked hopefully.

"No, I'll call you and let you know—if you'll give me your phone number."

"I have a cell phone." He gave her his number and said, "Do you have one? If you do, you could call me on the drive back."

"I have to have one in my business. I'll call you," she answered promptly and left the building, heading for the parking lot. The air was crisp, and she was glad for her warm jacket. Music from Temple Square resounded in the star- and light-filled night. She rejoiced in the beauty and peace of the area—a peace that was always present there, no matter how big the crowds. She felt a warm surge of gratitude for her world and said a silent prayer of thanks for her many blessings.

The drive to Park City was furious but uneventful, and she went to her hotel, still not certain whether to cozy in for the evening or to change and go with Gareth to the Music Café. When she looked about her room, she found she wasn't really ready for another lonely night, so she decided to call Jim. There was no answer so, disappointed, she paced for a moment, contemplating what to do.

Then, almost involuntarily, she called Gareth's cell phone number. If she found herself not enjoying the music or the company, she could walk back to the hotel, she reasoned.

She told Gareth that she'd meet him at the Elks Lodge's music café, thus ensuring that she could leave when she wanted to without feeling obligated to stay there with him. She changed into jeans, a kelly-green sweater, and walking boots, which she'd purchased the previous evening at a nearby boutique. Wearing her warm coat and gloves, she stepped out into the wintry night and walked downhill toward the Elks Lodge on Main Street. A festive atmosphere filled the streets, and she couldn't help rejoicing in the happy throngs of people whom she weaved through on the narrow sidewalks. The smells of good food made her hungry, so she stepped into a candy shop for a small bar of wonderful Swiss chocolate, which she munched on the remainder of the way to the Music Café.

When she found the historic Elks Lodge, she entered to find the Music Café filled to capacity with people standing and sitting in almost every available space in the room. A stage large enough to hold a full band was at one end of the room, but only a lone pop-rock singer accompanied himself with his guitar in a soulful melody. She saw a space against a wall and leaned back, enjoying this little-known but original singer-composer.

She'd almost forgotten about meeting Gareth, but he hadn't. He found her and said, "There you are. I've been looking for you."

"He's very good, isn't he?" she said, turning attention away from herself.

"Yes, the big names won't be playing until Saturday night, but these lesser-known musicians have nothing to apologize about. They're all good. The next guy sings a set of folk-rock songs. You'll like him, too," he said, squeezing in beside her.

"Would you like something to drink?" he asked.

"Well, I am thirsty. I ate a chocolate bar on the way," she confessed. "Could you get me a club soda?"

"Sure, sure. I'll be right back," he said, pushing through the crowd.

At that moment her eyes locked on a familiar face—Jim Shepherd was leaning on the wall across the room opposite her. She hoped that he hadn't seen her with Gareth, but he waved, smiled, and looked as if he were coming her way. Then Gareth returned with her soda, and she saw a change in expression on Jim's face. He turned away toward the singer then backed away to the wall. He avoided looking her way until the singer finished. Then, when she looked back, Jim had disappeared in the crowd. She should have stayed in Salt Lake as she'd planned to do. She was very angry with herself for having gone there with Gareth, but who would have thought that Jim would go there as well. Anyway, she tried to convince herself, *I have a right to go where and with whomever I wish—no strings attached.* But her inner arguments didn't work—she still felt bad at the possibility that even though it wasn't actually a date, she'd really hurt Jim by being seen there with Gareth.

She stayed on through one more singer, then excused herself to Gareth, saying that she was tired and would walk back to the hotel. He didn't protest, maybe deciding that she really did want to make up her own mind about things. He just said, "Okay, I'll see you later."

She said, "Bye," and walked slowly uphill to the Silver Princess, examining her conflicting emotions and unaware of the people or places along the way.

She readied for bed and kneeled to say her evening prayer, including a special prayer for the happiness and well-being of Jim and his family. She asked the Lord to help Jim find his way back to the Church. Then she prayed for guidance in sorting out her feelings for Jim.

On Friday she'd be free to do whatever she wished until it was time for an evening showing of a documentary entry in the Sundance Festival, *Daughter from Danang*, rumored to be an excellent candidate for a festival prize. Trying to put the evening's events out of mind and thinking of the prospect of seeing some exciting new films, she finally fell asleep.

CHAPTER 11

Friday and Saturday were lazy days. Lesley caught up on her rest, ate good food—avoiding the Silver Fork restaurant—and experienced selected films in the Sundance Festival. She stayed mainly with the documentaries, feeling safer about their subject matter, but she did see *Noon Blue Apples,* the story of a college student's confusing attempts to find the way between reality and paranoia.

Some films debuted in Park City, others in Salt Lake, and still others in nearby Ogden. She spent a few hours driving to and from these destinations, which gave her time to think and reflect on her future. She met a few acquaintances from past films she'd worked on and saw some of the stars who were attending the festival, but most often she felt very much alone and found herself thinking a lot about Jim and his family.

She *would* be staying in Utah because Heidi called to say that she'd firmed up the role in *Touched by an Angel* and would mail the contract. Lesley knew she couldn't afford to live the whole time at the Silver Princess, so she considered her options. Rent a studio apartment in the Salt Lake City area? Find a place in Park City? Weekly rates would probably be cheaper in Salt Lake, she decided.

Then she thought of her house. It had been made presentable enough to live in, but there was no heat, no water, and no electricity. Would the plumbing and wiring even work if she had utilities turned on? Would she have trouble with the roads if there were a lot of snow? And she'd need linens and personal items. She'd also need a car. Maybe she should fly back to L.A. and drive her old clunker back to Utah. All in all, the task of trying to make the house habitable seemed too formidable, and she still felt wary because of the unusual occurrences there earlier in the week. Anyway, she was booked at the Princess until after the Olympics. She'd have time to make some decisions before then. The car problem also would have to be solved later.

Thoughts of her house led to more thoughts of Jim. She decided she'd better call him on Saturday as she'd promised to do. She hoped that he would still be receptive to going with them to church and that she hadn't seriously damaged their growing friendship because of her Thursday night appearance with Gareth at the Music Café.

Saturday morning she braved the call to Jim. She dialed his number using her cell phone, rather than going through the possibly nosy hotel switchboard.

She had started to feel that everyone associated with the Silver Princess was far too interested in her personal affairs. Maybe it was just routine courtesy, but their interest seemed much too intense for that.

Carol answered, and Lesley said, "Carol, this is Lesley."

"Oh, how good to hear from you," she said. "Let me get Jim." She left before Lesley could say more.

It was several minutes before she heard him pick up the phone and take a deep breath. "Hullo, Lesley," he said in a neutral voice.

"Hullo, yourself," she answered. "I told you I'd call about the time of church services tomorrow." There was a brief silence, so she asked, "We still have a date, don't we?"

"Yes, I guess we do. I said I'd go and 'Ah'm a man of mah word.'" That made her feel better. At least his sense of humor hadn't changed—they could still laugh together, she hoped.

And she did laugh. "Well, I'm glad. I've been looking forward to Sunday," she said truthfully.

"Mom and Julie have been excited about it," he said.

"But you haven't?" she asked.

"I didn't say that. It's just that I'm going to find it—difficult—going back after so long. I guess I don't know what to expect—how people will react—how I'll react," he explained.

"We'll all be there together. I'm a stranger here too, remember. We'll be strangers together. Okay?" she urged, trying to bolster his decision to come back to church. "Is sacrament meeting at nine?"

"Yes, nine AM sharp. Mom hates going late, so better be here about eight thirty, unless you want me to come pick you up?"

"Well, I'd like that, but there's no need. I'll save you the trouble and drive to your place."

"Well, ma'am, there'd be no trouble in carryin' ya here in mah rig," he teased.

"Thanks, but I'll use 'mah own rig,'" she said, laughing. "I'll be there at eight thirty sharp."

"Ah'll be ready in mah best bib 'n' tucker."

"Okay," she said, laughing again. "Eight thirty it is." She paused a moment, then said, "I'm glad you're not upset with me."

"Why would I be upset?"

"Well, I've learned a little more about your reactions to Gareth Sanders. You saw me with him on Thursday night, and I was afraid you might be upset with me."

"No . . . I have no right to control who you see and don't see. That's your business. Has nothing to do with me," he said abruptly.

"Okay, then I didn't need to worry, I guess. Anyway, I can't wait to see you—all of you—tomorrow. Tell Carol I said thanks for the invitation," she urged.

"I'll tell her. See ya tomorrow morning," he said, and hung up.

She felt somewhat better after that conversation. He had said that he wasn't concerned about Gareth, but there was still something in his tone that suggested hurt. She resolved to be more careful of his feelings in the future.

Saturday night's experience with the movie *Gerry* was disappointing. She'd gone because it starred Matt Damon. She admired him for lending his star power to an independent filmmaker, but the movie was too artsy for her. When she got back to her room, she changed into her warm flannel night-gown then kneeled and said her prayers, including her concerns about Jim's relationship to the Church. Then she climbed under the snuggly down blanket and fell asleep looking forward to Sunday.

CHAPTER 12

Lesley dressed for church in a camel-tan, soft-wool skirt and jacket and an off-white blouse and then drove the few blocks to the Shepherds' house. There had been a light snow during the night, but the roads and sidewalks were still clear, so she walked toward the front door.

She didn't have time to knock. Julie, in a pretty powder-blue dress, held the door wide and said, "Hi, I couldn't wait till you got here."

"It's good to see you too," Lesley said, hugging her. "How have you been—since your experience at my house? Are you okay?"

"Yeah, I'm okay. I just—don't think about it," she said. "We're all ready. I'll tell Dad and Grandma you're here." She left Lesley standing in the entry.

Carol appeared first. "Didn't Julie offer you a chair?" she said, shaking her head.

"Well, no need, since we're headed out anyway. How are you this morning?"

"I'm all right. Just a bit of arthritis in my back and hips. Old-timers used to call it rheumatism, but I guess it's arthritis. Makes me feel older than I am. Anyway, I'll be fine once I get moving a little more," she said, smiling. "I think we've all recovered from our experiences with—seeing things. But how are you?" she asked, looking at her quizzically.

"I'm fine." She changed the subject. "You remember how you were so concerned that I was leaving the area so soon? Well, I got some good news—I'm going to be staying in Utah for a while. I've been offered a role in an episode of a locally produced television series."

"I'm so glad you won't be running off. What show is it?" she asked, and Julie appeared behind her.

"*Touched by an Angel*," Lesley answered. "Have you seen it?"

"Seen it? I love that show. Inspires me every time I watch it," she said.

"I watch it too, Lesley. When can we see you in it?" Julie questioned, excitedly circling round them and jumping up and down.

"Oh, it will be a while," she explained. "But maybe you could come watch the filming one day. I'll try to arrange it if your Grandma says it's okay."

"We'd love to do that. Jim will probably want to come too. Could we all come, do you think?" Carol asked.

"Well, I'll have to see. I don't know what their policy is about visitors on the set. But I'll look into it. Okay?"

"Okay," they said in unison.

Jim showed up right then, dragging his feet a bit. He looked as handsome as ever in a dark brown, western-cut suit, a tan tie, and shiny brown boots.

"Let's get going," Carol urged. "I don't want to be late."

"Told you, didn't I? Mom hates being late, and she gets very upset when others are," Jim repeated.

Carol said defensively, "Well, it's disrespectful to come late to meetings in the Lord's house, and it interrupts everything. Destroys the spirit."

"Now Mom, remember tolerance is a virtue," Jim teased, as they exited the house.

"Oh, I can tolerate it when someone's late once in a blue moon, but when they come late all the time, seems like laziness—just a bad habit," she said.

"Shall we go in my Navigator?" Lesley asked. "It's all warmed up."

"Sure, why not. Would you like me to drive or give you directions?" Jim asked.

"Why don't you drive? That seems easier," she answered.

The ward chapel was not far away. It was an older but charming building. The exterior had been designed to complement the Park City environment, with warm-colored brick and natural stone decorating the entry.

Lesley noticed that Jim was bringing up the rear, walking behind her, Carol, and Julie at a slow pace. She went back to him, took his arm, and said, "Remember, we're strangers here together."

He smiled wanly. "Oh, I'm all right. I just feel a little self-conscious."

"It will be okay. You'll see," she encouraged.

Carol and Julie had already entered the building. After looking back to see that Jim and Lesley were still coming, they waited in the foyer.

Everything went better than Lesley could have hoped. The greeter at the door welcomed her when Carol introduced her and then looked up to see Jim. "Well, old-timer," he said, pumping Jim's hand. "It's so good to see you here."

"Well—thanks," was all Jim could say.

Then they went down the aisle, and a big gray-haired man with a butch haircut left the rostrum and hurried toward them. "Jim, am I glad to see you," he said, shaking Jim's hand and patting him on the back. "I'm Bishop Jones," he said to Lesley, enveloping her hand in his mighty paw.

"I'm glad to meet you. I'm Lesley—Kern."

"She's our new friend, Bishop," Julie offered, smiling up at her possessively.

"Well, welcome to our ward—all of you. We hope you'll feel welcome here," he said.

She looked at Jim, who was smiling, and said, "I already do—we all do."

"Bishop Jones, it's good to see you too," Jim said. "Thanks—for the welcome."

The bishop left to talk with the arriving speakers, and the Shepherds and Lesley found a bench in the side section about halfway back.

They had just sat down when a mustached, dark-headed man about Jim's age stepped into the empty row behind them and placed his hands on Jim's shoulders. "Jim," he said. "I'm so glad you're here."

Jim turned and smiled his recognition. "Gary—it's good to see you too." Then he turned toward Lesley, "Gary, this is—our—new friend, Lesley Kern. Lesley, my old high school buddy, Gary Beck."

"Yes, we go way back," Gary said, smiling a warm smile that almost rivaled Jim's. "Glad to meet you, Lesley. Hope to see more of you—all of you. You'll be coming to our elders quorum meeting, Jim? I'll find you after Sunday School, and we'll go together. Okay?"

Jim thought for a moment, then said, "Well, I'll see, but—thanks, Gary."

Lesley thought silent thanks for answers to her prayers. Things couldn't have gone better. Everyone seemed so genuinely pleased to see Jim. They'd reacted exactly as President Hinckley suggested members should—with welcoming love and friendship. They had done as Christ would do in welcoming back a lost sheep. She looked at Carol and smiled. Carol smiled back but with a tear in her eye—a tear of gratitude.

They listened quietly to the peaceful organ prelude music, then at nine sharp, Bishop Jones stood to welcome the congregation and visitors and to make announcements, one of which mentioned that they had found enough volunteers for the Olympics. Jim whispered, "I've already volunteered for the games."

She smiled, realizing again that this was a giving man—he cared about so many things.

After the opening hymn and invocation, the congregation was asked to sustain several ward members in new positions, and then one of Lesley's favorite hymns, "I Stand All Amazed," was announced as the sacrament song. Jim joined in singing, but quietly. Still, she could hear his beautiful bass voice and sensed that he was really considering those wonderful words as he sang:

I think of his hands pierced and bleeding to pay the debt!
Such mercy, such love, and devotion can I forget?
No, no, I will praise and adore at the mercy seat,
Until at the glorified throne I kneel at his feet.

Jim seemed to be thinking deeply, with his head bowed, as the sacrament was blessed and administered. When the deacon came to their short row and held out the tray of broken bread, Jim looked up, hesitated for a moment, then decided quickly to take the sacrament. Lesley's heart softened when she imagined his serious thoughts of repentance and taking on the Savior's name.

When the sacrament service was over, Lesley looked at Jim and saw that he was smiling—a sweet smile of relief and joy.

Bishop Jones introduced two speakers, Brother and Sister Smith, a husband and wife new to the ward. A vocal solo would bridge the two speakers.

Sister Shirley Smith, a motherly lady in her late fifties, spoke first. She took a slightly different approach to the discussion of the Atonement, expressing the thought that the Atonement can only be accepted fully if people become forgiving toward their fellow human beings. She paraphrased Elder Richard G. Scott in saying as we forgive, we emulate Heavenly Father and His Son in Their forgiving—in Their love.

Lesley couldn't help feeling that those words were an answer to her prayers for Jim. The subject seemed tailor-made as a remedy for his problems.

Then an auburn-haired, teenage soprano sang, "As I have loved you, Love one another. This new commandment: Love one another . . ." Her voice so beautifully matched the words and melody that she brought tears from the congregation. Lesley looked over to see the eyes of Jim, Carol, and Julie sparkling too.

Brother Brent Smith, a thin, balding, slight man with glasses, reinforced his wife's message in retelling a story from an *Ensign* article of a sister who struggled to forgive her husband after he had confessed to betraying her. She had prayed long and deeply for comfort and gradually came to realize that the Atonement not only makes repentance possible for the wrong-doer, but also makes it possible for the victim to experience the sweet peace of forgiving.

He also quoted a statement by Elder Henry B. Eyring from another *Ensign* article: "The Atonement working in our lives will produce in us the love and tenderness we need."

The Smiths' sweet message of love and forgiveness was further emphasized in the words of the closing hymn: "Judge not, that ye be not judged, Was the counsel Jesus gave . . ."

If Lesley had organized the service herself, she couldn't have directed it more perfectly toward helping Jim. She thought, *The Lord hears and answers prayers.*

Jim remained seated after the benediction and after most of the congregation had exited. Lesley waited behind while Julie and Carol went up the aisle toward Sunday School classes. "Are you okay?" she asked Jim after a moment.

"Yeah, I'm okay. I just need to do some heavy thinking. I'm going to walk home," he said abruptly, and stood.

"Won't you stay for Sunday School? Gary will be looking for you to take you to elders quorum meeting," she reminded.

"No, just tell Mom and Julie that I'm kind of bursting over right now." He saw her concerned look and said, "It's okay. I'm happy I came. I just need to make some decisions. I need some time alone."

"Well, okay, I guess."

Carol stuck her head in the door and said, "Come on, I'll show you where Gospel Doctrine class meets."

Jim looked at Lesley again. "Just go on with Mom. I'm all right. Really. I'll see you at dinner," he said. "If Gary comes looking for me, tell him thanks for me and that I'll take a rain check on his offer."

"Well, if that's what you want." She couldn't hide her disappointment but understood his feelings. She walked toward Carol then looked back over her shoulder to see Jim going the opposite way, toward the foyer.

"He isn't coming?" Carol asked, alarmed.

"No, he says he's fine but needs some time alone—to think," she explained.

Carol sighed. "Well, that'll be good for him," she said. "Maybe he can sort out a few things."

"Yes, I'm sure that's it. He seemed very touched by the service."

They went to Sunday School and Relief Society meetings, and Lesley thought, *I could be very happy in this ward.* Everyone was so welcoming and courteous, and she loved being with Carol. She felt so comfortable with her that it was almost like being with her own mother.

After the meetings they found Julie, who was also looking anxiously for Jim. "Where's Dad?" she asked.

"Oh, he's in one of his silent moods," Carol said. "He's fine. He just wanted to go for a walk."

"Well, if you're sure he's okay," Julie said, sounding disappointed.

It was snowing, so they hurriedly climbed in the SUV and drove back to the house.

"How did you manage to cook dinner and still go to church?" Lesley asked.

"Oh, I've been practicing that for a long time," she said. "Of course, the microwave helps. It still scares me a little," she said, laughing at herself, "but it does help. The pot roast will be done, and everything else is ready in the refrigerator, waiting to be warmed up."

"I'm hungry," Julie said from the backseat.

"I am too," Lesley agreed. "Thanks for inviting me, Carol, and for making me feel so at home."

"I'm glad you feel that way—means we'll be seeing more of you," she said.

"Yeah, why don't you come for dinner every day?" Julie begged.

"Well, I couldn't do that to your grandmother, and I will be busy—the Olympics and my work," she explained. "But I'm glad you want me to, Julie."

"Okay, but we will see you some more, won't we?" she asked.

"Yes—I hope so," she said, thinking of Jim.

Inside they were greeted by the wonderful smell of beef pot roast, and she was relieved to see a smiling Jim, who had changed into jeans and a blue sweater that brought out the color of his eyes. "Everything okay?" she asked quietly.

"Yep, I've been thinking—and praying—and I've made up my mind about a few things," he said.

"Care to tell me what?"

"Later—after dinner," he suggested.

Carol took Lesley's coat, hung it in the entry, and ushered her back to a combination country kitchen, dining, and family room. A warming fire burned in a black stove with a glass door, and the peace of the Sabbath enveloped her. *I love this place and these people,* she thought.

"Can I help?" she asked Carol.

"No, it's ready—and Jim has set the table. Good boy," she said, like she was talking to her little boy—or a much-loved puppy.

Jim offered Lesley a rocking chair, and she felt as if she'd known this family for years instead of days.

When Carol announced all was ready, they joined hands at the table for a blessing. Carol asked Lesley to pray, and she gave thanks.

Dinner was delicious—pot roast, homemade Parker House rolls, mashed potatoes and gravy, buttered carrots, and a green salad—real down-home cooking. Lesley loved every bite. For dessert Carol had made an apple pie, served with a dollop of real whipped cream. Lesley felt she should have turned it down but couldn't resist. And she remembered Carol didn't like to cook for picky eaters. Well, Lesley didn't disappoint her.

After dinner she joined Carol and Julie in clearing and washing up. Jim volunteered to help too but was shooed away by his mother. He sat on a comfy-looking sofa before the fire.

When they finished, Carol said, "I'm ready for a little nap," and whispered, "Julie, don't you have something to do in your room?"

"Okay, Grandma," she said, winking knowingly. "But don't go away," Julie said to Lesley.

"Oh, I won't leave until you boot me out," she promised. "I definitely prefer your lovely home to my hotel room. Thanks for a wonderful day and a wonderful dinner."

Carol smiled. "You're welcome, dear. Anytime."

When Carol and Julie were out of sight, Jim said, "Come sit with me by the fire."

"Don't mind if I do," she said, cozying next to him on the sofa.

She broke the quiet moment. "You and your mother have made such a beautiful home here." She looked out the big windows on either side of the cast-iron stove. Big flakes of snow were falling gently. "The backyard is beautiful even in winter."

"Well, that's more Mom's doing than mine. She has the green thumb. I'm better with animals than green things."

"Then you're a good combination," she said. "Was this room part of the original house?"

"No, it's an add-on. I built it," he said proudly.

"You did? It's beautiful. You really are a jack-of-all-trades."

Jim just smiled his reaction to her praise.

"What do you burn in the stove?" she asked. "Doesn't look like wood."

"It isn't. It's recycled newspapers. Ah roll mah own," he said.

"You do? And it really heats?"

"Yes. I have a little device that rolls them into a log; then I cover them with a waxlike coating, and they burn—not as long as wood logs, but it's a way to reuse the paper and it doesn't pollute the air as much. Oh, by the way, I meant to tell you I found a home for the cat and her kittens," he said.

"Oh, that's wonderful. Thanks for doing that—for me—and for the cats," she said.

"An old dairy farmer wanted some cats to help with his mice problem, so they'll have a good home."

"You are a sweet man," she said, smiling at him.

Then they were silent. She really wanted to know what he was thinking about his experiences at church but didn't know how to bring it up without prying. So she sat quietly, enjoying the fire and the peace of the day.

Finally he said, "I've made some decisions—some resolutions."

"Want to share them?" she asked, pleased that he had brought up the subject.

"Yes, I've . . . decided I have to bury the past—let bygones be bygones."

"Care to elaborate?" she urged after another long pause in his revelations.

He leaned forward, elbows on his knees, fingers interlaced, and chin resting on his hands. "Well, I guess you know that I've been holding on to some bad feelings—about Jenny's accident."

"Your mother told me a little."

"I've decided I have to let it go—for my sake and for Julie's." He leaned back into the sofa, arms locked behind his head. "For too long I've been blaming someone—or something—for what happened to Jenny, and it's been eating me up inside. It's even begun to affect others."

"How do you mean?"

"Well, I saw you with Gareth Sanders and I resented it—resented that you would be with someone whom I've disliked for so long. I have no right to make those kinds of judgments," he explained.

She sympathized and understood but didn't want to preach or press for details. He was making his own good changes. Instinctively she kissed him on the cheek.

He reached out with one arm and hugged her. "Thanks," he said. "That meant more than you could know—you approve, then?"

"I approve. It takes real strength to unload a burden like you've been carrying, and I know you'll feel better for letting it go."

"That's what the sacrament meeting speakers said: '. . . experience the sweet peace of forgiving.' I thought about that all the way home. I prayed and then realized that my bitterness has hurt me—and Mom and Julie—more than anyone. I feel like a man let out of jail, to tell the truth. I'll never forget what happened, but I realize I don't have to dwell on it anymore."

"I'm so glad—for you and for your family," Lesley said sincerely.

"Yeah, a few years ago I heard some guy on TV say that you have to give permission for bad things or bad words or bad people to rent space in your head. I've been letting what happened rent space in my head for too long," he said. "I feel like a big weight's been lifted."

"I think you've overcome one of life's greatest challenges," she said. "Forgiving can be so hard to do. But you're right—you can actually feel the burden lift when you let it go."

He looked at her tenderly, then suddenly kissed her. "I haven't known you long, Lesley, but I feel very—good—when I'm with you."

"And I feel very comfortable with you," she said, thinking that this relationship was developing very rapidly, but though she'd known Jim for less than a week, it almost felt like a lifetime.

She considered asking more about his resolutions then realized she would have asked him to break them—to discuss what had been bothering him for years. Instead, he could quit thinking and quit talking about it. She did bring up another question. "How did you feel about getting back to church?" she asked directly.

"It felt okay—good."

"Then you'll go back—and stay for priesthood meeting?" She was pressuring him, she realized, but she really had to know—before she could let herself lose her heart to this man.

"Yeah, I'll be there next Sunday and yes, I'll stay. Gary made me feel that he'd be there to help me through. In fact, he called while you were in Relief Society, wondering where I'd gone."

"He did? That's sweet. I'm so glad you've crossed that bridge. It would mean a lot to me if . . ."

"Yes—if?" he asked.

"Nothing—it would just mean a lot to me. I want to go back to your ward too. I liked it, so if you'll allow me to come along again, I'll be there next Sunday."

Before he could respond, Julie peeked around the door frame and asked, "Is it okay to come back in now?"

"Sure it's okay, sweetheart," Jim said. "Come sit here between us." He slid over to make room and welcomed Julie into his waiting arms.

Lesley thought, *What a great father. Julie may have lost her mother, but she has plenty of love to make up for it.* It was warm and wonderful to sit together like a little family in this warm and cozy room. She realized then how hard, isolated, and lonely her life had become in the past few years. Alone in the city. The lyrics of an old song came to mind: "L.A. is a great, big freeway . . ."

"Lesley, have you decided when you want to finish up your house?" Jim asked.

"Oh, I've given it some thought. I told your mother and Julie that I have a job offer here—in Utah—a role in *Touched by an Angel*. I'm going to have to find someplace to live," she said.

"Why didn't you tell me?" he asked, sitting forward on the sofa and looking pleased. "That's great!"

"I didn't think about it until now. Maybe I was waiting for the right time."

"She says that we can watch her being filmed," Julie said excitedly.

"Well, I said I'll try to arrange it if you really would like to. Sometimes it can be rather boring—a lot of waiting—like being in the army," she warned.

"I wouldn't be bored," Julie said, and Jim added, "Neither would I. Sounds fun. When?"

"They don't start shooting the segment until after the Olympics. I don't know the particulars yet," she explained.

"Why don't you come and live with us?" Julie suggested.

Just then Carol popped her head around the corner. "Sounds like some big planning going on in here," she said, smiling.

"Why didn't you tell me that Lesley was going to stick around for a while?" Jim asked.

"I didn't have a chance. You left church. Then we had dinner. I was going to get around to telling you," Carol teased. "I know you were anxious about it."

"I want her to come live with us," Julie begged.

Lesley interrupted before Carol was forced to answer. "Oh, I couldn't do that. My hours will be so irregular, and this house is just right for the three of you. You don't need a week-long house guest."

"You'd be welcome," Carol said, sitting in the rocking chair across from everyone else.

"Thank you. I know you'd make me welcome, but I can't do that to you. I've been thinking more about living at my house, but I don't even know if that would be practical," she said.

Jim was deep in thought. "How soon do you have to make a decision—about where to live?"

"I'm booked at the Silver Princess until after the Olympics, so there isn't a great rush."

"What are your plans for this week?" Jim asked.

"Oh, I think I've seen enough of the film festival. I haven't really made definite plans for this week," she answered.

"Then why don't we go back to your house tomorrow and see what else needs to be done to make the place livable?" Jim proposed. "If you did decide to live there, it would be available for your future visits. Or you'd have a better chance of selling or renting it if you decide to do that."

"That reminds me—I had another message to call Silver Forks Realty. I put it in the round hole," she said.

"The round hole? What's that?" Julie asked, pulling a face.

"Oh, I'm sorry—the wastebasket, I should have said."

"That was the right reaction," Jim remarked. "Well, how about it? Shall we have another go at the house?"

"I don't know whether I want to go back there," Julie said quietly.

"Well, young lady, you'll be in school tomorrow anyway, so you won't have to worry about it. 'Sides, there won't be any more spooks up there," Carol predicted.

"I'm sure you're right," Lesley said, "but that has to be one of my considerations. It would be a pretty lonely place to live, I'm afraid."

"Oh, we'd see that you had company," Jim assured. "Let's cross that bridge when we come to it. Want to go back there tomorrow?"

"Okay, if you're sure you have time," she said.

"I have time . . . anyway, I was hoping you'd be available this week—to put me to work, I mean."

"If you go, I'm going to let you two go back there alone," Carol said. "I don't think you'll need this old chaperone—now that you know you can trust my son." She laughed. "'Sides, I've got a few things to catch up on here."

"Same time, same station?" Jim asked.

"Fine with me. Pick me up at eight." She was glad that they had a reason to be together.

On the way back to her hotel, Lesley felt a peace and happiness at the events of the day. Jim had begun to resolve his feelings about Jenny's death, and he'd made a commitment to continue attending church. *Maybe there's more than one reason that I came back to Park City,* she thought.

And she'd have a whole week to consider moving into her house or renting or selling it. She'd begun to feel that she didn't want to neglect it as she had in the past. Anyway, she had Jim and his knowledge to guide her in her decisions.

Just one occurrence spoiled the peace of the day. When she neared the Silver Princess and started to turn toward the garage, she saw the black Lincoln that seemed to shadow her wherever she went, pulling out of a parking space in front of the hotel.

When she opened the door to her room, she found another note on the floor inside. She opened it quickly and read:

It would be in your best interest to contact Silver Forks Realty on Monday.

She didn't like the change in the tone of this message from the previous efforts to contact her. It almost sounded like a threat. Silly paranoia, she thought. *I'll just ignore this message as I have the others.* She threw it in the wastebasket.

She went to bed early, after praying her thanks for the marvelous blessings of that day—and for the potential of her future. She also gave thanks that Jim had come back to the Church and that she had secured an acting job that would keep her in Utah.

CHAPTER 13

She was a little late coming down to the lobby next morning, and Jim was waiting for her there. He smiled that brilliant smile and walked toward the stairs when he saw Lesley descending. She couldn't help noticing that the front desk help, including Barnaby, were all eyes, but she concentrated on Jim all the way to his truck.

"Can you handle McDonald's again," he asked, "or would you rather go someplace else?"

"Oh, McDonald's is fine—for breakfast," she said. "Besides, it's fast." So they went there again but to the drive-thru. They pulled over to a parking place and ate in the warmth of the truck.

"This is kinda fun," she said. "Like a picnic."

"Yeah, a breakfast picnic in winter," he said, smiling.

His mood seemed upbeat, so she braved asking, "How are you feeling today—about the decisions you made yesterday?"

He paused and took a deep breath. "Oh, maybe like it won't be quite so easy to change as I thought. I've been in a rut and have to climb out, I guess."

"But like you said—it's worth it."

He wiped some stray ketchup off his lip with a napkin then sighed. "I know it—it's worth it, but old habits die hard."

"Old habits?" she asked.

"Yes, just the habit of thinking too much about the past, about things you can't change—and the habit of staying away from church."

Lesley started to say something, but he interrupted, "I know, I know. I promised, and like I told ya, 'Ah'm a man of muh word.' I'll be there bright-eyed and bushy-tailed next Sunday. Don't worry." He smiled at her then wiped a smear of yogurt from her upper lip with his napkin. "We seem to have the same problem—can't find our mouths. Anyway, enough about me," he said. "Let's talk about you. Have you given any more thought to what you want to do with your house?"

"Yes, but I still can't make up my mind. I found another note from Silver Forks Realty when I came back to the hotel last night. I didn't like the way it was worded."

He sat straight and looked directly at her. "What do you mean?"

"Well, it kinda sounded like a threat—or an ultimatum: 'It would be in your best interest to contact Silver Forks Realty on Monday.'"

"I guess you could take it that way, or they probably were suggesting they have a better offer for you to consider. Anyway, I wouldn't worry about it. The title to your place is clear, isn't it?"

"Well, yes, the property has been in my family since the house was built, and it was left to me in my father's will. It's mine," she said firmly.

"I guess that's why Sticky Finger—why Joe—is being so persuasive. I think he got his hands on everybody else's property up there without much resistance. You're probably the last hold out."

They finished their breakfast and deposited the remains in a trash receptacle near the parking lot exit. "Seems a waste to throw away all of this packaging," Jim said, as he pushed the garbage into the can. "Just our modern way of doing things. We think everything's expendable and replaceable, I guess."

Jim drove onto the freeway, which was clear of snow and ice, even though snow had fallen throughout the night.

"All of this snow's great for the Olympics," she said.

"Yes, and for the drought. Still isn't enough to take care of the long-range water problems, though. That's another area where we need to preserve and conserve," he said.

"You've made me more conscious of many things—many ways in which I waste. I'm driving a rented Navigator—guess if I ever buy a new car, I'll avoid a gas guzzler."

"Good girl. If everyone . . . I'm sorry. I'm on my soapbox again. I know that can get pretty tiring," he apologized.

"No, I agree with you. We need to think more about the environment in our choices. I think the Lord wants us to care for the earth He made for us. I really do."

She looked over at him, and he was grinning.

"As I said before, you're a girl after muh own heart."

She thought, *I believe I really am—after your heart.*

As they climbed higher, the snow was deeper, but the road from Silver Forks business district to her house was only dusted with snow. It was beginning to melt because of the rock product that had been spread on the road. "Who improved this road, do you suppose?"

"Well, the county might have done it, but I doubt it. I wouldn't be surprised if Joe Spencer had it done so he could access all of his property on Silver Forks Mountain."

"Really? Then he must have big plans for the place," she said.

"I'm sure he does, or he wouldn't be spending so much money and effort here. Guess we could try to find out what's going on," he suggested, "if you're really concerned about it, that is."

"I don't know whether to be concerned or not. I'm so uncertain about what to do with my place. Do you think I should consider Joe Spencer's offer? It almost seems the easy way out."

They were at the gates to her place and stopped. Jim breathed deeply before answering her question. "I really don't know how to advise you," he said. "I think the place is worth keeping—your own little piece of earth—but you do have to consider your work and need to travel. You're the only one who knows what's best for you."

She appreciated that he didn't just jump in and begin to lecture her about what she should do, especially since she knew that he had some definite opinions. "Maybe I should consider placing it on the market . . . looking for another buyer—not Joe." Without thinking, she said, "Gareth Sanders expressed an interest in the house for a bed and breakfast."

There was a long silence, and Jim got out to open the gate without responding. Immediately, she regretted bringing up Gareth and wanted to bite her tongue. Jim climbed in without saying anything.

She touched his arm. "I'm sorry. I didn't mean to mention him. Gareth just stated his interest in the place when I first met him on the plane. It just popped into my head. It's not something that I've discussed with him."

"Well, again, I'm not the one to advise you. Anything I say would seem tainted by my past feelings. Anyway, I've resolved not to get upset at the thought of Gareth Sanders. Look at me. I'm smiling." She did and saw his silly pasted-on grin.

"I'm forgiven, then?" she asked.

"You didn't do anything to forgive. I'm the one with the problem—but I'm working on it."

He drove down the lane to the front of the house, slipping and sliding a bit in the snow-filled ruts. "Want to go in?"

"Yes, I guess so, since that's why we came here." She had some reservations about reentering the house. Somehow the happy moments while cleaning the house had been overshadowed by the unforeseen and unexplainable experiences.

"Are you spooked?" he asked.

"Yes, I guess I am. Oh, I'm not really worrying about ghosts. It's just that three of us had such strange experiences—your mother, Julie, and I—and it seemed so real, like someone was really there trying to—communicate with us."

He laughed. "Well, let's go in and have a conversation. Maybe we can talk it out and settle that problem, too."

"Okay, but I'd rather keep the conversation between the two of us if you don't mind."

They trudged through the snow onto the porch, stamping their feet to get the snow off. Jim unlocked the front door. "Well, no one's been here. The place sure looks better than when we came here the first time," he said, looking around the lower level.

They sat in the parlor, and Lesley wished they'd brought the heater again. "It's so cold," she said. "We can't stay too long."

"No, just long enough to decide what needs to be done if you want to live here," he agreed.

"Well, how about utilities? Do you think the furnace will work? And how about the electricity and water? It all seems too difficult to take care of in the time we have."

"Hold on! Don't give up before we start," he said. "The furnace burns propane. We'd have to get someone to come up and fill the tank behind the house, and we may have to get a professional to check out the furnace. I could take a look at it, of course, but heating problems are not really my expertise. Any plumbing or electricity problems I could probably handle.

Of course, we'd have to get some heat first so that the pipes wouldn't freeze." He fished out a pad and pencil from his coat pocket and made some notes.

"I don't know the first thing about it. I've lived in apartments where the landlord or super takes care of everything," Lesley admitted. "I still don't know what I should do. Maybe I should sell." Her thinking was going in circles. "Guess I need to pray about it."

"Yeah, that might be a good idea. But remember, the Lord helps those who help themselves. He can guide you, but you have to take action. That's what I believe, anyway," he advised.

"Well, could you look into getting some propane delivered and having someone check out the furnace, since that's the first step?" she asked.

"Ah'd be glad tuh to do that fer ya, ma'am."

"I'll pay you of course, for your help."

"Sure, ma'am, that was the agreement," he said, "but it won't cost ya dearly. Today's estimates are free."

"No, you're here with me when you could be working at something else. I insist. I want to pay you for your help."

He sat beside her on the sofa. "Well, our arrangement began as strictly business, but it has changed a little, hasn't it? Or am I being too optimistic?"

"No, you're right. Our relationship isn't strictly business anymore. But you still have to make a living." She insisted again, "I won't let you do this unless you let me pay you for your time and work."

Further argument was interrupted by a startling knock at the front door. "Who in the world could that be?" she asked.

"Don't know. I'll find out," he said, standing and going to the door.

"Well hullo, Big Jim. Fancy meeting you here. Actually, I saw you drive by my office." Lesley recognized that braying voice at once—Connie Evans from Silver Forks Realty. "Is the lady of the house in?" she asked, undoubtedly thinking she was being funny.

"As a matter of fact, Connie, she is," Jim said, revealing that they were acquainted. "I bet I can guess what brought you up the mountain in this weather."

"Yeah, well, if Mohammed won't come to the mountain, the mountain will come to Mohammed—or maybe it's the other way around—I came to the mountain," she said, laughing uproariously at her very convoluted humor.

Lesley stood and prepared to meet the woman whom she'd known only through an obnoxious phone experience. Her appearance matched her voice—dyed red-purple hair, bejeweled glasses that reminded her of Elton John's, and long, dangling earrings. She was wrapped in a fake leopard coat and wore faux fur-topped boots.

"Guess who's here, Lesley," Jim said, leading Connie into the parlor.

"I hope I'm not intruding on—anything," Connie said, with a ridiculous wink.

"No," she said, "but I would have replied to your messages if I'd changed my mind. I told you on the phone that the house wasn't for sale." Saying it aloud made her realize that she really wasn't ready to sell. She needed more time to think about it.

"Yes, and I told you I'd see if they'd up their offer. They have, and you'd be a fool to turn this offer down," she said flatly. Lesley hadn't offered her a chair, but she sat down in the parlor anyway.

"Connie, you'll find I can be pretty stubborn. I haven't made up my mind what I want to do with my house. If I decide to sell it, I may contact you. Otherwise, please don't hassle me anymore," Lesley said, as kindly but as firmly as she could.

"Don't you even want to hear the offer?" she asked.

"I think the lady's spoken," Jim said.

Connie was not to be daunted. "But you can't turn down one and a half million dollars for this old place," she argued.

Lesley was speechless. One and a half million dollars would solve all her financial problems for the rest of her life. She could go on with her acting career without worrying about its lack of security. Or maybe she wouldn't have to work at all. These thoughts raced through her mind while Connie waited expectantly for her response.

She looked at Jim for help, but he just shrugged his shoulders and raised his eyebrows to suggest that it was up to her. And it was.

"That's a very tempting offer, I agree," she said, finding her voice. "But I still need some time to think about it—to make some decisions."

"But the buyer can't wait forever," she said, pushing to close the deal.

"And that's another thing. Who is this buyer you keep mentioning?" Lesley asked, certain of the answer.

"I still haven't been given liberty to reveal that, I'm afraid," Connie said apologetically, "but I assure you, it's a genuine deal, and he has the money—the cash," she revealed.

A cash deal? Lesley thought for a moment. "Well, contact me again when you can tell me who wants to buy my place. I won't deal with a nonentity," she said firmly.

"I think you have your answer, Connie," Jim said. "Now, if you don't mind, we have work to do."

"Yes, I'll bet you have," she said, standing and giving another wink as she moved to the door. "I'll be on my way, then. I'll talk with the buyer and get back to you. Can I reach you at your hotel? Will you take my call?" she asked.

Lesley followed her into the entry. "I'll take your call—or you can leave another message—but don't get your hopes up. I'm giving some serious thought to opening up my house again and living here," she warned.

"Oh, that would be so foolish, dear. You couldn't live up here alone. It's too far away from everything, especially in winter. It might even be dangerous for you," she added.

Is that a threat? Lesley wondered. "Well, that's my personal business and my decision, isn't it?" she said.

"Oh, I was only trying to point out the realities," she said. "I'd do that for anyone, of course."

"I'm sure you would. Well, thanks anyway," Lesley said, opening the door to urge her on her way.

"Okay, well you'll definitely be hearing from me," Connie announced.

I'm sure I will, Lesley thought. "Okay, bye now," she said, and closed the door, maybe a little too forcefully. "What do you think of that?" she asked, returning to the parlor, where Jim was looking very seriously out a window, watching Connie drive away.

He turned to look at her. "Well, that's quite a tempting offer," he said.

"Yes, it is. I don't know what to do."

"I can think of a worse dilemma," he added. "One and a half million dollars is a lot of money. It could set you up for life."

"Then why didn't I jump to accept it?" she thought aloud.

"You said that you wanted to pray about it. That's a great idea. Then after you've done that, sit down and separately list the positives and the negatives. That's what I do. See if one column overbalances the other. That may help you in your decision," he said. "But it is your decision. Don't let anyone else make it for you."

"Thanks, that's good advice." She sat on the sofa, thinking. "Do you think we could pray together—right here, right now?" she asked.

He paused for a moment. "Why not? Two prayers may be better than one," he said, coming directly to her and, without hesitation, kneeling by the sofa. She did the same.

"Will you pray?" she begged, aware that she was putting him in a difficult spot, since they'd known each other for such a short time.

He paused. "Okay. Sure. I'll pray for you," he agreed quietly.

They bowed their heads, and after a moment of silence, Jim prayed a simple prayer, telling Heavenly Father how grateful they were for all their blessings and for their meeting each other. Then he asked the Lord to bless Lesley in the decisions she had to make about her house and future. Jim asked that the Lord's will would be known to her and that she'd act accordingly. He closed in the name of Jesus Christ.

He does know how to pray, she thought. She had tears in her eyes when he finished, and he helped her stand. Then he looked at her and gently kissed her. "I didn't mean to make you cry," he said, smiling sweetly.

"I guess I felt the Lord's spirit in this room," she explained. "And your prayer touched me. Thank you. I feel better now."

They sat together, looking lovingly at each other. Then they both leaned back to watch the falling snow through the frosted window.

Instead of seeing a peaceful view, however, Lesley was shocked to see *WATER* etched in the window. Involuntarily they both ran to the door to get out of the house and also to look for the perpetrator of the hoax. Had Connie done it? Had someone besides Connie Evans followed them there and written on the outside of the glass?

There were no footprints in the new-fallen snow below the window, and they realized that the word wasn't written from outside the window. Rather, it had been written on the inside—while they were in the room.

"I don't want to go back in there right now," Lesley said, trying to catch her breath.

"Go to the truck. I'm going to take a look in there. Someone came in while we were praying. That's the only thing that makes sense," he said, going toward the front door.

"Be careful."

"I can handle myself," Jim assured her, and she didn't doubt that for a minute. *But,* she thought frantically, *what if the intruder isn't real, isn't—mortal?* She ran to the truck and hurriedly climbed inside, locking the doors behind. This couldn't be happening, she thought. Then Lesley remembered, *Julie also thought she'd heard that word from the little girl in the mirror. The girl said, "Water," Julie had insisted.*

Jim startled her when he tried the truck door. She reached over and unlocked it. "There's no one in there. I couldn't see any sign that anyone had come through the back door. There's no one upstairs or downstairs," he said, breathing hard from running through the house.

"Let's get out of here," she said. "Did you lock the front door?"

"Of course, and I agree, I don't want to hang around here right now. Let's get somewhere else, where we can think and talk," he said, starting the truck. The wheels spun as he dug out of the lane, stopping to lock the gate behind them.

They didn't speak until they were down the mountain and entering Silver Forks. Then Jim spoke first. "I don't know about you, but that was too surreal for me. Maybe your place is haunted," he said, laughing nervously.

"Maybe it is," she agreed quietly. Then she thought for a moment. "But there wasn't a bad feeling in the house. We supplied that in our reaction. Like your mother said, the word *water* is pretty harmless. We were frightened, but maybe it was just fear of the unknown."

"You're right, when you consider it logically, but my hair literally stood on end when I saw that word on the window. Up to that point, I have to admit, I'd thought all your experiences were hysterical reactions. I'm sorry now for doubting you—for doubting Mom and Julie. But what does it all mean?" he asked, almost to himself.

"I don't know. I wish I did. Again, maybe the experience itself wasn't so frightening. We supplied the fear. Anyway, let's drop it for now. I'm tired of thinking about my house, and I'm hungry," she said, wanting to return to a more everyday subject and mood.

"Okay, I guess ghosts make me hungry too," he agreed. "Can you wait till we get back to Park City?"

"Unless you can find something along the freeway. I want to go someplace and get warm, drink something warm, and eat to forget," she said.

"I know a little place in Midway. It'd be closer than Park City if you don't mind going that way."

They were at a crossroad in more than one way. "Yes, let's go there. Someplace different. Sounds good to me."

They drove into Wasatch County to the beautiful little hamlet named Midway. Lesley thought that she'd probably been there as a little girl but didn't remember it.

"Why is it called Midway?" she asked.

"I haven't thought much about it, but it might be because it's midway between Park City and Heber City. I really don't know. But it's a spot that Swiss immigrants chose to settle because it reminded them of their homeland. Their descendants have Swiss Days here every summer. It's fun. We'll have to come if you're still around then," he suggested.

"I'd like that—to still be around, I mean, and to go to Swiss Days," she said.

"You mean you still want to hang around here, even if you own a haunted house?" he half teased.

"Wanting to stay around doesn't mean that I want to live in my house. I still can't make up my mind about that. But the 'ghost,' as you called it, certainly doesn't make the house more appealing."

He pulled into the Midway Chalet, a small chalet-style restaurant at the side of the road. It looked inviting, and Lesley thought, *Bet they have good hot chocolate.*

They went inside and were greeted by a sweet, middle-aged lady with glasses, hair braided in wheels covering her ears, and wearing a Swiss costume. The dining room was decorated with white lace curtains, cuckoo clocks, photographs of the Swiss Alps, and wooden tables and chairs. A fire was crackling in the fireplace. Maybe it was because they were the only customers at this hour, but they received a very gracious welcome. The smell of scones wafted from the kitchen, and Lesley decided she had to have some. They ordered scones, honey, and hot chocolate and sat quietly in anticipation.

"This is fun," she said, "like stepping into a European village."

"Yeah, I love this area. There's a lot to see and do here."

They were purposely avoiding discussion of the happening at her house but realized they couldn't just forget it.

"Do you still want to me to inquire into getting the propane tank filled and the other utilities arranged for?" Jim asked.

She didn't respond immediately, so he asked, "Would you rather wait a while—need more time to think about it?"

"I don't know what to do. Maybe we should wait until I know more about the *Touched by an Angel* shooting schedule."

"That's true," he said, taking Lesley's hand across the table. "Frankly, I was hoping that opening the house would give you a reason to stick around a while longer—and to come back here when you're not working someplace else."

"Yes, I've been thinking that too. Maybe I should sell the place and buy another house—a smaller place, not so isolated," she thought aloud.

He seemed pleased at that thought and said, "Yeah, that would be another option. Do you really want to sell to Joe Spencer, though? I guess a cash deal would make a difference. He couldn't go back on that."

"Well, why don't we do this. You go ahead and look into the costs of filling the propane tank and getting someone to check out the furnace. Then maybe you could do the same for the electricity and plumbing. Then I'll have more information to help in my decisions. And keep track of the time you spend, so I can pay you," she insisted.

"Ah'd be glad to do that fer ya, ma'am," he said, smiling.

The same little woman who had greeted them arrived with a tray of wonderful-smelling scones and steaming hot chocolate, and they dug in ravenously. "This is delicious," Lesley said. "I'd come back again without hesitation. What a happy spot."

"Yeah, a true sensory experience, I agree," he said, rubbing his tummy.

She laughed. "You're like a little boy sometimes."

"Do you like little boys?" he asked. "If so, I'm glad."

"Yes, that's just one of your endearing qualities."

"I like you too." He smiled that beautiful smile that also shone in his eyes.

She thought, *My cold hands have thawed, and my heart is warming.*

The earlier fright was temporarily forgotten as they enjoyed that moment of closeness together. But the peace was interrupted by the ringing of Jim's cell phone.

He talked for a moment, then disconnected. "That was Mom. Apparently the County called. Animal Control needs my help with a moose that's come down into someone's yard. What they forget is that their house on the mountainside is really located in the moose's yard. Guess we better go," he suggested reluctantly.

"Guess we better. But I understand," she assured him. "After all, that's what wild animal specialists are supposed to do, isn't it? Help with wild animals?"

"Yes, but I hoped we'd have the whole day together."

They paid the check, left a tip, then headed for the truck.

"There'll be another day. How about tomorrow?" she asked.

"I've got a remodeling job in town that'll probably take me a couple of days. Maybe we could get together some evening— take in a Sundance Festival film?"

"I'd like that. Call me when you know you're free. I don't have many plans this week, as I told you."

"Okay. Kinda plan for tomorrow night, but I'll call to make sure," he said.

The drive back to Park City was peaceful. The roads were relatively free of traffic, and the sun was shining brightly. The world seemed refreshed and cleansed by the storm. Lesley thought of how much she'd missed the changing seasons while living in California.

More and more she began to feel that she could make Park City her home.

CHAPTER 14

Lesley awoke to the brilliant sun shining through the window and looked out at the snow-covered village and valley below. She knelt to thank the Lord for her blessings and prayed for His help in making the right decisions, particularly regarding her future in Utah.

She decided to spoil herself again by ordering a room service breakfast and sat on the comfortable chaise, catching up on her scripture reading while she ate. She felt less wary about the happenings at her house and the problems that she faced, but she still didn't know what to do about them.

She literally shook her head, trying to clear away her confused thoughts. But the experiences of the past week—shared by others, including Julie, a very young and innocent girl—were strange. There had to be some explanation, either scientifically rational or undeniably spiritual, for the things they'd all seen. If she'd been there alone experiencing those happenings, she'd have attributed them to silly hysteria or paranoia, but she wasn't alone. *Mass hysteria?* She didn't think so.

She dressed in jeans, a warm, white sweater, and her ever-ready, all-purpose boots. She had no specific plans for the day but felt herself drawn back to her house. She wasn't totally frightened, and she simply had to explore the mysteries of their experiences there. Maybe if she were there alone, she could figure out what was happening and why—and what she should do.

As usual, Barnaby was standing near the front desk when Lesley came downstairs. "Going to the movies again, Ms. Kern?" he asked.

"No, Barnaby, not today," she said, trying to hurry past him before he could question her further.

"I know you're not going out for breakfast, since someone took it to your room. So—where are you headed?" he asked too anxiously.

"Who wants to know?" she demanded.

"Oh, just wondering, so that if someone asks for you, we can tell them how to find you," he said.

"I'll ask again—who? Who wants to know?"

"Well, I guess I'd better fess up," he said guiltily. "Mr. Sanders was asking for you all day yesterday, and I had to tell him that I didn't know where you were."

"Good. You can tell him that again. You don't know where I am," she said, and went quickly down the hall and downstairs to the garage without waiting for Barnaby's reaction.

It was a beautiful day. Otherwise, she might have thought twice about driving alone to Silver Forks Mountain, but she simply felt that she must go there—alone—to think. She wouldn't stay long, because she wanted to get back in case Jim called about seeing a film that night. She was looking forward to that possibility.

The drive was pleasant until she turned in to Silver Forks. There, parked in front of Silver Forks Realty, was Joe Spencer's black Lincoln. She sped up and drove hurriedly across the creek bridge and up Silver Forks Mountain Road, hoping that nosy Connie wouldn't see her driving past. She supposed that

Connie was meeting with her boss to discuss Lesley's rejection of his current offer.

But she had other things on her mind that day. She wanted some answers about the unusual happenings at her house. She'd begun to feel less wary, less frightened of whatever it was going on there. She supposed she'd become more curious than spooked at that point.

She opened the gate and drove the Navigator through the now-familiar ruts in the lane.

Habitually locking the car, as she'd learned to do living in big cities, she stomped her boots on the porch and opened the front door to her house.

The sun had melted the frost on the parlor window where they had seen the word *WATER* written, and sunlight filled the parlor, taking some of the chill from the room. She sat in the parlor for a moment. Then, taking a deep breath and forcing herself to stand, she decided to go up the stairs, almost inviting in her mind another experience with the little girl in the mirror.

She climbed very slowly and carefully, stopping about three steps from the second floor landing. Then, breathing deeply, she took one slow step at a time, halting with one foot on the tread of the last step. She looked into the mirror, almost willing the image of the young girl to appear. She wasn't there, and Lesley was almost disappointed. Then something equally strange happened—the mirror began to swing slowly toward her like a hinged door. When it creaked open fully, she realized that it was indeed a door—a mirrored door to a dark opening.

She took a step backward, holding her breath and not knowing what would happen next. Then she heard it—from somewhere above her came a sweet, childlike voice humming an old but recognizable Primary hymn, "Can a Little Child

Like Me?" Mesmerized, Lesley walked toward the opening behind the mirror and saw a very narrow flight of stairs leading to what seemed to be an attic.

She hesitated before going up the steep stairs. *Should I wait until I'm not alone?* she wondered. Then the humming stopped for a moment and began again. She had to find its source. She slowly crept up the stairs. The area was dark except for a crack of daylight that appeared to be coming through a small window. She had never heard her parents speak of an attic. The stairs creaked as she climbed. The dusty and musty odors suggested that the area had been closed up for ages. She wondered if her parents even knew of the existence of the space—a secret room?

When she reached the top of the stairs, the humming stopped abruptly. In the dim light she strained to see someone, to find the source of the music. Unless the singer had a very good hiding place, there was no one up there.

Three old steamer trunks were stacked against one wall. A wooden rocker, a brass headboard, an old baby bed, several small tables, and an antique tricycle were stored where they'd probably been left many decades before. Near the low window, in what she figured from the octagonal walls must be the interior of one of the turrets on the roof, she saw a small child's desk. An open book—a photo album or a scrapbook— lay on the desk. She knelt to see it better and became aware of the dusty floor and dust everywhere—except on the book— which was as clean as if it had just been placed there.

She picked it up and moved closer to the small window. As she had suspected, the book was a photo album. It was open to what appeared to be a family picture—a man, a woman, a boy, and a girl—the girl she'd seen in the mirror! They wore late nineteenth-century, best-dress clothing. Upon closer examination, she realized that the picture was of her great-grandparents, their only child, a son—her grandfather—and a girl, taller and older than the boy. Who was she? She looked beneath the picture to find there was no identification of those in the sepia-toned photograph.

She turned, suddenly needing frantically to escape the dusty, claustrophobic enclosure. Despite her panic, she had the presence of mind to grab the photo album. As she started down the stairs, the mirror door at the foot began to close. She raced to the bottom and shoved the door outward before it closed completely. She stepped out into the welcoming fresh air and light of the house proper and then heard it again—humming from the room behind her. She slammed the mirror door shut and flew down the stairs. She ran through the snow toward the car, clutching the photo album in her arms.

Fumbling with the car keys, she managed to get inside, then pressed the automatic lock to shield her from—from what? All she knew at that point was that she wanted off the mountain. She'd try to figure out exactly what was happening in her house when she wasn't alone. She had been foolish to come there without Jim.

She started the car, then drove to the gate, almost crashing head-on into Joe Spencer's black Lincoln, which was turning into her gateway. She slammed on the brakes, and the Navigator skidded to a stop. She was already shocked and breathless from her harrowing experience at the house, but the near crash sent her into a shaking fit.

The next thing she knew, Connie was climbing out of the Lincoln's passenger-side front seat and rushing toward her car. She rolled down the window. "Are you all right? You look white as a sheet," Connie said. "You're not hurt, are you?" she questioned.

"No, I'm not—hurt. Just shook up. I hadn't expected anyone to be entering my gate," she explained.

"Well, you were certainly in a hurry. You were acting like you'd seen a ghost," she said, laughing at her ridiculous suggestion.

"No, I . . . I just have to get back to town," Lesley said truthfully. She wanted to get back to the safety of the crowds in bustling Park City. "What are you doing here?"

"Oh, I saw you drive past my office. Ya see, my desk sits so I can look right out the front window. Coincidentally, I was meeting with someone about your request—to know the identity of the buyer. Well, he not only gave permission for that, he's come to tell you himself." She gestured a "come-here" toward Joe Spencer's car. A wizened, sallow-complexioned, older man with a pencil-thin mustache, rimless glasses, and a crumpled, dark business suit and a gray fedora hat climbed slowly out of the car. Lesley assumed he was the infamous Joe Spencer, the last person she wanted to meet at that moment.

He seemed irritated at having to trudge through the snow but came over to Connie, changing his countenance to suggest a genial, agreeable gentleman. "Ms. Kern, this is Mr. Joe Spencer, the buyer of your property," Connie gushed, as if introducing a royal personage.

"Mr. Spencer," Lesley said, nodding her head out the window, without extending her hand to meet his proffered handshake. "But I have to correct your assumption, Connie. At this point, no one is the *buyer* of my property. I haven't agreed to sell it—yet."

"Oh, I'm sorry. I didn't mean to suggest that. I meant that Mr. Spencer is the party who wants to buy your property. He's come all this way up the mountain to meet you and to answer any questions you might have," she said, trying to salvage the situation. "I'm sure that . . ."

"Ms. Kern," Spencer interrupted, "I wanted to reassure you that the offer for your property is a bona fide offer—one and a half million dollars, payable by certified check at the closing. Could we go back to the realty office and discuss the matter?"

"Well, no, I . . ."

"Perhaps this isn't a convenient time. You seem in a hurry to go someplace," he said, smiling what he must have thought was a warm, inviting smile but that came off as a vampirish leer through his worn and stained teeth.

"Yes, yes, I have to get back to town—to Park City—at once," Lesley said, wanting to avoid any further contact with these people that day.

"Well, then, could we make an appointment with you at a more suitable time?" Connie asked, obviously drooling over her anticipated commission and even more obviously wanting to please Joe Spencer.

"I'll—I'll see," Lesley said. "Call me—and I'll see."

"Well, I wish that we could set up an appointment right now," she said, pressing the sale.

Joe Spencer stepped in, displaying the fawning, obsequious manner which he'd undoubtedly perfected in his numerous wheelings and dealings. "If this isn't a good time, let's do that, Connie. Call Ms. Kern and set up an appointment at her convenience. I assure you, I'll make myself available."

"Well, all right. Could I call you this afternoon?" Connie asked.

"No, I'll be busy all afternoon and evening," Lesley said. "Just call me tomorrow morning—not too early." She wanted to get away from them and from her house and was willing to agree to another meeting just to get rid of them.

"We'll do that," Spencer said. "Come along, Connie. Let's move the car out of Ms. Kern's way. Glad to have met you Ms. Kern," he said, tipping his hat and walking toward his car.

"I'll call," Connie said wistfully, seeming disappointed at her failure in clinching the deal. "Thanks, anyway." She climbed in the front seat, and Spencer backed slowly out of the gate and turned onto the main road.

Lesley sat there for a moment, seeing the photo album, which she was still clutching, and trying to comprehend all that had happened in the past hour. Then she rallied, drove through the gateway, and concentrated solely on not overtaking Joe Spencer's car.

CHAPTER 15

Secure behind the locked door of her hotel room, she snuggled beneath a comforter, trying to remove the chill from her bones—a chill caused not only by the weather but by all that had happened that morning.

Was the humming voice real? Had she imagined it? She was almost beginning to doubt her sanity when she saw the photo album beside her and was reminded that it was definitely real. And the attic beyond the hidden mirror door was real, too.

She opened the album, searching for that photograph of her great-grandparents, their son—their only child—and the unidentified girl. In a better light and without emotion, she wanted to determine if the girl in the picture was really the same girl she'd seen in the mirror. *Should I show the picture to Julie?* she questioned. Would Julie say that it was the girl she also saw—the girl who spoke to her?

Lesley looked through the other photos in the album to see if there was another picture of the girl. There wasn't. Who was she? How could she find her identity? *Of course, where better!* she thought. *The Family History Center in Salt Lake.* Maybe the girl in the picture was a relative, a foster child, or a live-in at her great-grandparents' home. She thought of Jim's reminder that the Lord helps those who help themselves—who do something.

Breakfast seemed a long while back. She was hungry but didn't want to order from room service again, so she decided to put on her coat and gloves and find a place for a quick lunch. Then she'd return and wait for Jim's call. Maybe she could convince him to go with her to the Family History Center.

She had managed to dodge Barnaby on her return from Silver Forks Mountain and hoped to do it again. No such luck. He was standing at the foot of the stairs.

"You're back already," he said, "and going out again?"

"Yes, going out again—for lunch," she said, trying to keep the information general.

"Well, the Silver Fork has an excellent lunch menu," he suggested with a silly grin and a wink.

"You never give up, do you?"

"Well, can't blame a guy for trying, as Mr. Sanders says. He called again this morning. Said that I should invite you to come back to his restaurant."

"Thanks, Barnaby, but I saw a little hamburger place closer to the hotel. I'm in a hurry," she said, realizing she'd revealed more than she intended.

"Yeah, I know the place—Great Burgers. I eat there all the time. Well, okay, have a great lunch," he said, heading for the front desk and, she was sure, the phone.

She went out into the sunny but still crisp day, breathing deeply in the cold mountain air. Main Street was crowded, and she had to weave her way along the narrow sidewalk. She could have found the hamburger place by simply following her nose—frying onions wafted through the air outside the small café.

She went inside to find a hungry mob chattering noisily, but there was one empty, two-person wooden booth near the rear exit, and she made her way to it, pushing through the crowd.

She found a well-used menu in a wire rack on the table—a rack which also held a small jar of chili sauce, a jar of pickle relish, a squeeze bottle of Dijon mustard, and a bottle of ketchup.

She was perusing the huge variety of "great" burgers, when she heard a familiar voice behind her. "Well, fancy meeting you here," Gareth Sanders quipped.

Almost in disgust, she looked up as he leaned on the edge of her table.

"Yes, just another coincidence, I suppose," she said.

"No, as you probably realize, Barnaby told me where you'd be. Also, I haven't had lunch and it's a good idea to check out the competition once in a while. Would you mind if I join you?" he asked, almost too politely.

"Oh, not really, but I'm just staying long enough to order and eat, so don't expect a lengthy conversation." She was purposely preparing for her exit even before finding out what he had in mind.

"You know, we began quite amicably," he said, sliding into the seat across from her. "What did I do to create this icy feeling between us now?"

"Oh, don't worry about it. I've just—had a lot on my mind and a lot to do this past week. Of course, I did tell you that I didn't like your tactics in finding me and following me—and here you are again," she reminded him. She thought again of Jim's family and their feelings about him—feelings that she had at least begun to understand, if not share.

"Well, you can't blame . . ."

"I know. 'You can't blame a guy for trying.' You've said that before. But I don't know what you're really after. An acquaintance can develop slowly into a friendship—but it can't be forced." She tried to smile at him, but her smile seemed forced, validating her words.

A long-haired, youthful waiter with an earring loop, a tattoo, and a not-too-clean white apron arrived to take their orders. "Welcome to Great Burgers," he said, not too enthusiastically. "I'm Tom. I'll be your server." The formality of this announcement was as incongruous as the whole situation in which she found herself. Despite her hunger, she just wanted out of there.

Gareth asked, "Are you ready to order, Lesley?"

"Have you been here before?"

"Yes, and I can recommend the chili burger if you like chili." He looked at her inquisitively.

"I do, but it doesn't like me. Just give me a plain hamburger—no onions—they don't like me, either," she told the waiter, "and a Sprite."

"Okay, and do you want the chili burger, sir?" the waiter asked, obviously trying to hurry the momentous decision so that he could get on with his work.

"Yes, a chili burger and a Coke," Gareth said.

The waiter went without another word, and Lesley was left trying to decide where to direct her eyes and what to say. She had created a wall between them, and conversation had dried up.

Gareth cleared his throat. "I've heard you've been going up to your house on Silver Forks Mountain rather often."

"Oh, you have, have you? And I'll bet I can guess who's been your informant—the grinning boy who loves your tips—for his tips?" she asked sarcastically.

"Well yes, but someone else said that you were considering selling your house. Are you?"

"This *is* a small town," she said. "Actually, I'm looking into refurbishing it a bit and possibly living there myself."

He looked very surprised. "You are? What would make you want to do that, I wonder, after forgetting it for so long?" His foxy smile belied his question, suggesting that he knew more than he was revealing.

"I have a job—a role in a *Touched by an Angel* episode. I'll have to stick around for it, and I'll need a place to stay. I've been thinking about opening my house and using it as a home base while I travel doing my acting jobs."

The waiter came with their food, and she had to admit it looked and smelled good.

She had just taken a big bite when Gareth started asking questions. "Well, you actually could live in the hotel—do you really want to live that far out of town? Where will the filming be done?"

She tried to talk with her mouth full. "I don't really know that yet, but I'd guess it would be shot in Salt Lake. Anyway, as I said, I'm just trying to decide what's best to do. I haven't made any firm decisions."

"I like a girl who likes to eat," he said, smiling at her attempts to eat and talk at the same time. "I also heard that someone made an offer to buy your house. Was the offer—at all tempting?"

"Why are you so interested in that? Do you know more about it than you're pretending?" she asked point-blank.

"Well, there is something I've been hiding—something I haven't told you," he explained. He looked down at his hands, then said, "I own—or rather my corporation owns—the Silver Princess." He looked up for her reaction. "That's the reason I know so much about what goes on there. I heard that both Connie Evans and Joe Spencer have been leaving messages for you, and I just put two and two together. I should have told you, but I didn't want to make you uncomfortable about staying there. I could arrange it so that you could stay on—indefinitely."

"So Barnaby isn't only your informant—he's your *stooge*," she said angrily.

"No, no, he isn't exactly carrying out any orders from me. You already know that he was trying to get us together at my urging, but it was all very innocent."

She took another bite of her hamburger and didn't respond immediately.

"Are you mad—about my owning the hotel and not telling you?" he asked.

"No, not exactly, but I can't understand why you didn't mention it on the plane when you were telling me about your restaurant. It would have seemed the natural thing to do," she suggested, looking him in the eye and feeling less trustful of Gareth than ever.

"But you were so reluctant to tell me where you were staying," he explained. "When you finally told me you were staying at the Silver Princess, it just seemed best not to worry you about my connections there. I don't really know why I didn't tell you. Later, when you became upset about my shadowing you and about Barnaby's nosiness, I didn't dare tell you, frankly."

"Was I that witchy about it?"

"No, but I got some definite negative signals from you. I didn't want to give you any other reasons for rejecting me," he said, looking down at his untouched chili burger.

"Your food's getting cold."

"Yes, but I'm not really hungry. I actually came here to try to—patch things up between us—not to eat," he admitted.

"Well, no harm's done, I suppose, but I have to say again that I'd prefer that you communicate rather than just showing up where I'm going. I have a right to privacy, even if you do own the hotel."

"Yes, you do, and I apologize. Will you take my calls if I try to phone you?" he asked.

"Of course. You're as tenacious as Connie Evans—whom you seem to know, right?"

"Right. I do know her and Joe Spencer. As I told you, I've spent a lot of time in the Silver Forks area, and it's a very small town. News travels as fast as Connie and the general store employees can talk."

She finished her burger, but he hadn't eaten a bite. "Well, I have to go," she said. "Where's that waiter when you need him?" She looked around, trying to catch his eye.

"Don't worry about the check. I'll take care of it."

"Well, thank you—again—for feeding me." She stood and started to get her coat.

Gareth stood to help her with it and said, "I'm glad we had this little talk. Are things okay between us now?"

She paused before answering. "Yes—okay. Just give me some elbow room, *please*," she emphasized. "See you when I see you, and thanks for lunch." She turned and left him standing there watching her leave.

She was actually glad for the meeting since they'd cleared the air, and she hoped she'd experience less interest in her affairs from the hotel staff—and from Gareth Sanders. But he had revealed that the Silver Forks people were also watching her every move, which was rather disconcerting. She went back to the hotel feeling somehow less comfortable there. She entered her room thinking of Gareth's revelation and of the sneaking suspicion that he had known beforehand that she was to stay at the Silver Princess. She tried to dismiss these disturbing thoughts and to concentrate, instead, on her anticipation of Jim's call.

CHAPTER 16

Lesley fell asleep on her bed while looking at the photo album and was awakened at about five PM by the ringing phone. She fumbled for it without really opening her eyes and said a sleepy, "Hello."

"Well, sleepy head, seems I woke you from your late afternoon beauty nap," Jim said. "I'm sorry."

She sat right up at the sound of his voice. "No, no, don't be. I didn't plan to take a nap. I can't seem to catch up on my rest. Maybe it's the higher altitude here. But I'm glad you woke me."

"Well, I promised I'd call. The remodeling turned out to be a one-day job, so I'm all yours tonight and tomorrow if you still want to do something."

"Oh, I do. I was hoping you'd call. Something happened . . ."

"What do you mean? Are you okay?" He sounded very worried.

"Yes, I'm okay, but I decided to go back to my house today—alone. I'm not sure it was a good idea."

"I'm coming right over to get you," Jim insisted.

"No, there's nothing wrong—but I would like to talk to you about it."

"I'm coming. I need to shower and change. Then I'll be right there. Six o'clock okay?" he asked.

"Yes, I'll be ready. Where are we going?"

"I'm hungry. If you are too, let's get something to eat. Then after we talk, want to see a movie?"

"Sounds fun, but I don't think we'll be able to get tickets to any of the Sundance films this late in the day. Maybe we should save that for tomorrow," she suggested.

"Okay, we'll go someplace for dinner, then talk."

"I'll meet you out front," she said, "at six."

"Ah'll be there in mah best rig to git ya," he said.

As usual she laughed and said, "I'm glad you're coming. I really am." Then she hung up.

She freshened up, put on her coat and gloves, and started for the door. Then she remembered the photo album and went back to the bed for it. She wanted to show the old photograph to Jim and tell him what had happened at her house.

Fortunately, Barnaby was off duty, so no one bothered her while she waited in the lobby for Jim's arrival. She sat near a window where she could see his truck when he came. She thought, *Maybe Gareth called off his employees' snooping.* She hoped so. The fire in the fireplace was warm and cheery, and she began to feel less tense about everything.

When Jim pulled up, she stood and hurried out the front doors, almost running to his truck. But he jumped out and opened the truck door for her. "Nice to see you," he said.

"It's so good to see you. I've looked forward to this all day," Lesley revealed, not hiding her growing feelings for him and looking up at those smiling blue eyes that had so fascinated her from their first meeting.

"What's that?" he asked, pointing to the album.

"It's a photo album. I found it at my house. That's part of the reason I need to talk with you, but let's wait until after dinner. I know you're always very hungry after working," she said.

"Okay, if you're sure you're all right. What sounds good to you—a steak?" he asked.

"No, I haven't had a vegetable for days. How about a good salad?" she suggested.

"Vegetables? How about Chinese? There's a very good Chinese restaurant on Main Street. In fact, there are several Chinese cafés around—holdovers from the old Park City Chinatown—miners who came here from China and then went into other businesses. We could walk to any one of them—wouldn't have to find another parking place."

"Yes, that sounds good. Let's walk," she said, swinging her legs out of the truck.

He helped her down, locking the doors behind him.

"It's cold, but it's a pretty night," he said, taking a deep breath and leading her back to the sidewalk.

"It is. I've really enjoyed that part of my stay here—the weather and the setting."

They joined the happy crowds on the sidewalk, then jaywalked to the other side of Main Street to a promising Chinese restaurant. Inside, a tall, thin Chinese headwaiter with a scraggly chin beard greeted them in the auspicious entrance decorated in gilded oriental sculptures and black lacquer paint. He led them to a table by a window overlooking Main Street. Red linens contrasted with the gold and black decor, creating an elegant dining room.

The head waiter seated them, presented large, shiny black menus with gold lettering, and announced, "Pang be your waitress. Hope you enjoy."

The restaurant was crowded, but the thick carpeting absorbed most of the sound, making it a great place for conversation. The petite Asian waitress, her hair in a bun atop her head and wearing native Chinese dress, arrived and took their order. Jim chose a combination dinner with beef pea pods, egg foo-yong, and Oriental chicken. Lesley asked for the steamed vegetables. While they waited for their Chinese-American dinners, Jim suggested, "Might as well tell me about your day."

"Okay, but I feel kinda silly about my reactions to what happened. I probably shouldn't have gone back there alone, but I felt I had to . . . and I had a free day . . . so . . ."

"I wish you'd waited until I could go back with you. Were you hurt?" he asked with real concern.

"No, it wasn't that. I just had another strange experience in the house, which actually made me doubt my sanity for a moment. If you'd been there, I might have responded differently," she explained. "And you could have corroborated what happened—I wouldn't have wondered if I was losing it."

"Well, I know what I saw personally. It was real, so I wouldn't be so likely to doubt you as I might have been earlier. Go on," he urged, reaching across the table to hold her hand.

"I drove up there in the morning. It was pleasant until I passed Silver Forks Realty—Joe Spencer's car was parked there, so I hurried past. When I went in my house, I sat for a while in the parlor. Then I felt drawn to go upstairs. I didn't know what to expect but found—a real surprise . . ."

"Yes, go on."

"At the top of the stairs, I stopped, actually thinking I might see the girl in the mirror again, but instead the mirror opened by itself, like a door. It's a hinged door, and it leads to another flight of stairs and an attic. I'd never heard of the doorway, the stairs, or the attic. I even wonder if my folks knew about it."

"Whew, that is spooky," he said. She was relieved that he was treating the matter seriously. He wasn't mocking her.

The waitress brought their food, so Lesley's story was put on hold. The plates were already heaped, but she also brought a covered bowl of rice. Jim dug in, as hungry as he'd said he was. Lesley toyed with her food at first but found it so good that her appetite improved.

"Well, tell me the rest. You've got me hooked," Jim said.

She had to swallow a mouthful before she could talk. "I was afraid to go into the dark opening. Then I heard—this is the part that's hard to believe—I heard a little sweet voice humming an old Primary song."

Jim said nothing but looked at Lesley incredulously with raised eyebrows.

"I know, it's hard to accept, but I did hear it. I went up the narrow stairway but found just what you'd expect to find in an attic—old furniture and junk, covered in dust. No one was there, and the humming had stopped. But then I found this album open to an old photograph."

He'd stopped eating, concentrating on her story. "Who's in the photograph?"

"It's a group photo, a family photo, of my great-grandparents, their son—my grandfather—and a girl just older than he."

"A girl?" he asked expectantly.

"Yes, a girl—it's the girl I thought I saw in the mirror. Here, let me show you." She reached down for the photo album, which she'd placed at the side of her chair, and thumbed through the pages to the photograph she wanted him to see. She displayed it for him.

"You're sure that's the same girl—the one you saw?" he asked, still unbelieving.

"Yes, I'm sure, but if you think it would be all right, I'd like to show the picture to Julie—to see if she recognizes the girl as the one she saw," she suggested tentatively.

"Well, I guess it would be okay, but Julie was rather spooked by that experience. I'm hesitant to put her through that again. Let me ask her about it—see how she'd feel about looking at it, okay?"

"Sure, sure. I understand and I won't insist. I guess I'm searching for some kind of reinforcement that I'm not imagining things."

"That's understandable. You have no idea who the girl was?"

"None. I've never heard of another girl in our family line. The other children were all boys. I'm the first girl born in my father's line going back to my great-grandparents."

"You're food's getting cold," he pointed out.

"Yes, and cold, cooked vegetables are pretty nasty," she agreed. "I'll quit talking and eat."

"Okay, then I'll talk for a minute. Just nod your answers—yes or no. Did the humming start up again?" She nodded yes. "Did you completely search the attic?" Again she nodded. "Did you stay in the attic for a while?" She shook her head.

Then she interrupted the silly process. "I can't keep quiet," she said, laughing. "I felt claustrophobic in that dark little attic and ran down the stairs with the photo album clutched in my arms. The humming started up again, and I slammed the mirror door closed. Then I ran to the car."

"I wish you hadn't gone there alone," he said.

"I do too. But there's more. I was racing out the lane and almost ran into Joe Spencer's car."

"You're kidding? Was it him? Did he come up there?"

"Yes, with Connie Evans. She'd seen me drive past the realty office and talked Joe Spencer into following me to my house."

"What did they want?"

"Connie came to my car first. Then Joe Spencer followed. They both tried to pressure me into a meeting to close the sale of my house, but I resisted."

"Good for you. What did you think about Joe?" he asked, looking directly at her.

She paused for a moment, trying to find words to explain her reaction. "Well, I didn't feel—comfortable with him. Frankly, I was repelled by his oily manner. I just wanted to get away—to get back here to safety."

"I think your instincts were good," Jim said. "So you didn't agree to meet with him?"

"Not exactly. Connie's going to call me. But I don't have to meet with them if I decide I don't want to."

"Has all of this made you want to sell the house?" he asked, remembering his dinner and taking another bite.

She hesitated before answering. "I still haven't made a firm decision, but since you've asked, yes, I think I want to sell—but possibly not to Joe Spencer. I really don't feel good about doing business with him. But I don't really think I could live there alone. Too much has happened. And I have to figure out what's going on—what it all means."

"I agree, if you can. Then what's your plan?"

"I've been praying about it. I want to go to the Family History Center in Salt Lake and see if I can find out anything about the girl in the photo. I've been wondering if she was a foster child or if my great-grandparents had adopted her."

"Want to go tomorrow?" he asked.

"Yes, could we? I'd be so grateful if you'd come with me. Maybe I'll find some answers, but even if I don't, I have to try."

"Let's do it. I'd like to go to the Museum of Church History and Art next to the library, and maybe we could see a movie after and then go to Temple Square at night to see the lights. How about it?"

"Sounds wonderful, Jim," she said, relieved that he'd agreed to go with her and excited at the plans for an eventful day in the city.

Jim had managed to eat most of his dinner while she left half of hers behind. They left the restaurant and walked up the hill to her hotel.

He insisted on walking Lesley to her room. On the way they agreed to take her rental car in the morning and to make a nine o'clock departure. Then he kissed her at her door, wished her good night, and went away toward the stairs. Watching him leave, she leaned back against the door, feeling a little light-headed. She told herself to regain her objectivity and recover from her silly swoon. But she was happy in the reassurance that he wanted to help her. She thought, *I will sleep well tonight*—and she did.

CHAPTER 17

Lesley wore a beige cashmere sweater and her warm, brown wool pants since they would be walking outside in Salt Lake City and going from building to building in and around Temple Square. She knelt for her morning prayer, thanking the Lord for her blessings and asking for safety in their travel and assistance in her search for the identity of the young girl in the picture. Then she took the stairs to the lower-level garage, found the Navigator, and drove to Jim's house.

On the way she remembered that she'd told Connie to call her later that day. *Anyway, no matter,* she thought. *If she tries to call, I guess she'll get the message that I'm not too anxious to sell my house to Joe Spencer.*

She debated about simply honking the horn for Jim, but the decision was made for her—he was watching for her and came running out of the house. He looked handsome in a dark brown leather coat, a light brown turtleneck, and khaki Dockers. Without planning it, they were color coordinated for the day.

He jumped in beside her in the passenger seat.

"Hi," she said. "Do you want to drive?"

"No, you drive. I'll sit back and relax," he said, smiling.

"Maybe you won't relax. You haven't been my passenger on a long trip," she warned. "I'm a speed demon."

"Well, if you need me to, I'll tell you how to drive," he offered, laughing.

"Don't you dare. I can't stand backseat drivers—even from the front seat."

"I trust you," he said, touching Lesley's hand, and she knew that he meant it.

"And—I trust you," she said. Saying it and meaning it was a nice feeling.

"Okay, let's be off—oh wait, I had an idea. Where were your great-grandparents buried?" he asked.

"Well, my parents were buried in a newer cemetery—Mt. Olivet Cemetery—just south of the University of Utah, across from the Olympic Stadium, but I'm not really sure about my great-grandparents and my grandparents. I think they were probably buried in the old Salt Lake City Cemetery. They both moved from Silver Forks into Salt Lake. My great-grandfather built a big Victorian house just off South Temple—or Brigham Street it was called back then. He built in the area now called the Avenues, near the cemetery. I don't know whether his house is still there, but I think I could find the cemetery."

"I know exactly where it is. I've been there before—to a funeral," he said. "Anyway, I thought that we might look for your great-grandparents' graves on the off chance that the young girl could be buried there. What d'ya think?"

"It's a long shot, but I think it's a great idea. If she is there, her name might be on a headstone."

"Yeah, it may be just a wild goose chase, but it's worth a try. If we can't find the graves, we'll go on to the Family History Center and dig there. Oops, I guess that wasn't a very good way to put it," he apologized.

She laughed and started the car. "Well, we won't be doing any digging at the cemetery. I can guarantee that." As she was about to drive off, she saw Carol from the corner of her eye coming out the front door, waving.

"Oh, it's your mother." Lesley rolled down the window and called, "Hi, Carol. I should have come in to say hello, but your son was raring to go."

"It's okay, I just wanted to wave. Drop by when you bring my big boy back, if it's not too late," she called.

"I will. Thanks. It's nice to see you," Lesley said and waved good-bye.

Carol waved again and stepped back into the warmth of her cozy home.

"I like your mother so much," Lesley said, driving toward the freeway access road.

"She likes you. In fact, we all like you—Julie included. She keeps asking about you. Wants to know why I haven't brought you home again."

She smiled, thinking of the connotations of that phrase: "brought you home again." The somewhat remote potential of that idea was becoming rather important to her. She realized that she already felt more at home with the Shepherd family than she had anytime or anywhere in her life.

They waited until they were in the city to get breakfast, and she turned off Foothill Boulevard at the same pancake house where she'd stopped after her flight to Salt Lake. The restaurant served breakfast all day, of course, and they both ate heartily.

Then they drove downtown, passing the University of Utah and turning west on South Temple. Jim said, "Turn right here."

"Turn right—right here, you mean?"

"Yes, that's what I mean," he said, laughing. After they turned the corner, he directed, "Stop here for a second. That red brick, two-story house a few houses down was David O.

McKay's home." He pointed to a lovely but modest two-story bungalow on South Temple.

"Really?"

"Yes, really."

"My parents loved David O. McKay, and I love reading his words. Apparently he had a wonderful regard for his wife," she said.

"Yes, I've heard that too. Somebody—I think it might have been President Monson—told a story about his kindness to everyone. Apparently President McKay drove a big car—a Buick, I believe—and was headed along South Temple to the office when he saw a woman trying to cross the street at a crosswalk. He stopped for her, of course, and a man behind him began honking his horn. As the story goes, after he helped the woman cross safely, President McKay stopped by his car, took off his hat, bowed to the man, and then got back in his car and drove away—a real example of patience and courtesy."

"How did you hear that story?" she asked, impressed that Jim had paid that kind of attention to a prophet's life.

"Oh, I've frequently watched conference and the Church station—even though I haven't attended church meetings. It always gives me a real boost." He paused. "But I guess the Lord sent you along to give me another boost—the will to do something more than *think* about going back. I'm grateful for that," he said, smiling at Lesley. And she believed him.

Just then a driver behind her honked, and she realized she was blocking the street by stopping after turning. She thought it more than coincidence that she now had the challenge of being patient and kind in her response. Lesley pulled over out of the way, rolled down her window, and waved, mouthing the words, "I'm sorry." Then the lady smiled, drove past, and went on her way. They followed her up the hill until they almost reached Eighth Avenue and could see that they'd taken the right route to the cemetery.

There was snow on the ground, but the roads inside the cemetery had been cleared. Lesley's winter driving skills had returned during the short week she'd been back in Utah, but she had yet to meet a real driving test—the roads had been good everywhere she'd been.

Rather than driving all over the cemetery looking for the Kern plot, they found the sexton's office and stopped for directions. A stout, middle-aged lady with thick glasses consulted her files and said, "Yes, here it is. Kern." She brought out a map and pointed out the route as she spoke. "Just continue up that main drive, where you entered. Then turn right at the next main road. It's located about fifty feet east of that intersection," she said helpfully.

They thanked her, and Lesley drove up the hill, following the directions she'd been given and slowing to try to read the names on headstones. They found the Kern plot about fifty feet from the intersection, just as the lady had said they would.

"Here it is—the Kern plot," Jim said, and she braked. "Are you ready for this? To learn more about the unknown girl?"

"Yes, cemeteries don't bother me in the daylight. Actually, I usually feel a sense of peace there," she explained. "I've thought sometimes that the presence of the Holy Ghost is there as a comforter."

"I hadn't thought about it that way, but you're probably right. Makes sense." He opened his door and came around to open hers.

"You're taking very good care of me," she said appreciatively.

"Well, it pleasures me, ma'am," he said, smiling and taking Lesley's hand.

The large granite monument that designated the plot as belonging to the Kern family was very impressive. *It must have been purchased in my great-grandfather's wealthy period,* she thought. Smaller headstones delineated the resting places of her great-grandparents and her grandparents, but there appeared to be no markers for the other graves. She was rather disappointed but not surprised. "Looks as if this was a wild goose chase," she said.

"Well, we still have the history center," Jim reminded. "Don't give up yet."

They returned to the car. Lesley sat behind the wheel again but didn't start the car.

Jim slid in beside her and said, "I know it's been a letdown, but don't give up. Coming to the cemetery may not have been such a good idea. Let's go to the history center, like you wanted to do in the first place."

"No, I really feel like there's something here—something I need." They sat quietly for a moment. Then Lesley said, "Let's just look around a little more. Maybe there's another Kern plot nearby," she said, opening the car door again.

"Okay, if you feel that way, let's look some more," Jim agreed, and got out on his side.

They walked together toward the main Kern monument, and paused to look around. The plots on either side, next to the Kern graves, were designated by monuments of other families, so that approach failed.

Lesley said, "Well, that's it, I guess. Let's go on to the history center. I'm sorry I made you come out in the cold." She moved to return to the car and stubbed her toe on something buried just beneath the snow, almost falling down. She righted herself then crouched and brushed away the snow with her gloved hand, revealing the tiny marker that read simply:

RACHEL
BORN 1900
DIED 1908

There was no surname. Whoever Rachel was, she had died at the tender age of eight. Lesley thought, *Was Rachel the ghost they had seen at her house?*

"Do you think that's your answer?" Jim asked, echoing her thoughts. "If Rachel is the girl in the photograph, she must have been at least accepted as a family member. Otherwise, she wouldn't have been buried here."

"You're right, but how can I find out her full name?"

Jim led her to the car. "Maybe the history center will have some answers. At least maybe we have her given name. We can start by looking for Rachel Kern," he said, pointing out the positive result of their search.

"Yes, at least now we have something to go on," she agreed, smiling.

They drove out of the cemetery and discussed what they'd learned, then they retraced the route back to South Temple and turned north on West Temple to the Family History Center. Lesley had to park in a lot on the north side of the library, so they had a short walk to the library and the nearby museum.

"These are impressive buildings," she said. "I remember when the genealogy center was in the Joseph Smith Building, the old Hotel Utah."

"Yes, and the only Church museum was the one on Temple Square," Jim pointed out. "This art museum is really something. Wait'll you see it."

"Okay, but first things first. Let's tackle the research on Rachel." She headed for the library and history center with Jim on her heels.

The genial senior missionary at the information desk directed them to the computers in a large area on the main floor and said that someone would come to help them if they didn't have computer skills. Jim assured her that they did, and Lesley looked at him to suggest, "Speak for yourself."

"I'm good at computers," Jim said with a cocky grin.

"Well, I'm glad, because I'm not," she admitted.

They found a vacant computer desk and two chairs, and Jim opened the Family Search program. He asked, "What was your great-grandfather's given name?"

"Lewis Edward Kern. My grandfather was named after him, as was my father," she volunteered.

"All had the same middle name?" he asked, surprised.

"No, they all had Lewis as their first name."

He entered Lewis Edward Kern in the space for NAME and pressed ENTER.

The results appeared on screen, revealing his birth date, birthplace, marriage, marriage date and place, and date and place of death. Following that were notes indicating the sources of information as census and other vital information records. For further information, the notes suggested consultation of the Family History Library Catalog.

Then Jim made another entry, and only one child's name appeared on the screen: Lewis Merrill Kern—Lesley's grandfather. "Well, this was a dead end," he said. "What now?"

"Maybe we should do what the notes suggested—consult the Family History Library Catalog."

"Good idea," he agreed and sought out another missionary aid, who explained how to access the catalog. Time moved swiftly while they were involved in the research. They found many interesting items from news media regarding her great-grandfather's time in Park City, some of which made them sympathize with the difficult life experienced by early miners and their families. Health problems abounded, and many miners died too young. One item was particularly distressing— in the first decade of the twentieth century, many children died of cholera, tuberculosis, and other diseases. A picture of a group of Primary-age school children made the reality of their deaths very poignant.

And, of course, this led Lesley to think of Rachel. She had died at eight years of age. *Why? One of the communicable or environmental diseases?* she wondered.

Then Jim found a gem. "There's a diary in the special collections section—a diary of Grace Amanda Clark Kern. Is she a relative?"

"Yes, yes. In fact, she was my great-grandmother. Is the actual diary here?" she asked, overjoyed at the prospect.

"Apparently so. Here's an accession number. Let's look for it," he suggested, seeming as excited as Lesley was.

With the help of another senior missionary, they found her great-grandmother's worn and yellowed diary. Lesley wanted to hold it in her arms, bringing close a woman she'd never known and knew little about. "Oh, Jim, this is very precious to me," she said, sitting at a table and opening the aging book.

Jim asked, "Didn't your folks know about the diary being here?"

"If they did, they never mentioned it. My parents weren't at all involved in family history or genealogy, so they probably didn't even know the diary was here," she said.

Lesley began reading, consumed by her great-grandmother's tales of her early life in Coalville, a Summit County mining town near Park City.

A half hour passed. "Are you going to try to read the whole thing today?" Jim asked, watching her patiently.

"No, I'm sorry. I just got lost in her story. I'll come back another time to read the whole thing. I'll get on with our objective," she said, turning dated pages until she came to the year 1908, the year of Rachel's death. An entry in the last week of January read as follows:

> *Our darling daughter Rachel died today after a lingering illness during which she became weaker day by day. The doctor couldn't tell us what it was or why she died so young, so we have to accept her going as the will of Providence.*
>
> *But I am not sure I can bear the loss. Rachel was never the same after she was hurt by that stranger—a very young miner who, for some unknown reason, my husband befriended. Of course, we told no one about it. That kind of thing has to be kept as a private family matter. The young miner who attacked Rachel has disappeared, but I will always wonder if that attack on Rachel contributed to her eventual death. My husband says that it would be best to just forget the whole matter and forget that Rachel was ours. We must just go on, he says, but I'm writing of her here, so that her short life on this earth will not simply be erased—disgrace or no disgrace—she was ours, she was mine.*
>
> *I must leave this house. I can't live with the memories. We are moving to live in Salt Lake City as soon as our house there can be finished. We will bury Rachel there, in Salt Lake City, where I may visit her, and away from the prying eyes of those who knew her and of her disgrace, as my husband calls it.*

Lesley slowly closed the diary, so choked up, so moved, that she was unable to speak for a few moments.

Jim had been reading with her, standing behind her and looking over her shoulder. "Are you okay?" He placed comforting hands on her shoulders.

Lesley reached back and touched his hand. "Yes . . . I'm okay. I guess I'm glad we found the truth about Rachel—at least part of it—but it's a sad revelation. I can't help feeling for Rachel and for my great-grandmother." Lesley's voice caught, and she fought to control her tears. Finally she said, "But the diary explains a lot of things. I think my great-grandmother Kern purposely placed her diary in the Church's genealogy library so that someday someone would know about Rachel. I really do."

"Well, you've found what you were looking for—explanations. But I know that knowledge can hurt. Maybe it hurts too much, and we shouldn't have gone digging for it," he suggested.

"No." Lesley sighed and took a deep breath, resolving, "Ignorance is not bliss. I hope that we've moved beyond the attitudes of that time: blame and hide the victim of the crime and hush it up at all costs."

"Yes, I hope we have," Jim said, "but there're still too many instances and places where that happens."

"My heart goes out to Rachel . . ." Lesley fought her tears, then continued. "She was the victim of that man and of society's ignorance. But I had to know about her, even if it hurts, especially after all that has happened recently at my house."

"But now that you know about Rachel, you still have to determine if she's the one—visiting your house," Jim reminded.

"Yes, yes, I do." Lesley squared her shoulders, and controlling her voice, she said, "If she is coming here, I have to find out what she wants—what she wants me to do. And what does water symbolize—why did she write it on the window and say that word to Julie?

It was difficult, but Lesley tried to put the emotions of the morning behind her when they left the history center and went to the Museum of Church History and Art. The featured exhibit was "Mormon Works of Art," selected for the current show from entries of Mormon artists worldwide. Lesley loved the works inspired by the Book of Mormon, several of which interpreted Lehi's dream of the tree of life. They both enjoyed the works that related to the family— done in oils, watercolors, sculpture, and even soft sculpture and quilting.

Also impressive were the portraits of the latter-day prophets, many of which were excellent. Lesley especially enjoyed the work of Alvin Gittins, an artist formerly from the University of Utah, who had painted David O. McKay's portrait.

Children's groups were everywhere in the museum, and volunteers and senior missionaries were directing them in their experience with Mormon art.

"This is as magnificent as you promised it would be," Lesley said.

"I know. Mom brought Julie and me here, and I couldn't believe the skills that so many Mormon artists have. It really is inspiring," Jim agreed.

They spent several hours in the museum and could have stayed all day. But they had other plans and left the museum to cross West Temple toward Temple Square. Church hymns were broadcast throughout the square, and the spirit of peace in that holy place descended on them. "I love it here," Lesley said.

"I do too."

Without thinking of the possible implications of her next remark, she let slip, "I'd like to be married here someday." Immediately she was embarrassed, thinking that it sounded too much like a hint.

Jim thought for a moment, then said, "I would too." He spared her the embarrassment of kidding her about what sounded like a proposal and instead was very sincere, as if he'd really thought about it before.

They noted that the choir and a large group of actors, singers, and dancers would be presenting a special production for the Olympics called *Light of the World* in the new Conference Center. They both wanted to see it.

They left Temple Square and went looking for tickets to a Sundance Film Festival movie, but all shows were sold out for that date, so they gave up on the movie idea. Walking down the rather deserted Main Street, with its vacant shops and buildings, they found an inviting restaurant with an art-deco atmosphere. Lesley remembered having gone there as a teenager with her parents and was surprised to find it basically unchanged and still in business.

They returned to Temple Square to enjoy the magical Christmas lighting display, left in place for the Olympics. Then Jim drove them back to Park City and his family's cozy home. On the way they reviewed what they had learned about Rachel from Lesley's great-grandmother's diary.

Then Lesley napped, satisfied to set aside all worry and to let the fun and the findings of their adventure fill her thoughts. She laid her head on Jim's shoulder the rest of the way home.

CHAPTER 18

They arrived at Jim's house at about nine PM, and Lesley awoke to see him looking at her tenderly. Yawning and stretching, she said, "Oh, I didn't mean to fall asleep. It's probably too late to intrude on your mother tonight."

"Are you kidding?" Jim asked. "There'll be heck to pay if I don't bring you in." He climbed out of the car and came around to open her door. "Just come in for a while. We won't make you stay all night."

They walked arm in arm to the front door through lightly falling snow and were greeted anxiously by Carol and Julie. "We've been waiting forever," Julie said, smiling up at Lesley and taking her hand. "We thought you'd never come."

"Thanks," Lesley said. "You always make me feel so welcome."

"You are welcome," Carol said, ushering her in and taking her coat and gloves. "Come in by the fire."

"Hey, what am I? Chopped liver?" Jim asked, laughing. "No one acts very happy to see me." He removed his coat and hung it beside Lesley's on the entry coat rack.

"Well, we're glad you came home," Carol said. "You're not chopped liver, but you are old shoes—we're used to you."

"Yeah, Dad," Julie teased affectionately.

"Okay, just so you recognize that I'm here too," he said, smiling.

Jim and Lesley sat on the sofa by the fire, and Julie curled up next to her. Carol was busy in the kitchen. "I'm fixing some hot chocolate and cookies," she said.

"Sounds wonderful," Lesley responded.

The fire was crackling, the snow was falling softly outside the window, and the warmth and comfort that she'd felt before in this house surrounded them. She thought, *I'm more content here than I've ever been anywhere.*

Carol asked, "Well, what did you do today? Anything exciting?"

"Yeah, tell us what you did," Julie echoed.

Jim changed the mood somewhat, trying to relate the events of the day. "Well, it may not have qualified as exciting, but first we went to the Salt Lake City Cemetery."

"What in the world did you go there for?" Carol asked, bringing a tray laden with steaming mugs of cocoa and a plate piled high with chocolate chip cookies.

"Maybe Lesley ought to tell the story," Jim suggested, looking at her.

Lesley took a mug and a big cookie from the tray. "Thanks, Carol." She paused to phrase her response to Jim's request. "Well, okay, I'll make a long story short. I went back to my house yesterday and found an old family photo album in an attic room—an area that I didn't know existed."

"Really?" Carol said. "Where is the room? How did you find it?"

Lesley had tried to gloss over the experience with the mirror door and the unidentified humming voice, but Jim urged, "You might as well tell the whole story just as you told it to me."

"Okay, but I don't want to stir up any—bad memories. Are you sure?" she asked, looking at Jim.

"I don't know how else you can explain it. Go ahead and tell what happened."

She recounted her experience in deciding to go upstairs in her house and seeing the mirror door mysteriously swing open. Still worrying about Julie's possible reaction, she told of the childlike humming voice and of her being drawn up the narrow attic stairs to find nothing there but stored items and the open photo album. She paused to sense Julie's and Carol's reactions. Julie was wide-eyed but didn't appear frightened, and Carol seemed mesmerized by Lesley's tale, urging her on.

"I became rather claustrophobic, feeling I had to get out of the attic. After examining the old photograph on the open page, I ran downstairs, taking the album with me. It was a photo of my great-grandparents; their son, my grandfather; and—a girl."

"A . . . a girl?" Julie asked hesitantly.

"Yes, a girl whom I'd never heard of. You see, I'd always thought that my great-grandparents, like my grandparents, had only one child. And they were boys."

"Could we see the picture?" Carol asked.

"Oh, I left the album in the car," she remembered.

"Give me your keys. I'll get it," Jim offered, standing up.

"They're in my coat pocket, I believe."

He headed toward the coat rack and found the keys in the coat pocket. He was gone before Lesley could question the wisdom of showing Carol and Julie the photo.

"How old was the girl?" Julie asked suspiciously.

"She was about eight years old in the picture, I would guess."

Julie bowed her head for a moment, then sighed and looked up at Lesley. "Was she—was she the girl we saw in the mirror?"

Lesley didn't answer at once, pausing to think what she should tell her.

"She was, wasn't she?" Julie asked, determined to get an answer.

Jim returned with the album before she could reply. "Here it is, open to the family photograph," he said, handing the album to Lesley.

She set her mug on a side table and spread the album on her lap so that Julie had a full view of the photograph. "It's her," Julie said without any prompting. "It's the girl I saw in the mirror!" Lesley was relieved that Julie seemed more amazed than frightened.

"Is it?" Carol asked, astonished.

Lesley tried to phrase her next words cautiously. "I *thought* it might be the girl that I had seen, but I wasn't sure that Julie would think so too. I hope I haven't done the wrong thing in bringing the album here," she said, still worrying about its effect on Julie.

Julie reacted before Lesley could say more. "I'm glad you brought it. Now I know she was really somebody—not just a ghost—she was real . . ." She actually seemed relieved.

"Then that doesn't upset you?" Lesley asked. "I didn't want to bring back the fears you'd felt after you saw her."

"No, I feel better now—not worse," she explained. "I—I don't think I'm afraid of her—if she was real."

Carol brought them back to her original question. "Then, is the photo the reason you went to the cemetery?"

Jim responded. "Yeah, I had the idea that we could find Lesley's great-grandparents' graves and might also find a clue about the girl."

"It was a good idea," Lesley added. "We found the Kern plot and, at first, found only the graves of my known relatives.

Then we almost had given up when I literally stumbled on a little grave marker just beneath the snow. It was the grave of a Rachel—no surname—and she died when she was only eight."

"No last name, huh?" Carol mused.

"No, that's what led us to go on to the Family History Center, where we'd originally planned to go. We went to see if a Rachel Kern was listed as a child, or even as an adopted or foster child, of my great-grandparents."

"And . . . ?" Carol urged.

"There was no record of her in my forefathers' genealogy, but we did find my great-grandmother's diary."

"How wonderful," Carol said. "Were you thrilled?"

"I was—I am. The diary confirms what we'd suspected— Rachel was my great-grandparents' daughter. She died at age eight, as I mentioned. But there was more." Lesley quickly decided she shouldn't mention, with Julie present, the story of the stranger abusing Rachel. So she said, "For some reason— they had chosen to keep her existence secret."

"Your grandparents or your parents never mentioned her?" Carol asked.

"No." She thought, *I'll explain to Carol later.*

There was a silence, all of them just thinking of the ramifications of the new information. Jim broke it. "Well, now you have to decide what to do about Rachel's visits."

"I think Julie's right," Lesley said. "Rachel was real, and I believe she must have a purpose in appearing or that she has a message for me. That may sound unlikely, but how else could we explain her attempts at communication? We've already agreed we didn't imagine that."

Carol said, "No, we didn't."

"So what do you propose we do now?" Jim asked, always the practical "fix-it" man.

"I don't know. I guess we could go back there—all of us—and see if she tries to communicate with one of us again. Would that upset you?" Lesley asked, directing her question to both Julie and Carol.

"I—I don't think I'd be afraid to go back there now," Julie said. "In the daytime."

"Do you think I'm being silly—or sacrilegious—in even thinking that Rachel might have a message for me?"

"Well, no. Anyway, I don't see what harm going up there again could do. If we don't have another experience with Rachel, you can dismiss it as a mystery and try to forget it. If she does try to communicate again, you'll know that your suspicions were right," Jim said.

"Well, do you think we should go back?" Lesley asked.

"Jim, it's up to you," Carol said. "You're the working man—when could you go?"

"How about Saturday? I do have another job or two this week. And, of course, Julie would be out of school on Saturday," he pointed out.

"Well, I'm not really anxious to go back there, but any day's all right with me," Lesley said. "All I'm doing right now is waiting for the Sundance awards ceremony and the Olympics to begin."

"Saturday would be good for us," Carol agreed, looking to Julie for confirmation.

Julie nodded affirmatively.

"Okay, a Saturday excursion to Silver Forks Mountain. We'll have breakfast before we go and eat out for lunch this time," Jim suggested.

"Okay, if you're sure. Anyway, thanks to all of you. I don't know what I would have done—would do—without your help," Lesley said honestly. "Well, it's getting late. I'd best go home—I mean, I'd better go back to my hotel."

"Oh, you don't need to leave on our account," Carol said. "It's our bedtime, Julie's and mine, but Jim's a night owl."

"I usually am too, but all that walking around and the impact of what we learned has made me one tired cookie—oh, I don't mean I'm tired of cookies. I could eat those all night," she explained, laughing.

"Do you want me to follow you in my truck to the hotel?" Jim asked.

"No, thank you. I don't think the roads will be too bad yet. You could walk me to the car if you'd like," she said, smiling. "Thanks, Carol. Julie, it's so nice to be with you again."

"Me too," Julie said, hugging Lesley.

Jim helped her with her coat, she said her good-byes, and then he walked her to the car.

"Thanks, Jim, for your help today. I'm relieved about what I've learned, too. And I had a very nice day and evening."

He didn't say anything—just took her in his arms and kissed her good night.

She drove to her hotel with stars in her eyes, though there were none visible in the sky.

As she drove into the hotel garage, she realized that she'd left the photo album behind. *Oh well,* she thought, *better not to dwell on that problem tonight.*

The hotel night clerk stopped her before she reached the elevator. "Oh, Ms. Kern, there are several messages for you." He turned to a box and retrieved three small envelopes.

"Thank you," Lesley said, taking the messages and going to the elevator. She decided to wait to read them in her room.

Snug in her terry robe and furry slippers, but feeling rather lonely, she curled up on the chaise. All the envelopes were hotel stationery, suggesting that front desk personnel had received and recorded them.

She chose one envelope at random and tore it open. As she'd guessed, Connie had called at around noon regarding a meeting to talk about selling her house. "Urgent!" had been written by the clerk, she was sure at Connie's request. She set it aside.

The contents of the second envelope were equally expected—a message from Gareth Sanders, asking that she return his call or come by the Silver Fork for dinner.

The third message was more intriguing. Lesley's agent, Heidi, had called: "Imperative that you call me, Wednesday AM," giving the number of her agency in California. That would be Lesley's first action next morning.

She prepared for bed, then kneeled and thanked the Lord for bringing the Shepherd family—and especially Jim—into her life. She prayed that Jim would have the strength to follow through with his resolve to return to the Church.

CHAPTER 19

At ten AM Lesley ordered breakfast from room service and, still lounging in her robe, called her agent, Heidi, forgetting the difference in their time zones. However, now back in her California office, Heidi answered immediately: "Heidi Sigurd; I work for you."

"Well, Heidi, that makes me happy. This is Lesley."

"Oh, I'm so glad you returned my call. They want you in Salt Lake tomorrow for a preliminary script reading and conference on your *Angel* role. You have to be there," she said.

"Well, I can make it, I guess. What time and where?"

She gave Lesley the address of the *Touched by an Angel* production office and then added, "Be there at ten. Oh, I almost forgot. Their locations people are looking for an old house as the setting for the episode. Hope you don't mind; I told them about your house near Park City. They might want to see it," she said.

"Well, I suppose it would be all right, but there's no electricity, heat, or working plumbing there."

"Oh, as you know, they're used to working on location. Trucks, vans, and honey wagons take care of all those problems," she said, laughing.

"Okay. Well, thanks. I'll go to the meeting. And thanks for your efforts," Lesley added.

"You know it will cost you," she said, laughing again. "Bye!"

She hung up, leaving Lesley with the reminder of Heidi's fifteen-percent cut from her earnings. *Oh well, she's doing her job—at least I have work,* Lesley thought.

Room service, in the person of Barnaby, interrupted her thoughts. "Barnaby, I haven't seen you for a while," she said after opening the door.

"Yeah, I had a day off yesterday," he said, wheeling the cart into the room.

"Just leave the food there on the table." She found her purse and fished for his expected tip.

"Thanks, Ms. Kern. Anything else I can do for you?" he asked, grinning that knowing grin.

"No thanks, Barnaby. Not today." She backed him toward the door.

"Well, can't blame . . ."

"Don't say it."

"Okay, I'll be on my way, then," he said, turning red. "Thank you, ma'am."

She ate the scrambled eggs and bacon, skipping the toast. *I've been eating too much this trip,* she thought. *If I keep it up, I'll look like a cherub in my* Angel *role.* That caused her to think of last night's chocolate chip cookies and the warm happiness she'd felt with the Shepherds.

Then she had to decide whether to respond to Connie's and Gareth's messages. Her inclination was to ignore them, but she remembered that she'd told both of them they could call. She decided that courtesy demanded a response. Calling Gareth seemed the less complicated of the calls, so she punched in his number first.

"Silver Fork. May I help you?" a pleasant male voice asked.

"Yes, I'm returning a call from Gareth Sanders. This is Lesley Kern."

"Oh, Ms. Kern. I'm sorry, but Mr. Sanders is away today. He said that if you called, I should ask where he could reach you."

"Did he tell you where *I* could reach *him*?" she asked.

"Well, not officially, but—I think he went to Silver Forks for some kind of meeting," he revealed reluctantly.

"Hmmm. That's interesting. Well, tell him to leave a message at the Silver Princess if I'm not here. Thanks." Then she hung up, actually relieved that she didn't have to deal with Gareth that day but also more than curious about what business he could have at Silver Forks.

Now to call Connie, she thought. *But what am I going to tell her?* She waited six rings for Connie to answer the Silver Forks Realty phone and was about to hang up when Connie answered, obviously out of breath, "Hello, Silver Forks Realty. Connie speaking."

"Connie, you sound like you've been running," she said. "This is Lesley Kern returning your call."

"Oh, I'm sorry, I was outside talking to Jim . . . Shepherd. Sorry I made you wait," Connie said, trying to catch her breath. "Well, can we meet today?" she asked, hurriedly changing the subject and getting right to her objective.

Lesley didn't answer immediately because she was so startled by Connie's indication that Jim was in Silver Forks talking with her.

"Lesley, are you still there?"

"Yes, did I hear you correctly? Jim Shepherd is there?"

"Yes, dear, he's here on some kind of—errand, I guess," she explained. "Now, how about our getting together?"

"But I really haven't made up my mind about selling my place," Lesley said honestly. "Until I do, a meeting would be premature." She couldn't think straight because of Connie's slip about Jim's being there. This definitely wasn't the time to make a major decision like selling a house.

"Lesley?" she asked.

"I'm—I'm sorry. I'm just trying to decide whether to meet with you or not."

"But Joe—Mr. Spencer promised you a cash deal. Surely you can't turn that down," she urged. "There's nothing that could go wrong with the sale—you'd get a cashier's check for the full sum—at the closing."

"Don't you mean the full sum minus your commission?" Lesley asked, somehow feeling even less friendly toward her.

"Well, of course, but we've already planned to waive any other charges—title insurance and so forth. You'll only have to pay the commission—for my representing your interests in the sale."

Lesley laughed. "But you're not representing my interests. You're representing Joe Spencer," she reminded her.

"Well, of course I understand that, and since you hadn't actually listed your place for sale, I wouldn't expect the full six percent commission—*only* three percent," she offered magnanimously.

"Only three percent?"

"Yes," she said, as if it were a real bargain.

"I figure that amounts to about forty-five thousand dollars. That's quite a commission," Lesley stated frankly.

"Well, I know, but that kind of commission doesn't come along everyday. I have to make a living too," she reasoned in a whining voice. "Joe Spencer's offer is a great offer for that property. You won't get a better one, and my advice is that you grab it before he withdraws it," she said, making it sound as threatening as she could.

"There are some problems—some personal matters—at my house that I have to resolve before I can make a decision about selling it. Also, I'm still looking into the possibility of—living there myself. I have to investigate the costs involved in making it livable. Until I can do that, I can't make an informed decision. I'm sorry, but I need some time. If Mr. Spencer can't wait, just tell him that I'm not interested, then." She thought, *There, that should be firm enough and will buy me some time if nothing else.*

"Well, that disappoints me," Connie said, "and I'm sure Mr. Spencer will be very disappointed too—but if you're sure, I'll tell him you haven't said 'no' but you need a little more time. How much time do you need?" she asked, still pressuring Lesley.

"As much time as it takes," Lesley answered. "I'll call you—don't call me." *This timeworn, show-business audition comeback works well in business matters too,* Lesley realized. "Bye." She hung up with nothing resolved about the sale of her house but with the satisfaction that she didn't have to rush into anything.

Then she sat back trying to fathom the unlikely coincidence in both Gareth and Jim going to Silver Forks that morning. *What is going on?* Lesley wondered. Apparently Gareth was in a meeting of some kind, but with whom? And Jim had told her that he had several jobs to do before the weekend. Why would he be in Silver Forks, and why would he be talking with Connie? Why should she be so concerned that Connie had mentioned Jim's being there? Lesley was very disturbed and wished that she hadn't made either phone call.

She prayed for guidance in her decisions and read her scriptures, trying to catch up on neglected study and hoping for some inspiration to remedy her confusion about Jim and about selling her house. Then she dressed casually but warmly in jeans and a beige sweater.

Without a definite destination in mind, she decided to go for a drive to clear her head. She'd made no conscious decision about it but found herself driving out of Park City and turning toward Silver Forks. She hadn't planned to go there that day, but a compulsion to satisfy her curiosity about Jim's and Gareth's activities seemed to push her in that direction. *What am I doing?* she questioned. *Am I planning to spy on Jim? On Gareth? No,* she told herself, *I have a perfect right to go to my house.* Anyway, she knew that she *was* going to Silver Forks and would try to avoid being seen. What did she expect to learn in going there? She didn't know—but she *had* to go.

When she turned off into Silver Forks, there appeared to be more going on than she'd seen there previously. Several heavy-duty trucks and other heavy equipment vehicles were moving in a slow caravan through Silver Forks and up Silver Forks Mountain Road. The in-town traffic suggested something big happening on Silver Forks Mountain. *What's going on?* she wondered.

Near Silver Forks Creek bridge, she pulled over behind some tall evergreens, providing a good vantage point from which to watch the activity in town without being observed.

Most of the big equipment had moved out of sight when she saw Joe Spencer's black Lincoln come down the mountain road going in the opposite direction from the caravan. The unknown driver turned in to the spa driveway, as she'd expected he would. *Had Joe Spencer or one of his cronies been back to her house?* she wondered.

She waited for a few minutes, deciding whether to drive to her place. Then she saw Joe Spencer's Lincoln reappear and head up Silver Forks Mountain Road again. And after a few minutes, she was startled to see Jim's truck come out of the spa driveway and also head up Silver Forks Mountain Road.

She was more confused and concerned by the minute. *Why was Jim at the spa, and where was he going now?* To add to her confusion, Gareth Sanders came out of Silver Forks Realty, climbed into a Silver Fork Restaurant van, drove in to the spa, and then came back and also drove up Silver Forks Mountain Road.

Why had she come there? She was more puzzled than ever, and her observations provided no answers to her questions about Jim's and Gareth's activities. *Should I follow Jim and confront him? No,* she thought, *he'll think I don't trust him—that I'm spying on him. I am spying on him,* she realized, ashamed.

It could be that Jim had some perfectly legitimate reason for being in Silver Forks, she supposed. Anyway, from what she had observed, Jim and Gareth weren't there together. It was just coincidence that they were both there, she reasoned. She decided she should probably just go back to Park City and let sleeping dogs lie—let things alone—rather than investigating further. But even as she decided that, she started the Navigator and headed up Silver Forks Mountain Road.

She fully expected to see Jim's truck in the lane in front of her house. But when she drove up, she was surprised to find the gate unlocked and open, and the only vehicle in her driveway belonged to none other than Joe Spencer. She panicked at the thought, *Did I lock the front door when I fled my house after my last visit?*

She drove cautiously toward the front porch, trying to avoid crossing the tire tracks left there earlier. She didn't know why she'd done that—possibly she was remembering Jim's joking suggestion that they could be detectives, comparing the tire tracks to Joe Spencer's tires. But Joe Spencer's car was there—no need to play detective. *But why is he here?* she wondered.

She parked, locked the car door, and went up the porch stairs to the front entry. As she'd feared, the front door wasn't locked. On her earlier visit, she must have left it unlocked in her haste to get away. But when she quietly and cautiously stepped inside, there was no indication that anyone had been there or was there now. She silently closed the door. It was totally quiet. She was relieved to find the house interior just as she'd left it. She'd begun to relax when there was a loud knock at the front door. She turned around, and her first thought was to find a place to hide. But the door opened slowly, and Mr. Joe Spencer Jr. eased his head in.

When he saw her, he said, "Oh, my dear Ms. Kern, I came by to see if you might be here. I knocked earlier but no one answered, so I just went round to the back to see if you might be there. I'm so glad I found you," he said, stepping in and closing the door behind him. He tipped his hat and smiled that nasty leer.

Lesley was startled and frightened, but she found the courage to confront him. "Mr. Spencer, I'm concerned that you—and some of your employees—have been entering my property illegally. I want it stopped!"

Sticky Finger removed his hat. "But, my dear, I don't know what on earth you're talking about. I've been on the up and up in all my dealings with you. I've made legitimate offers to buy your property, but you keep avoiding me—you refuse to meet even to discuss the matter. That's why I came here looking for you," he explained, stepping uncomfortably close to her.

She backed away a few steps. "I'm not talking only about today. I know that you've entered my property on several occasions, possibly when I wasn't even in Utah—before I came back here."

"That's nonsense, dear. It's true that one or two of my associates might have come by the place to look at its general condition before I made an offer to buy it. Surely that was a legitimate thing to do."

"No, it wasn't—not if it involved breaking and entering," she insisted.

"But I assure you that we wouldn't stoop to that—there'd be no reason to approach the matter that way. Perhaps the gate and doors were left open, as they were today?" he suggested condescendingly.

"I don't think so, but I've changed the locks, and I assure you that I won't leave them unlocked in the future." She braved a step toward him, thinking, *After all, he's an older man. He can't harm me physically.* "Now, I'll appreciate it if you will leave my property. When—and if—I decide to sell my property, I may let you know. Until then, please quit hounding me—and call off Connie too."

He seemed undaunted by her words. Straightening his back and appearing somehow much taller and more physically fit, he looked directly into Lesley's eyes with a hate that shook her to her toes. "I have tried to be patient, my dear, but that patience isn't unbounded. I'll give you one more opportunity to sell me your property—then I'll have to . . ."

"Have to what? Are you threatening me?"

"No, no, of course not, dear." He began to back toward the door. "I'm simply saying that I'll talk with you once more—that's all." He paused, as if to let his words sink in, then said, "I'll be off now. Think about my—offer. Good day, my dear." He left, closing the door softly behind him.

Lesley was unable to move. She'd never had an experience like that. She'd never actually been threatened. In fact, she'd never met anyone quite like Joe Spencer. She wished she'd never had anything to do with him.

Then she heard a noise from the rear of the house. She called out, "Is anybody there?" There was no response. She walked cautiously down the hall toward the rooms at the rear and heard a scuffling sound in—the basement. *Another animal or one of Joe Spencer's men?* she questioned. Then she panicked and backed away from the basement entrance toward the stairway leading to the second floor.

Quietly she climbed the stairs, looking nervously behind her and trying to distance herself from whoever or whatever was in the basement. She prayed for safety. She was very apprehensive as she approached the mirror door, but no ghost appeared in the mirror to frighten her further. Still, her imagination was working overtime. She tried the mirror door, actually thinking that she could sneak into the attic and hide behind the secret door in that secret room. If a prowler were in her house, he wouldn't know to look for her there. She felt both afraid and foolish.

Then she told herself, *This is my house. I'm not the trespasser here. But what if this intruder isn't—mortal? What if—Rachel— is up to her antics, trying to lure me to the basement—to show me something else?*

She tried again to open the mirror door, pulling on it with all her strength, but it wouldn't budge, as if it had been nailed shut or as if someone or something was holding it closed from the other side. She began to wonder if she had imagined the whole thing—the mirror door and the secret attic. Then she remembered the photo album—it was *real*—which she had left at Jim's.

She stealthily looked in all the upstairs rooms and found no indication that an intruder had been there, then she started downstairs. She heard hurried, heavy footsteps on the basement stairs and the opening and slamming of a door—the rear outside door. She raced to the foot of the stairs and toward the back door, flinging it open. There was no one in sight, but there were large, widely spaced footprints in the snow as if someone had run away from the house and toward a bank of evergreen trees. She considered running after the trespasser to confront him but realized that would be foolhardy. She couldn't run that fast in the snow, and if she were to catch him, what could she do?

She firmly closed the rear door and locked it, cursing herself for being so stupid in leaving the front door unlocked—an open invitation to a thief or a vagrant. But who unlocked the gate, she wondered. *Had I forgotten to lock that too?* She realized that she must have forgotten in her hurry to get away. *What good are new locks if you don't use them, dummy!*

Should I go downstairs? she questioned. *What had the intruder been doing down in the basement?* She opened the basement door and realized it was totally dark in the stairwell and in the furnace room. She didn't dare go there without some kind of light.

Suddenly she had to get out of her house. She really didn't feel safe there alone. She hurried out the front door, double-checking the lock behind her this time, and rushed to her car, peeling out of the lane and stopping only long enough to lock the padlock on the gate.

Close calls were becoming habit on Silver Forks Mountain—she almost rammed into Jim's truck as she shot out of her property. Jim saw her SUV just in time, slammed on his brakes, looked at her with shocked surprise, turned off his engine, and walked slowly toward her car.

"Whew! You almost got me," he said, after she rolled down her window. "Where are you going in such a hurry? What are you doing up here?"

"I'm sorry I almost hit you. I'm so used to no one being on this road," she explained, upset, embarrassed, and trying to justify her lack of caution.

"You're forgiven—but I'm glad my brakes work. Now, how come you're up here?" he asked.

"Well, I might ask you the same thing. I thought you had work to do," she said accusingly.

"I did and I do," he answered. "I had a job to do for Sticky—for Joe Spencer—at the spa. Earlier I saw all this heavy equipment coming up this road and decided to follow Joe to see what was going on. I didn't find Joe, but I did find something else. Now, how about you? I thought you weren't going to come back here alone after what happened the last time," he chastised. Then he looked at her more closely. "You're shaking. Are you all right?"

"No, I don't know if I'll ever be all right again. I'm sorry, but I followed you up here, thinking you were going to my house . . ."

"And . . . ?"

"I didn't find you—but I did find Joe Spencer. My gate and door were unlocked. I went inside, and Joe came in to—to threaten me."

"Threaten you?" he asked, showing an anger that she'd never seen in him.

"Well—not really. But he *seemed* threatening. I don't like him. He said I'd have only one more chance to sell my property to him, or . . ."

"Or what?"

"I don't know—that's all. But I told him that I might call him if or when I decide to sell my place—and I asked him to leave me alone and to call off Connie."

"Well, I don't think you should have any more to do with him," Jim said. "I warned you about him."

"I know you did."

"But why did you come to Silver Forks anyway? I thought you weren't ever going to come up here alone."

"Oh, I know, but I had nothing to do and somehow felt compelled to come here. Actually," she admitted, "I returned Connie's call, and she let it slip that she was talking with you. I guess curiosity got the best of me. I wondered what you were doing up here." She didn't explain that she was also drawn to find out why Gareth had come there too.

"Checking up on me?" he asked, smiling for the first time.

"Well, not exactly, but—yes, I suppose I was," she confessed.

"I guess I should be flattered that you're that interested in my work. That is what you mean, isn't it? You're not suggesting that you don't trust me?" he asked half-seriously.

"No, no. It isn't that. But why were you talking to Connie Evans—at Silver Forks Realty?" she asked bluntly.

"Well, actually, *she* was talking to *me*. I stopped at the general store for some materials and had to park in front of the realty. She saw my truck and came out to persuade me to use my influence to get you to sell to Joe. That's what she was trying to do when you called. I told her that I had no influence—that it was your decision. Satisfied?"

"I'm sorry. She mentioned that she was talking to you and then acted so cagey about it that I couldn't help wondering why. Oh, can we go somewhere else, where we can talk? Right now I don't want to be here," she said truthfully.

"I finished the job for Joe, but I have another one in Midway. If you're okay now, why don't you follow me—at a safe distance," he teased, "and we'll go back to that little Swiss place in Midway for lunch if you feel all right."

"Oh, I feel all right—now. Are you sure you want to go there? I'm so sorry about all of this, and I really don't want to interfere with your work," she said.

"Well, I have to eat lunch. Why not join me? Besides, I have a few things to tell you—a few thoughts I've had about what's going on at your house. And I want to get the whole story about Joe Spencer."

Intrigued by his announcement, she said, "Okay, I'll follow you—at a safe distance." She was also relieved to know that she could tell him about the other intruder at her house, though what he could do about it she didn't know.

He caressed her cheek, blew her a kiss, and went to his truck. She followed him back to Silver Forks, where she saw Joe Spencer's car pulling out of the spa driveway and heading toward Park City. Jim obviously saw him too, because he stopped at a stop sign then turned his head toward Lesley and pointed at Joe's retreating Lincoln.

CHAPTER 20

Lesley had a lot to think about while following Jim to the Midway Chalet, where they'd previously eaten. What had Jim learned about her house? What was Joe Spencer threatening to do if she didn't sell? What had Jim found out about the heavy equipment heading up Silver Forks Mountain? What was Gareth doing up there? She also worried how she'd tell him about the intruder in her house. And she still wondered why Gareth was in Silver Forks—at the realty office, at Joe Spencer's spa, and on Silver Forks Mountain.

The Midway Chalet was busier than on their last visit, but they were still able to find a table in a quiet corner away from the other customers. The same sweet, costumed hostess gave them a menu, and they ordered sandwiches made with scones instead of ordinary bread. Lesley relaxed for the first time that day, taking a deep breath and sinking into her chair.

Then they both started talking at once, so Lesley said, "You go first. What about my house?"

"Well, I've been thinking and—praying—about your problems," he said, looking at her to see her reaction. "Are you surprised?"

"Yes, yes I am, but I'm grateful, too. And pleased," she admitted.

"Well, I prayed long and hard about it. Also, I'd been thinking about our recurring experience with the mysterious *water* message. I couldn't figure out why that word should be important—why it would have a special meaning. As Mom said, *water* doesn't seem too frightening or too unusual a word. I decided you were right—we supplied the fear rather than Rachel bringing it with her. Maybe all she did was strive to communicate to us in any way she could."

"Well, I have to confess, I've tried to put those events out of my mind. They frightened me—not because of the word but just because they happened," Lesley said, shuddering at the memory of the personage in the mirror, of the word appearing on the window—twice—and of Rachel's speaking it to Julie.

"Yeah, I was spooked too, but I came to agree with you. Rachel must be—must have been trying to communicate something with that word. That's the only thing that makes sense. So I thought about it, and I think I have the answer—or at least a possible answer."

After all that had happened that morning and all that she now had on her mind, Lesley was rather leery of hearing his explanation of the events but urged him on anyway. "Okay, what was she trying to say—beyond the literal meaning of *water?*"

The gray-haired lady brought their food, delaying Jim's answer.

They thanked her and couldn't ignore the delicious look and aroma of the hot sandwiches.

Jim moved to take a bite of his, and Lesley said, "Don't you dare fill your mouth until you give me an answer. What do you think Rachel was trying to tell us?"

"Okay, okay. I still don't know if I'm right, but there's a way we can find out," he said, still delaying his answer.

"Spit it out—not your food—the answer," she said, half laughing and half-crazed by the waiting.

He laughed. "Okay, let's get serious. Here it is. Because of her early death and the early deaths of your other relatives who had lived in your house, I think that Rachel was driven to warn you that something is wrong with the water—the *culinary* water—in that house—your house."

"But how could that be? People have lived there before. I'm sure there's never been any indication that the water was unsafe," she insisted.

"But didn't you say that no one lived there for long? Also, as I said, I've been thinking about your statement that your ancestors had short lives. And what about Rachel's unexplained early death?"

Lesley's mouth was open—not to eat—but because she realized that Jim really may have come up with something—a plausible explanation for Rachel's death, at least: *poison* in the water.

"Well, what do you think?" he urged.

"I don't know. It's an incredible thought. But how could we go about proving it?" she asked.

"I've had a great idea, and I've researched the procedures for getting water tested. The Utah Division of Water Quality in Salt Lake uses a private laboratory certified for environmental testing—also in Salt Lake. We could take some water samples to them to test for toxins—for trace minerals and substances that might be polluting the water."

"But how could we get samples? The water is shut off."

"Hold on. Remember, I'm the handyman. I've already looked into that. You don't have water piped into your house from Silver Forks Water Company. You have a well. The water at your house comes right out of the ground without being treated."

"You see how little I know about the place. I just assumed that the water was city water. The man I had shut it off must have known, but he didn't explain that to me."

"I'll look for the well or the main valve that controls the pipes from the well, and we can easily get a sample." He stopped to take a bite. "Better start eating or your hot sandwich will be a cold sandwich."

"Somehow food doesn't seem too important right now," she said, but tasted the sandwich anyway. It was delicious, so she took another bite.

"And that's not all," Jim said. "While I was at the health spa doing some repairs on their roof, I sneaked a water sample from the hot springs. It's in a plastic vial in my truck."

"But why did you do that?" she asked.

"Well, wouldn't it be something if Joe Spencer's health spa turned out to be a polluted spa instead? The water comes from the same source—underground water from the same soil—as the water at your house. In fact, Joe may already be aware that the water's polluted. That may be another reason that he wants control of all the property up there, including yours. Anyway, I just had to do it as long as I was there. I think I may have come up with the answer, Lesley. Anyway, it can't hurt to find out."

"No, no, it can't hurt. I'm glad—I'm grateful for your concern about my problems," she said.

"After I finish the job here, I could go back to your house and try to get a sample of the water there," he suggested, "if you feel okay about it."

"Yes. Anyway, I'd like to know about how to turn on the water—even though I feel now that I could never live there."

"You've definitely made up your mind, then? Is Joe Spencer's threat the reason?"

"Oh, I don't know what to do. Should I sell it? It seems the easiest way to solve all the problems." She covered her eyes and leaned her head on her hand.

He reached across the table, took her hand away, and held it. "I've said before that it's up to you. Frankly, I'd like to keep you around, but selling it may be the best choice for you. Either way, we need to find out about the safety of the water."

"There may be alternative ways to keep me around," she hinted. "Anyway, thanks for the advice. And thanks for caring so much, for praying so hard for a solution to my problems," she said, looking into his loving eyes. "Oh, but what did you find out about those trucks and equipment that were going up Silver Forks Mountain?" she asked, shifting the focus away from her own problems.

"I didn't actually talk to anyone. I just drove up to sneak a look," he said.

"And . . . ?"

"I'm just guessing," Jim said, "but I pulled off the road and hid my truck behind some trees and bushes, and I saw Joe Spencer there for just a minute. Then Gareth Sanders came up and started talking with him and Joe left in a hurry. I suppose he was returning to your place. It looks to me like they're starting some construction up there—maybe condominiums? There's a lot of lumber stacked around in various places, and they've started to dig out the hillside, like they're grading property for buildings. What Gareth Sanders was doing up there, I don't know."

"Then Joe Spencer's behind the building project?" she asked.

"I'm sure it's him. As I said, I think he owns all the property up there. But there's not a spot nicer than yours, so he probably wants to divide your acres into condo lots too," he surmised.

"Well, I wouldn't want that. It would totally spoil the beauty of my property."

"Yes . . . and help to spoil the environment. Soon there won't be any unspoiled places left," he said wistfully.

"Could we find out if Joe's behind the construction? If he is, that would help me make up my mind about selling."

"We could probably find out—building permits and property titles are public records. I'll research it if you'd like."

"It seems I'm always asking favors of you," she said.

"But I told you—it'll cost you," he said, laughing. He finished his sandwich. "Guess I'd better get going. I told the guy in Midway I'd be there by two." He stood, then noted that she'd eaten only half her sandwich. "Oh, you haven't finished," he said.

"No, but I'm full. I had a big breakfast—rather late." She stood too. "Let me pay the check."

"No, this one's on me," he said, leaving a tip on the table and walking her toward the cashier.

"Thank you for coming back," the hostess said. "I remember you from your previous visit—such a handsome couple. Hope you'll come again."

"Thanks, we will," Jim said, and Lesley smiled her apprecia-tion for the compliment.

They walked into the sunny crisp beauty of the mountain-ringed valley and to Jim's truck. "Smell that air," Jim said, taking a deep breath and stretching.

"Yes, invigorating," she agreed, following his example of breathing in the fresh mountain air. "It's certainly different from L.A., where I've been for so long. This is a bit of heaven. At least, I thought it was—before today."

"You mean before your run-in with Joe?"

"Well, there's more, but it can wait till later."

"Are you sure? Are you really all right now?"

"Yes, I'm okay. I'll just enjoy all this beauty on my drive back to Park City. I'll try to concentrate on that instead of my worries."

"Good idea," he said. "It is a beautiful area. Hope we can keep it that way—for Julie—and for others who'll follow us." He opened the truck door and climbed in. "Well, enough of my preaching. Got to get back to reality—to work. Sorry." He kissed her through the open window. "I'll call you later if you're going to be at the hotel."

"I plan to be. Tomorrow I have to go to Salt Lake for a meeting with the *Touched by an Angel* staff, but I have no plans for tonight."

"Then it's back to reality for you too—you'll be going to work soon." He sounded rather dejected at the thought.

"Yes, but not till after the Olympics—I'm still on vacation—supposedly." She sighed. "Life isn't predictable, is it? I hadn't thought I'd become so involved with my house—and all the problems related to it."

"Well, I'm glad you did—otherwise, you wouldn't have called the Woodpecker Man," he said, laughing.

"Yes, as I said, life isn't predictable. Who could have known that a week or so ago I'd meet you—and my life would change."

"For the better, I hope," he said, looking into Lesley's eyes.

"Yes—for the better, where you're concerned." That moment of truth was broken, when she remembered, "Oh, I did have something else to tell you, but I won't keep you any longer."

"Is it important?"

"Well, I'll make it short. There was someone else in the basement of my house when I finished talking with Joe Spencer this morning."

He looked alarmed. "How did they get in—a break-in?"

"No, I hate to admit it—I forgot to lock the gate and the front door when I was there last time." Jim raised his eyebrows. "I know, unlocked locks don't work. I was so upset that day that I simply forgot. There was no need for a break-in. Both Joe Spencer and the other intruder had an open invitation to walk right in."

He looked directly at her. "You weren't hurt, were you?"

"No, I didn't even see him. After Spencer left, I heard a noise downstairs in the basement, and I called out—foolishly warning him, I guess. Then I crept upstairs to hide in the attic, but I couldn't open the attic door. I heard the back door slam and ran down, but he was gone—his footprints led into the trees."

"I don't want you to go there alone. I mean it this time," he said.

"Is that an order?"

"No, of course not. But you could have been hurt. You don't know who it was or what he was doing," he said. "Besides, I thought you were going to wait until Saturday to go there, when all of us could go with you." He reached out for Lesley's hand. "Lesley, you need to take this seriously. I don't like what's going on. If Joe Spencer's involved, it could be dangerous," he warned.

"Dangerous?"

"Yes. He's used to getting his way. You've been an obstacle to his plans, and frankly I wouldn't put anything past him."

"Then why did you work for him today?" she said impertinently.

"Well, It was the same kind of deal he's offered you—cash—and it was an honest job—roof repair," he said defensively.

"I'm sorry. I didn't really mean to question your honesty. I was just surprised to see you there—at the spa—knowing your opinion of Joe."

"Oh, forget it. I often have to work for people I don't like. Don't you? Anyway, I'm really not bothered about that. I'm worried about you—and what's happening with your house."

"I know, and I'm grateful," she said, squeezing his hand. "I've caused you a lot of trouble."

"Well, Ah said it before—it pleasures me tuh help ya, ma'am."

Lesley was glad to see his sense of humor still intact. "I know—and that fact pleases me. Go on—do your job—and call me later. I'll be waiting."

"Good. I am going up to your house on my way back. I'll try to get a water sample, and I'll see if I can see what that prowler was doing in your basement."

"Thanks." She waited until he drove off in his truck, waving as he passed her.

Then she drove to Park City with no further concern about Jim's actions, but she still wondered why Gareth Sanders was in Silver Forks, why he was meeting with Joe Spencer, and why the intruder had been in her house.

CHAPTER 21

As usual, upon Lesley's return, Barnaby greeted Lesley in the hotel lobby. "Mr. Sanders called a few minutes ago. He asked me to tell you he'd called," he said cautiously.

"Thanks, Barnaby," was her only reply, leaving him guessing at her reaction.

She took the stairs to her room, still ruminating on her problems. *In a way, I will be glad to get back to work,* she thought. Her vacation had been interesting, and in several instances fun, but she hadn't anticipated the problems her house would bring. She had too much time to think about them, she realized.

She heard the phone ringing. Fumbling with her keys, she opened the door and rushed to the bedside table. "Hello?"

"Hi, it's Gareth," he said, with his customary forced joviality. "I heard that you called the restaurant earlier. Sorry I missed you."

"I was just returning your call, so . . ."

"So . . . what did I want? Right?" He laughed.

"Yes, right," she said, suddenly irritated by his phony, upbeat manner.

"Well, I have an invitation for you. Please note, I'm asking *formally* this time." He paused, she guessed for her response, but she said nothing. "Anyway, I have two tickets for the

Olympics opening ceremony and wondered if you'd like to go with me."

"That's a nice invitation, Gareth, but I already have a ticket. I ordered it as part of my Olympics package."

"You could sell it. I know a good scalper. Might even make some money on it," he suggested. When she didn't respond, he added, "Just kidding, but I could get your money back. These tickets are in demand. Well, how about it?"

Her thinking was confused, and she fought for an answer. Finally, she decided to bring an end to the game. "No, I don't think so, Gareth," she said as politely as she could.

"But the ceremony's a few weeks away, so you could take your time deciding. I've been a very patient man," he said rather bitterly.

That comment made her realize that she possibly hadn't been very nice to Gareth, always responding curtly to all his attempts to contact her—although he had become more than annoying, and she'd become wary of encouraging him further. But she did have a question for him. "What were you doing in Silver Forks today?"

"Oh, how did you know I was there?" he asked, sounding caught off guard.

"Well, one of your employees mentioned that's where you were. Then I came up later and saw you leave Silver Forks Realty, drive to the spa, and then come out and go up Silver Forks Mountain."

"Were you spying on me?" he said, sounding irritated.

"Not really. I was just there, and I saw what I saw."

"I told you at our first meeting that I spend a lot of time up there and know many people there," he hastily explained.

"And those people include Connie Evans and Joe Spencer," she stated more than asked.

"Yes, what of it?" he asked, obviously angry. "I'd already told you I know them. So what?"

She realized that he wasn't going to tell her more and that she was no longer interested in his business. She was no longer attracted to him in any way. There was no use in keeping up the charade.

"Well, how about it. Won't you reconsider?" he asked insistently after her long silence.

She paused again, then made a final decision. "No, Gareth, I really see no reason to continue leading you on. I don't think there can ever be anything between us. I'd like to be friends, but you seem to want our relationship to be more than that. I'm sorry, but it can't be. I'll be returning to my work and my life, and you have yours. It's been nice to have become acquainted with you, but as I told you when me met on the plane, that's often where these things end—a brief acquaintance. Again, I'm sorry—but that's the way it is. And would you please call off Barnaby. He's become much too interested in my every move." She finished, wondering if she'd said too much or too little.

There was a very long pause on Gareth's end. She heard him take a deep breath, as if trying to control his response. Then he said in a sarcastic and biting tone she hadn't heard him use before, "Well, my dear, you may find that Gareth Sanders is not that easy to get rid of. I've done nothing but try to help you and show you a good time. In return, you've been very standoffish to say the least. I won't be treated that way. Your kind always think they're too good for the likes of me. I *did* want more from you—but *not* in the way you seem to *think*," he said, and slammed the receiver down.

"Thanks—for calling," Lesley said into the dead phone. Then she thought, *I guess I haven't been very nice to him.*

Reading the scriptures and then napping seemed the best way to try to escape her feelings after the confrontation with Gareth and after the other challenges of the day.

She thought about the happenings with Rachel at her house. Then, deliberating on these occurrences, she remembered an instance when the five-year-old daughter of a good friend had contracted leukemia. Her father had held the little girl in his arms in the last moments of her life. Earlier the child had told her parents that a kind lady had come to see her in the hospital. As the child took her last breaths, she said to her father, "Look, Daddy, there's that nice lady who came to see me. She's come to get me." And then she died. Her parents interpreted the experience, believing that their child was so pure in heart that she could see angels or spirits—and one had come for her.

Lesley realized that she had never doubted the existence of influences from the other side. Pondering this experience, she fell asleep with visions of Rachel haunting her dreams.

CHAPTER 22

She was embarrassed to be caught catnapping when she awakened to answer the ringing phone. *If it's Jim, he'll think all I do is sleep.* She cleared her throat, trying not to sound groggy this time. "Hello?"

"Hello. This is you-know-who—your slave," Jim said, laughing.

"Oh, come on. I haven't treated you like a slave, I hope—maybe a servant?"

"Well, your errand boy, at least. Any plans for tonight?"

"Only if you have some for us. I'm glad you called."

"You know I'm always hungry," he said. "Have you eaten dinner?"

"No, and I'm hungry too. You'll remember that I didn't finish my sandwich at lunch."

"Well, I'm clean, but I'm not dressed up. How about a return trip to the Burger Barn?" he proposed.

"Why not? After all, that's where it all began," she said, giggling like a teenager.

"Should I come pick you up?" he asked.

"No, I'll meet you there—just like old times."

"Yes—it does feel like I've known you for a long time," he agreed. "I'm still grateful to that woodpecker and those cats for bringing us together."

"I am too. But maybe we had a stronger hand pushing us. It feels almost that way to me," she said, wondering if she assumed too much.

"When can you be there?" he asked.

"Thirty minutes?"

"Okay, I'll be there first this time and have our booth all picked out. I have a few things to tell you—about your house."

"I can't wait. I've become curiouser and curiouser." *It's time to end this conversation,* she thought, *before it gets any sillier.* "See you there."

"Okay, bye," he said, and smacked his lips in a kissing sound. "Oh, I almost forgot. I'd be in deep trouble with Mom and Julie if I didn't invite you to come to Sunday dinner."

"Are you sure? They've been so good to me already," she said, not wanting to wear out her welcome.

"Yes, I'm sure. As I said, you have to come, or I'll never hear the end of it," he persuaded.

"Okay, and tell them thanks. I'll come after we *all* go to church," she emphasized.

"Yeah, yeah, I know. Sounds good to me. And we're still planning to go back to your house on Saturday?" he asked.

"Yes—for a . . . final investigation, I guess we could call it."

"Well, then we're all booked up for the weekend, and I'll see you in a few minutes at the Burger Barn. Bye."

"Bye," she said and hung up, happy at the prospect of seeing him tonight and on the weekend.

She didn't change but fixed her makeup and hair, then took the elevator down to the garage level. Someone had parked so close to the driver's side of her SUV that she couldn't get in. She went to the passenger side and had to climb over the seats. Irritated, she backed out slowly and headed up the exit ramp and out into the crisp, beautiful Park City night. The stars shone brightly, and she thought again how much she loved this smog-free area.

The Sundance Festival crowds had thinned somewhat, but the town was still busy enough that she was forced to creep down Main Street. After that, traffic was lighter, so she made it to the Burger Barn in good time—on time. She saw Jim's old truck in the parking lot and pulled up beside it. He had already gone inside, as he'd said he would, and stood to wave at her when she entered.

She made her way to the booth and his smiling greeting. "Hello," he said, giving her a hug.

"Hello, yourself."

She sat, and he slid in across from her. "Let's order," he said. "I'm starved. What would you like?"

"I guess the occasion—the anniversary of our meeting—requires the same gourmet meal, the Burger Barn Special."

"Hoped you'd say that," he said, and signaled the teenage waitress—not Clara's daughter this time—that they were ready to order.

"What can I get for you?" the waitress asked, between chomps of her gum, taking a pencil from behind her ear and brushing back wisps of unruly brown hair that were keeping her from seeing.

"Two Burger Barn Specials—fried onions on mine—and a Sprite," he said, and looked to Lesley.

"No fried onions for me, thanks. And water is fine."

"Don't know what you're missing," he said.

"Oh, yes I do—being up all night. Onions and I don't get on too well."

The waitress left, and Lesley dived right in with her question about her house. "You said that you had more to tell me about my house?"

C. Paul Andersen

"Yes, but can't we wait on that?" he asked, holding her hand across the table.

"No, it can't wait. What did you find in my basement?" she asked insistently.

"Not much, really. Someone was down there, but you must have frightened him away before he could do whatever he may have come there to do. He'd moved some boxes around, and I could see footprints in the remaining dust, all around the furnace room, but I didn't find any damage done. More like he was surveying the space."

"Well, that's both disappointing and a relief," she said, "but I thought maybe you'd find something that would lead us to the identity of the prowler."

"Not unless you like the idea of checking footprints against shoes."

"I know—or tire tracks against tires. We already decided that approach to detective work is beyond us."

"But I did locate something else—the main water valve. It was in a cubbyhole in the basement wall under the stairs. It wasn't outside, I'm glad to say. I turned it and opened a spigot in the water line. I let it run into a bucket for a while to clear the line. Then I took a water sample and turned it off."

"So you did some detective work after all. What do you plan to do with the samples, then?"

"You said that you're going to Salt Lake tomorrow? What time?" he asked.

"My meeting starts at ten am, but I'd like to get there a few minutes early," she answered.

"Well, if you wouldn't mind, we could drive to Salt Lake together," he suggested. "I could take the samples to the water testing laboratory and then spend some time researching the ownership of the properties that surround your house. I may also look into some of the business affiliations—some of the corporations—in the area. Sometimes the main players in corporations aren't evident from records of incorporation— blind ownership, intentionally hidden from prying eyes. But I think I might learn some things that have concerned me even before you came into the picture. I'd like to know who owns what in our area."

"Well, I don't know how long my meeting will last," she said, "but I'd be glad to have your company on the drive if you don't mind waiting in case the meeting is lengthy."

"I think I can keep busy. Take your cell phone, and I'll take mine. Then you can call me when you're done. Okay?"

"Okay, sounds like a plan."

The waitress brought their food, as if on cue, and they both ate hungrily, saying little in the process.

Afterward, Jim walked her to her car, kissed her, and asked, "What time do you want to leave?"

"Oh, about eight thirty. It may take some time to find the production office," she suggested.

"Okay. I'll drive—not my old truck—the new one. I'll be at your hotel at eight thirty then." He opened her car door, kissed her again, and waved good-bye from his truck. He drove off, and Lesley sat there for a while, thinking about how they were spending a lot of time together. She said a quiet prayer, thanking the Lord for the blessing of the Shepherd family in her life and asking Him to guide her in this very rapidly growing relationship with Jim, in decisions related to her house, and in her attempts to understand the significance of Rachel's appearances.

CHAPTER 23

The pre-job jitters took over the next morning as Lesley contemplated the challenges of meeting new people and the stresses of creating her role in *Touched by an Angel.*

She hadn't played a blind person, so in spare moments she had reviewed her training for this difficult characterization. She'd already rehearsed blindfolded the requirements of walking and gesturing without really seeing. The senses of hearing and touch would become even more important in this role. Also, the natural response of a seeing person—the eyes move first—would have to be avoided.

She kneeled to say her morning prayers and thanked the Lord for this new and exciting opportunity and asked His help in her attempts to meet the demands of the assignment. Then she prayed for Carol, Julie, and Jim, all of whom had become very important to her.

She chose a taupe cashmere sweater and pants in a contrasting brown and automatically completed her hair and makeup. She was consumed by worries about the coming day.

She checked her purse for her keys, a notebook, a pencil, and a pen before leaving her room and going toward the stairs to meet Jim.

Happily, he was coming up the stairs to get her. He looked as handsome in his dark leather coat and khaki Dockers as he had on their previous visit to Salt Lake. "You're ready—right on time," he said.

Her response was, "I'm always on time. Late to work isn't appreciated in show business, contrary to the stories about actors being undependable and always late."

"Hold on—I didn't say that you're always late. I was just making conversation. Actually, I meant it as a compliment— some women I've known do make it part of their routine. You know, keep 'em waiting," he said, trying to lighten the mood.

"Well, I'm not 'some women,' and I don't play those kind of games," she said, starting down the wide stairway to the lobby.

He followed, hurrying to catch up. "You're really on one this morning," he observed, laughing a little nervously.

She stopped. "Oh, I'm always like this at the start of a new role. I'm sorry. I don't mean to be short tempered. I'm just uptight, I guess."

"Understandable. I get the same way when I have a new challenge," he said with a genuine sympathy that made her feel better.

She saw Barnaby gawking at them from his station, leaning on the front desk, but she ignored him. She wondered if Gareth had told him to back off as she'd requested.

Jim held the heavy hotel door and led her to his clean and shining Chevy truck. "Have you had breakfast?" he asked.

"No, but I'm not sure I can eat anything. Nervous stomach."

He closed the door and then climbed in the driver's side. "But you should eat something," he said.

"Oh, they always have food at these kinds of meetings. They'll have some fruit and pastries at least. I'll wait for that."

"Okay, if you're sure," he said driving downhill and toward the freeway access road.

"But what about you?" she asked, trying to sound unselfish but not really wanting to take time to stop to eat. "You should eat."

"Oh, I can eat after I drop you off. Let's get you where you're going; then maybe you can relax."

They talked about his plans for the day—going to the water testing laboratory and doing some research on corporations and property ownership in Summit County—and she told him the little she knew about her TV role.

"That's fascinating," he said. "I sometimes forget I'm keeping company with a famous actress."

"Famous I'm not, but aspiring I have been. Every role seems more important than the last. I feel a real need to make each performance better than the last one. I guess I'm driven—without really setting out to be."

"Part of being an artist, I guess. You have to care to do your best," he said wisely.

"Thanks for understanding," she said, touching his hand. "Sometimes I feel that it matters too much—that I should stop acting. I really don't want it to consume my entire life. I want . . . a real life too."

"Well, don't wait too long for that real life," he advised. "Real life, as you've put it, can pass you by while you're chasing your dreams."

"You're quite the philosopher today," she said.

"Yeah, sorry. As you've noticed, I tend to get on a soapbox real often," he apologized.

"No, no. I do too. I like the fact that you feel strongly about so many things. It makes you much more human—much more interesting—because of your passions," she said honestly.

They were quiet then, having got past discussion of her nervous fears and his earnest persuasions.

Jim found the *Touched by an Angel* production office without trouble, proving his acquaintance with the greater Salt Lake area. After stopping the car, he moved to get out, but Lesley stopped him. "I'll just find my way from here. Thanks, Jim."

He seemed a little hurt, misinterpreting her intent. "Guess you don't want the country boy tagging along."

"That's not what I meant. Oh, I'm sorry you have to see this side of me. I didn't mean what you thought I meant. I'm just—nervous. And when I'm this way, I have to be alone to get it all together."

"It's okay—I understand," he said, smiling, but without the usual gleam. "Call me on your cell phone when you're ready to be picked up."

"I will, and thanks, Jim, for everything."

He didn't reply, so she kissed his cheek and then climbed out of the car and hurried toward an entry door. She looked back to see him watching her until she went inside. Then he drove off.

A receptionist greeted her, and Lesley told her who she was. "Yes, Ms. Kern. Welcome. Your meeting will be in the conference room. I'll show you the way." She led her down a hall and stopped halfway to open a door. "Just take a seat anywhere," she suggested. "The others should be along soon."

"Thank you," Lesley said, and selected a chair on the side of the long conference table and opposite the door, so that she could see people as they entered. *Why do I always have to be the type-A personality who arrives first?* she thought, wishing that she'd come later to make a grand entrance—or at least a less conspicuous display of early-arrival anxiety.

A producer, whom she recognized from photos in trade magazines, entered first and introduced herself. She seemed to know who Lesley was and said that they were pleased that she'd accepted the role. Others followed, including the actors who regularly appeared on the series and some other production staff members, not the least of which was the director for the episode. The producer introduced Lesley, the only newcomer, as the guest artist for the segment, and she felt tremendous pressure from that title. The others talked genially with each other, having become a TV family through their years of working together.

Finally, all sat down for a preliminary script reading, during which Lesley learned that the blind girl whom she would portray was about her age—type casting—and had not been blind from birth. Her blindness had come after a fall down a flight of stairs in her house and a resultant severe blow to the head. She was experiencing great anguish in trying to adjust to this unforeseen circumstance. Alone in her world, she was almost suicidal in her despair. Hence, the arrival of the angels—Monica and Tess—who would try to help her "see" that she still had much to live for and that God was watching out for her and would help and protect her. Andrew, in his role as the angel of death, was lurking about in the event that Heather, the girl whom Lesley would play, tried to take her life.

Lesley liked the character, the themes, and the challenges of the role, and left this initial production meeting with great anticipation. She also liked the people with whom she'd be working. A great spirit of graciousness and cooperation was evident in the company.

Shooting would begin after the Olympic Games were over. Grant Pack, a locations man for the company, had asked about Lesley's house as a possible locale for the segment, and they arranged to meet there—at her house—the next week.

All in all, she was very happy with this experience and was anxious to share her news with Jim. She sat in the foyer and called him on her cell phone.

"Hey, done already?" he asked.

"Yes, we only took time to read the script and plan the production schedule," she explained.

"Did you get something to eat?" he asked, always concerned for her welfare.

"No, I didn't even think of eating. I was too nervous and excited," she said.

"Well, did it go well?"

"Yes, yes, but I'll tell you all about it when you pick me up. How about you? Did you accomplish what you'd planned?"

"Yes and no. I'll tell you about it when I get there. Should take me about fifteen minutes. I haven't eaten, either, so let's grab a late lunch," he suggested.

"Sounds good. I'll watch for you," she said. "Bye."

"Bye," and he disconnected.

She was in a much better mood than at their earlier meeting. When Jim drove up, she hurried out to his truck. Then throughout lunch she did most of the talking, telling him about the script, the other actors, and the total experience of her morning. He listened patiently. Then she reflected on how those who live around actors have to be willing listeners, since actors tended to get very caught up in themselves and their creative projects.

On the way back to Park City, she finally got around to asking him about his day and what he had learned. "All we've talked about is my day," she admitted apologetically. "Now, tell me about yours."

"Well, my day was all about you too," he said.

"I know. You've been so good to me. I do appreciate it, and I'm sorry about my bad temper this morning."

"Guess we're even, then. You forgave me for one of my sulks last week," he said, smiling.

"Yes, okay, we're even, and I'll try not to get so uptight again," she promised.

"Me too."

"So, what did you find out?" she asked.

"I took the water samples to the laboratory. They charged me up front to do the testing and said the results would be available early next week."

"Oh, I'd hoped they could do it while you waited."

"Nope, they're pretty busy, I guess."

She urged him on. "So what about the rest of your research?"

"Not very successful, either. I finally decided I needed some help, so I went to see a lawyer friend of mine. He's going to look into the title holders of the Silver Forks Mountain properties and the structure of several corporations. All of this is getting a little expensive, but I didn't know what else to do."

"I told you I wanted it done, and I'm prepared to pay for it. By the way, I've written a check for your work for me this past week," she said, fishing into her purse for it.

"I feel like I want to just do this for you," he said.

"No, we had an agreement. You're spending time helping me that you could use working for someone else. So no further argument. Okay?" She handed him the check, and reluctantly he took it and stuffed it into his jacket pocket.

"My attorney friend said he could report to me next week," he said. "I'm sorry I had to go to him, but it's just a matter that he can look into easier than I. He'll have to go to the Summit County and Wasatch County recorders' offices to get what we need. I should have realized that."

"Well, you're a jack-of-all-trades, but you're not a lawyer, are you?"

"No, I'm not." He was silent for a moment.

"Is something wrong?" she asked.

"Oh, after this morning I've been wondering how you really feel about—what I do for a living."

"What made you think of that?" she asked.

"I guess I realized that what you do is pretty important," he said. "I just wondered if maybe you'd be—ashamed—of hanging around with a fix-it man."

"But you're more than that, unless you want to call your work with animals fix-it work. That's pretty important work to my way of thinking. And it never crossed my mind to feel ashamed of you—quite the contrary, in fact," she said, looking at his movie-star profile.

"You're sure about that? 'Cause I kinda got the feeling this morning that you didn't want me to be a part of your—professional world."

"I know I gave you that impression. But that wasn't it at all. I tried to explain that I have to be alone to get centered—to get it all together—before I reenter that world. Frankly, I'm not always comfortable there. I feel like everybody's more important or more talented or more skilled than I am. That's why I was behaving that way. It certainly had nothing to do with you or with what you do," she tried to assure him. "It's just that I almost have to force myself to go to each new acting assignment."

"Well, I guess I'm a little insecure too. My life isn't exactly what I'd planned it to be. As I told you when we first met, I really wanted to be a veterinarian—but things just didn't work out. My life changed when Jenny was killed."

Lesley didn't know what to say that wouldn't sound patronizing, but she jumped in with advice anyway. "I know that, but it's not too late. You could start some night classes through the University of Utah or even on the Internet," she suggested.

"But it seems like such a big step, and I'm too old to start college," he said.

"No, you're not. You'd be surprised how many students your age and much older are in university classes. A lot of people are having to retrain because they've lost jobs. You wouldn't feel at all out of place," she encouraged. "You just have to take that first small step—get admitted to the university and then take a class or two. You've been helping me—let me help you with this," she said, excited at the prospect of doing something for him.

"Hold on. I haven't said I'd do it," Jim said hesitantly.

"Well, I'm all excited about it. I want to help you get started. At least think about it."

"Oh, I have, believe me. But that's all I've done is think about it—kinda like my thoughts about going back to church. You gave me the boost I needed, and you're still here pushing me along. Guess I've come to need you, Lesley," he said, without looking at her.

"Well, as I'm sure you've realized, the feeling is mutual. I've come to . . . need you too, Jim."

At that moment they reached the turnoff to Park City, and Jim turned then found a spot by the entrance road. He stopped the truck, turned to Lesley, and kissed her. *I am falling in love with this man,* she thought, but didn't tell him so.

His duty done, Jim pulled out into the traffic and drove Lesley back to her hotel. "I'll walk you in," he said after parking the truck. She knew better than to suggest that she didn't want him to.

He took her upstairs to her door, then said, "Eight thirty in the morning, then?"

"Yes, my car or yours?"

"We'll all come by and pick you up. Good night." She watched him go down the hall to the stairs, thanking the Lord for another interesting day.

CHAPTER 24

Jim, Carol, and Julie were waiting in the truck when Lesley came out of the hotel at eight thirty in the morning. Jim hurried to meet her and led her to the truck, opening the door for her as he always did. Julie and Carol were in the backseat.

"Morning, everybody," Lesley said. "Thanks for doing this."

Carol spoke first. "We're glad to see you, Lesley."

"Yeah, we've been missing you," Julie added, touching her shoulder affectionately.

Lesley reached back and squeezed her hand. *What sweet, dear people,* she thought again. "I've missed you."

"I haven't missed you," Jim said, laughing. "Because I've been with you—I mean."

"It's good you added that," she said, smiling and jabbing him with her elbow.

They went to breakfast at McDonald's again, almost making it a regular routine. Then Jim drove them to Silver Forks. The day was overcast, but the roads were clear.

"Guess there's enough snow for the Olympics," Lesley said, making conversation.

"Yes, they'll supplement it with their snowmaking machines, of course, but I still worry about the drought. We've gone too many years without good winters," Jim said.

"Guess we'd better start fasting and praying," Carol said, meaning it.

"Yes, it wouldn't hurt," Lesley agreed. "Sometimes the prophet calls for a Churchwide fast. I wonder if that will happen."

"I don't know, but it seems like a good idea," Jim said sincerely.

"We don't have to wait to be told," Carol said brusquely. "We can do it on our own. We've already been told that it works."

"Well, you're right, of course," Lesley said, and realized once again that this feisty little woman had a strong faith.

Changing the subject, Jim said, "Now, what I want to know is what we're planning to do today—when we get to your place." He smiled, then asked, "Lesley, what are your plans?"

"I don't really know. I guess we'll see if Rachel's ghost wants to contact us again," she said facetiously. "Oh, I forgot to get that photo album from you. I left it at your house the other night."

"Have no fear," Carol said, holding up the album. "I knew you'd probably want it."

"Thanks, Carol. You always think of everything."

"Well, so what shall we do?" Jim asked.

"Are you sure you want to go back there?" Lesley asked them.

"Yeah, I told you I'm not afraid, now that I know she's real," Julie explained.

"We're not turning back now," Carol said emphatically.

Lesley said, "Maybe we can also look around the house a little more to make sure no one's disturbed anything."

"Yes, Jim told us you had a prowler. You shouldn't go up there alone anymore," Carol scolded.

"Your son has made that very clear," Lesley said, turning and smiling at her. She smiled back knowingly.

When they came to her place, the gate was locked and there was no evidence of new tire tracks in the snowy drive. They parked and went inside, keeping their coats on since they didn't have a heater this time.

They sat quietly in the parlor, which was colder than usual that day because the sun was behind the clouds. "Brrrr," Lesley said. "We can't stay here very long in this cold."

After a long silence, Julie stood slowly and left the room. They watched her go but didn't follow. They could hear her climbing the stairs, and Lesley moved to stand, but Carol reached out and touched her arm, restraining her. *What if something happens to her?* she thought, but didn't say it out loud.

There was more silence. Then they heard a door opening, and as one, they hurried to the foot of the stairs, looking up to see Julie entering the attic stairway. The childlike humming that Lesley had heard on that earlier occasion began. Julie was being drawn toward the voice as if hypnotized. Jim protectively bounded up the stairs when suddenly the mirror door closed. He ran up the remaining steps, followed by Carol and Lesley. He tugged at the frame of the mirror but couldn't get the door to open, echoing Lesley's experience at her last visit.

"Julie," Jim called. "Come back down here, please." There was no response. "I'm going to my truck for a crowbar," he said frantically. "We've got to get that door open." He moved past them down the stairs and ran out the front door. Carol and Lesley remained motionless and speechless, waiting for his return, their eyes fixed on the mirror door. He returned with a crowbar in hand and took the stairs two by two.

They stepped aside, letting him go to work, but as he positioned the crowbar to pry the door open, it softly opened, and Julie stepped out, a little dazed but smiling.

Jim threw his arms around her. "You scared us to death," he said. "We shouldn't have let you go off alone like that."

"But I wasn't afraid. Rachel was calling me—with her music," Julie said calmly.

Carol put her arm around Julie's shoulders and led her back downstairs to the parlor. Taking her to the sofa and sitting beside her, Carol said nothing, and Jim and Lesley followed her example, also sitting quietly.

Finally Julie sat upright, as if she were awakening, and said, "Rachel chose me because I'm a child and because I'm like her. Rachel told me something. She didn't actually talk but helped me understand that the creek that runs through your property is not in its true path. It was changed to run through the mine waste, and the water is poisoned. Rachel knew I would believe in her and her message. Then she left—went away. I—I don't think she'll come back," she added.

Again the adults were speechless. None of them wanted to contradict Julie or make light of what she'd said because she was so certain of it. They all had heard the music this time and had witnessed the operation of the mirror door. They were neither in position nor were they inclined to tell Julie that she was just imagining things.

Jim looked at them and nodded, as if to say, "You see, I was right about the water," but he didn't say it aloud. They were in silent agreement on the matter, and Lesley expected that the analysis of the water samples would corroborate Rachel's message.

Carol broke the silence. "Well, that's the answer, then. But what can we do about it?"

Jim answered her. "I've already done two things—the water samples are at the laboratory for analysis. When we get that scientific proof, we'll have more to go on. And my attorney is checking on the ownership of all the property on Silver Forks Mountain. If Joe Spencer owns all of it, as I've thought, we'll confront him with the problem and demand that he do something about it. If he won't, we'll turn our findings over to the State Water Department. He won't want his plans for condos on the mountain or expansion of his health spa to be sidetracked by the revelation that there's poison in the water."

"Okay," Lesley said. "I'm so glad that you thought of the water problem and took action. Now that we have confirmation from Rachel, we know that you were right, Jim."

"Let's go home," Julie said. "I'm tired and hungry."

"Yes, let's go home," Carol agreed. "I think we've accomplished what we came here for—and then some," she said, laughing nervously.

They all agreed and moved toward the front door, when Lesley remembered she'd left the photo album in the parlor and went back for it. "The photo album's gone," she said.

They hurriedly returned. "It was right there on the table," Jim said.

They looked all over, under the sofas and everywhere, but it wasn't to be found.

"Maybe Rachel took it with her," Julie offered simply.

"Maybe she did," Lesley said. At that point she refused to let her thoughts go to other possibilities for the album's disappearance. The events of the day had already been too exciting—too revealing. "Let's go home."

CHAPTER 25

The Sunday morning eight thirty appointment was still in force. When Lesley drove to the Shepherd home, arriving on time, they all came out to the car before she could honk or go in to get them. Since she now knew where the chapel was located, she drove them.

Jim seemed a little more relaxed that morning than he had been on the previous Sunday, thanks to the warm greeting he'd received from the ward members. Lesley said a quiet prayer that this Sunday would go as well.

She needn't have been concerned, however, because the bishopric was greeting at the door and expressed their pleasure at Jim's return. Then Gary Beck, Jim's friend from high school and now the elders quorum president, was right there to invite him once again to go to priesthood meeting.

They sat together on a side bench, and Julie made certain she was sitting by Lesley, who was becoming very fond of this sweet and caring little girl and who couldn't help responding to Julie's acceptance of her. Lesley's heart was full with thanks for what was happening to all of them.

The speakers' subject was the basic principles of the gospel—faith, repentance, and baptism. Comments regarding the necessity of baptism led Lesley to think of Rachel.

She had died at age eight, but was she ever baptized? Then she thought of Julie, sitting there beside her. Because of Jim's inactivity, she wondered if Julie had been baptized. She'd ask Carol when the opportunity arose.

That opportunity came before Relief Society opening exercises. Lesley leaned over to Carol and whispered, "By the way, has Julie been baptized?"

"Yes, I made certain she was ready, and she was baptized when she was eight. Of course, Jim couldn't participate, but he came and sat proudly while she accepted full membership."

Then Lesley shared another concern with Carol. "I've also been wondering if Rachel was baptized." Carol didn't have time to respond because the Relief Society president began the meeting, but Lesley could tell that she was seriously considering the question.

Jim had stayed for Sunday School and elders quorum, and when they gathered afterward in the foyer, Lesley was anxious to hear his response to the experience. But all she had to do was look at him—he was beaming from ear to ear, making her think of the glow that she'd often seen surrounding just-called or just-returned missionaries. The sight filled her—and she could see it filled Julie and Carol—with joy.

Dinner was as delicious as on the previous Sunday, and the warmth of the fire and of the Shepherd family enveloped them in the peace of the Sabbath. Without discussing it, they all avoided reference to Saturday's experiences. There seemed to be consensus that they'd take that up another day.

Jim announced that he had several jobs that would keep him busy on Monday and Tuesday. Lesley planned to go to the Sundance awards ceremony and to meet with Grant Pack, the *Touched by an Angel* locations man, at her house on Wednesday morning. Julie would be in school, and Carol would return to her everyday duties. So Lesley assumed that she wouldn't see Jim again until the latter part of the week.

She said her parting thanks to Carol and Julie, and Jim walked her to her car. He told her that he'd call when he heard something from the water testing laboratory and from his attorney.

Finally, Lesley had the opportunity to ask him how he was feeling about his return to church.

"Right now I feel like a new man," he answered. "Thanks, Lesley, for helping me along. I love you for it."

"Well, thank you, but I can't take the credit. I think the Holy Spirit had most to do with it. He knew your heart. Maybe I was sent to help you along, but you were already on your way back. I'm sure of that."

Nevertheless, his declaration both warmed and perplexed her. He hadn't actually declared his love for *her* but for her *part* in helping him to change his life. And that was good enough for now.

CHAPTER 26

On Monday morning Lesley read from Alma in the Book of Mormon. She reviewed chapter 4, wherein Alma and his followers baptize thousands of converts, and also chapter 5, where Alma exhorts both his followers and his detractors to remember their fathers, who had experienced a change in their hearts after their acceptance of Christ and after their baptisms.

That concept of changing hearts led her to think of Jim, of Julie, who had been baptized fairly recently, and then of Rachel. She began to wonder if Rachel, the unacknowledged daughter of her great-grandparents, had ever been baptized. Would there be mention in her great-grandmother's diary of that ordinance having been performed? She was determined to find out. She also intended to look again for the photo album that had so strangely disappeared on their last visit to her house.

Setting the scriptures aside, she began to work on memorizing her lines for her role in *Touched by an Angel.* Knowing that the script was subject to change many times before completion of the shooting, she still wanted to show them that she was a professional—ready for the role.

She ended up working most of Monday and Tuesday on her lines and on moving and responding as a blind person.

The Eighteenth Annual Sundance Film Festival closed with top honors awarded to *Personal Velocity* and to the documentary *Daughter from Danang,* both of which she'd seen. She was particularly pleased at the recognition for the documentary. The Sundance experience behind her, she was looking forward to the Olympics.

On Wednesday morning she set out to meet Grant Pack, the locations man, at her house. She had given him directions to Silver Forks and then to Silver Forks Mountain Road. She told him that he couldn't miss seeing her house since it was the only house up there.

They agreed to meet there at ten AM. She had a few qualms about returning there, but since she wouldn't be there alone and because the matter of Rachel might have been resolved, she was able to go.

When she drove into her place, she left the gate open for Grant and then cautiously went inside. The house was a little warmer that day because the sun was shining brightly outside and through the parlor window. She sat in the parlor waiting for Grant's arrival, noting that it was already ten o'clock. Had he had trouble locating her house?

She decided to look around again for the photo album, which had so mysteriously disappeared on Saturday. She had thought it was in the parlor, but maybe someone had carried it to another room. She searched the first floor without result. Then she started upstairs, not even thinking about her previous experiences there but concentrating on the possibilities and problems that her house might present as a location for the TV episode.

She was startled from these thoughts by the sound of humming from the top of the stairs. This humming was quite different, however, in that it seemed less distant and more direct, and she couldn't recognize the melody. As she reached the upstairs landing, a sudden light appeared, almost as a halo, in the mirror door. There was a difference in the appearance of this phenomenon—the apparition that then appeared was Rachel as she had looked in the old photograph, but this time her appearance was less hazy—more defined. Nevertheless, Lesley was breathless and frightened at Rachel's reappearance, having thought that Rachel had finished with her—with them—in communicating her urgent message. Involuntarily, she turned down the stairs but stopped when she heard Rachel speak three words of warning: "Sell your house!" Frightened, she almost fell down the stairs in her haste to get away.

She ran out onto the porch, having forgotten about the imminent arrival of Grant Pack, who was just then driving through her gateway in a white van. She tried to calm herself, not wanting to alarm him or scare him away from the prospect of using her house.

Grant was about forty, she guessed, and was bundled against the cold with a heavy khaki parka and a warm hat with earflaps. He removed his glasses and wiped them on a hand-kerchief. Then he saw her and smiled his genial greeting. "Sorry I'm late. I had a little trouble finding the Silver Forks Mountain Road after the Silver Forks turnoff. I stopped at a gas station but couldn't find anyone on duty there."

"Oh, that's not unusual. Out to lunch or breakfast, I guess. Well, welcome. This is my place," she said, gesturing toward the house and the spread around it.

He had brought along a video camera and a clipboard. "Thanks for taking time to show me your house," he said. "It really is out here in the boondocks, isn't it?"

"Yes, would that be a problem? Is it too far for the production company to come?"

"Oh, I don't think so, but I hadn't been this far from Park City before. This is beautiful country, even in winter, I guess. Ya see, I'm a California boy, so I have to work to convince myself that anything having to do with winter is pleasant."

"Well, that accounts for your warm clothes," she said. "But you may not need them today. It's pretty nice, really."

"I guess so, if you consider forty degrees nice. I get cold when the temperature hits fifty."

Meeting Grant had somewhat lessened her reaction to Rachel's reappearance. "If you have any questions, I'll try to be helpful."

"I do have a few questions. Are the electricity and plumbing working in your house?"

"No, they aren't. I might be able to arrange to get electricity turned on and the water lines opened, if necessary."

"Well, no, it isn't absolutely necessary. In fact, I was assuming we'd have to generate our own electricity and provide our own plumbing. But how would you feel about having vans and trucks parked all around the house for a week?"

"Oh, I can't see any real problem in that. The driveway and the areas around the front porch are available. Those areas are covered with gravel under the snow, so I don't think any harm would be done."

"Well, good. Let's take a look inside, then," he suggested.

"Okay," she said, opening the front door and ushering him inside. She was hesitant to go back inside but braved it, saying, "Feel free to look around the house. I'll follow you and . . . answer any questions you have."

"Well, the entry is large enough and lighted enough that we could set up here for the stairway scenes." He looked left toward the parlor. "Oh, this room is great—period stuff. Our art director and the camera people will eat this up. It fits very well with my vision of the setting. Could we see the kitchen?"

"Yes, right this way," she said, leading him along the center hall to the kitchen and dining room while avoiding looking up the stairs.

"Yes, the dining room will be great also," Grant said. "The rooms are big, so the camera and lighting crews can move about easily." They went into the hallway again. "We probably wouldn't use the upstairs rooms, but just in case, could I take a look?"

"Of course. Just go up yourself," she said, still somewhat shaken by her experience just a few minutes back. She didn't want to go up there right then.

He examined the handrail as he ascended. "Just checking to see if we could hide some wiring here if we need to run power to the upstairs," he explained. "What's this?" he asked, kneeling down to look more carefully. He peeled off something with his fingers, then returning down the stairs, he presented it on his open palm.

"I have no idea," she said truthfully.

"Well, I do. It's a bug. There are several of them stuck along the bottom of the handrail. Someone has planted some listening devices in your house. Do you have any idea who—or why?"

She was astounded. "Listening devices? What do you mean?"

"I mean, your place has been bugged so that someone could listen to everything that's said or done here. You weren't aware of that?" he asked.

"No, of course not, and I can't think who would have done . . ." She stopped midsentence, thinking back to the first day she had returned to her house and of the footprints in the hallway dust, beside the handrail, and of the fact that the handrail was clean of dust, when everything else was filthy. "They must have—must have planted them there before I came back here from California," she said, confused at the realization.

He bent down and examined further the underside of the handrail. "And there's some wiring here, imbedded in a seam between the decorative wood and the framing of the banister. Do you have any idea what it's for?"

"No, I can't think that it was original to the house or that it would have been necessary to add it to run household power to the upstairs," she said incredulously.

"Well, it's too new for that." He removed his cap, revealing a rim of sandy-colored, thinning hair, and scratched his head, puzzled at what he'd found. "You have no idea why anyone would want to bug your place or rewire it?"

"I have no idea who might have done it or why it was done," she said, looking for a place to sit down.

He followed her into the parlor. "Well, then, I'd remove all those bugs and look elsewhere for more. Someone has obviously been wanting to eavesdrop on the goings-on in your house." He sat across from her. "I'm sorry that upsets you, but it may be a good thing that I came here today. Do you want me to look for more bugs?" he asked.

"Yes, yes, would you? I wouldn't know where to look. I still can't believe it," she said.

He found a bug under the fireplace mantel in the parlor, another under the dining room table, and still another under the kitchen sink. "It wouldn't matter where you were in the downstairs or near the stairway; whoever placed these bugs could hear everything that was said here. Maybe you ought to report this to the police," he suggested.

"I'll talk it over with my friends—get their advice. They're from this area and would know the county sheriff, I'm sure."

She was dumbfounded at Grant's discovery, and her mind was racing, trying to think of who might be responsible and what their motivations were.

"Well, you need to take some kind of action. Somebody really wanted to know what was being said here," he advised.

"Yes, thank you. I'm glad you came today before I—before we . . ."

She was going to say, "before we did or said something that would reveal our private actions or conversations," but she realized that it was too late for that. Someone had heard everything that had been said or done here since the day she returned to her house.

"Lesley, are you okay?" Grant asked.

"Yes, I'm okay. I'm just puzzled," she answered.

"Then do you mind if I videotape some of the areas that we might use, so that the director can see the possible settings?"

"No, not at all. If you still think you want to come here, under the circumstances."

"Well, what we've found here concerns you more than it does me. We wouldn't want the segment recorded, of course, but since the bugs have been removed, that wouldn't be a problem."

"Just go ahead and do whatever you need to do," she said, remaining in the parlor, away from the stairs.

Grant made some notes correlating with his videotaping. He took some measurements in various places. Then he went upstairs to survey the second floor and then outside to look at the porch and areas surrounding the house.

She had time to worry anxiously about the implications of the discoveries Grant had made. She remembered again that someone had been in her house before she came in the first time. She reviewed her memory of the footprints in the dust and the contrasting dust-free banister. The bugs had probably been placed before her first visit. But what about the wiring hidden under the banister? When had it been installed and what was its purpose? She remembered having accused Joe Spencer of breaking and entering.

Did the intruder who came into her house when she'd left it unlocked do more than Jim had thought? Had he installed the wiring, completing his work before she chased him out? And ultimately, who was responsible for all of this? Who would want to gather information from her—about her? Of course, her thoughts then went again to Joe Spencer and Jim's warning that he could be dangerous.

Grant returned, interrupting her frantic thinking. "I checked for bugs upstairs but couldn't find any." He paused, then said, "Well, I have what I need, Lesley. Just for your information, I'll probably recommend that we use your house for the show. They'll pay you for that, of course, but it may be a rather nominal rent."

"Oh, I'm not worried about that. My only concern would be that they leave the house as they found it—minus the bugs of course," she said, trying to laugh about the very serious discovery.

"They'll take very good care of it. They cover the floors, so that the dollies and light trees don't ruin them, and they won't be driving nails or using screws or anything in the walls or woodwork."

"Well, okay. I guess we're done here." She wanted to get out of the house, which had become more than frightening to her—it seemed sullied or ravaged, as if a burglar had broken in. But this was even worse—someone had intruded on her privacy in a distinctly criminal way.

"Guess you can find your way back okay?" she asked.

"Yes, now that I've come here once, there's no trouble finding my way back. Thanks, Lesley, for taking the time to come here today. And I'm sorry about—what I found."

"Oh, I'm so grateful you found the bugs. It's very disconcerting, but at least, thanks to you, I won't have any more invasions into my privacy."

"Well, you should probably report it to the police," he said. "I'll be on my way."

"Okay, I'll be right behind you."

Grant took his leave, and Lesley went back to make certain the rear door was locked. It wasn't. She opened it and looked outside. The footprints leading away from her house were still there, but this time, there were also footprints leading from the evergreens toward the house. She hurriedly slammed the door and turned the dead bolt. She wondered if Grant had unlocked the door during his survey of the house. Then she heard it—a scuffling sound of footsteps from above. Someone was upstairs. But Grant had just been there. Then it hit her—someone was in the attic room.

She didn't stop to investigate. Lesley realized she could never live there as she ran toward the front door, locked it behind her, raced to her car, stopped to lock the gate, and shot down the mountain to get away from her house. Too much had happened for her to ever feel like it was home.

CHAPTER 27

That evening, Lesley received a much-anticipated call from Jim. "I have a lot to tell you," he said. "I heard from the water lab and from my attorney friend. Can we get together tonight?"

"I'm so glad you called. I've had quite a day too."

"Hold on, don't say any more. Let's talk face-to-face. I don't want any listening ears to hear what I've learned," he said.

"Well, from what I've learned, you have every right to suspect that," she said. She heard a click, as if someone had hung up an extension. "Did you hear that? We did have an eavesdropper."

"Yes, I heard it. From now on we'll have to be more careful. I'll use my cell phone to call yours."

"Good idea."

"Have you had dinner?" he asked.

"No, and I didn't eat lunch, either. I was too upset to eat."

"I'll come there. Meet me in the lobby?" he proposed.

"I'll be there. Let's find a quiet place where we can have a long talk and resolve some things."

"I know just the spot. I'll be there in fifteen minutes."

"I'll be downstairs watching for you. And thanks, Jim," she said.

"For what?"

"For everything—for being here for me."

"I'm coming. Bye."

She hurriedly changed into a light blue, cashmere sweater and jeans and freshened up a bit. Then she grabbed her coat and purse, locked her door, and rushed downstairs to the lobby.

Barnaby was not at his usual post, she was glad to see. *Maybe he's hidden away, listening in on people's conversations. Or maybe Gareth did call him off,* she hoped.

She walked out onto the porch of the Silver Princess just as Jim pulled up in his truck. She climbed in before he had time to get out to greet her. "I'm so glad you're here," she repeated.

"I'm glad I'm here too, but I'm a messenger with some bad news—or good news, depending on how you take it." He backed out of the parking place and headed down the hill, using an alternate road instead of Main Street to avoid the crowds.

"Well, I need some good news. Where are we going?"

"There's a little steak house along Highway 80 going toward Coalville. It's kind of a roadhouse, but it'll be quiet this time of day. The truckers will be snoozing or stopped for the night or on the road. But the food's good, and the atmosphere is dim and soothing. Sound okay?"

"Does it ever. I need an escape for a little while."

Heading for the freeway, Jim asked, "Do you want to hear about the water analysis report?"

"Okay, shoot. Let's hear the bad news first."

"The bad news is that the water on Silver Forks Mountain and in the Silver Forks Spa is laced with arsenic from the mine tailings. It's in small enough concentration to cause death in an adult over a fairly lengthy exposure time, but a child could die from drinking it in just a few years, according to the water testing lab. I asked specifically about that, since you were so concerned about what might have happened to Rachel."

"So what do we do now?" she asked quietly.

"When we give the okay, the water testing lab plans to report their findings to the State Division of Drinking Water and the State Division of Water Quality."

"What do you think will happen when they hear about it?"

"Well, I'm pretty certain they'll close down the health spa and put a stop to the condo construction—at least temporarily—until they can do something to make the water safe."

"What would that take?" she asked.

"First thing I'm sure they'll insist on is diverting the course of the Silver Forks Creek to its natural course. Then they'll probably follow up with more testing after that."

"What does that mean for my place?" she asked hesitantly.

He paused for a moment, as if carefully considering his reply. "I'm afraid the groundwater around your place is so heavily laced with arsenic and other harmful trace minerals that it will be years before the water's potable."

"So I couldn't live there—even if I wanted to."

"I'm sorry—that's probably true." He reached over and tightly clasped her hand.

"Well, it's okay, because I've already decided I never want to live there anyway."

"You have? What happened to make you so certain?"

"I—I went back there today . . ."

"You went back there again—alone?" he said angrily.

"No, I wasn't alone the whole time. Don't you remember that I had to meet the television show locations man?" she asked.

"You mentioned it, but I didn't know when."

"Well, I met him up there—but before he came . . . Rachel appeared again . . . in the mirror."

He seemed shocked. "Are you sure?"

"Yes, I'm sure," she said forcefully. "I'm past the imagining stage in all this. It happened—again."

"Okay, I'm sorry. I'm not doubting your word. I'm just very surprised that she came back."

"I was surprised too. Apparently Julie received the impression from Rachel that she wouldn't come back. I thought she'd done what she came to do. But there's more."

"What? Tell me," he said, all ears.

"Oh, it seems so unbelievable to me—but Grant, the locations man, found bugs planted throughout the first floor."

"Bugs?"

"Yes, that's what he called them—bugs. They're listening devices. I think they've been there since the first time I went back to my house."

"You're kidding!"

"No, you remember that I was so surprised that the footprints were all over in the dust in the hall but that the handrail was dust free? It didn't make sense then, but now it does. Grant found bugs under the banister—then more in the parlor, dining room, and kitchen."

"I can't believe it. Then . . ."

She knew what Jim was about to say and cut him off. "Yes, then someone has been eavesdropping since day one. Whoever it is heard everything that was said and done while we've been there."

"I'm trying to take all this in—to remember if we talked about the water—and about Rachel," he said.

"Yes, I think we did. They would have heard all our discussion about selling the house and—about Rachel."

"Hmmm. That suggests some—frightening possibilities."

"Possibilities?"

"Oh, never mind right now. I'd want to investigate at your house before I say more—before I make any accusations."

"There's more. Grant made another discovery," she said.

"What?"

"Well, first tell me about your lawyer friend's findings. Were you right? Does Joe Spencer own all of Silver Forks Mountain—except my place?"

"Yes—and no."

"What does that mean?"

"He owns it—but my lawyer thinks there's something more involved."

"You're being too cryptic for me. I don't understand," she said, frustrated.

"Well, I have to hold off on any accusations till I'm sure. I don't want to—tell tales out of church."

"What?"

"Oh, that's one of Mom's sayings. It means don't repeat anything that you're not sure of—or that shouldn't be said."

"But why can't you tell me? I won't repeat it."

"I—I don't want to make charges till I'm sure. Anyway, rest assured that Joe Spencer's involved somehow."

"Do you think he might have had my house bugged?"

"I wouldn't put it past him if he believed it would help him get what he wants—your property. But we'll need more evidence before we can make charges," he cautioned.

"Grant Pack said that I should report the bugging to the police."

"I agree. We should. I'll call the sheriff's office later on tonight."

"I haven't told you what else Grant found. Under the . . ."

Jim looked to the right and interrupted her. "There's the roadhouse," he said, turning at a freeway off-ramp.

"You didn't let me finish."

"Let's wait until we get inside," he suggested. "I can't take much more on an empty stomach." He pulled up in front of the rather nondescript building. Small windows were hung with neon signs and covered from the inside. A solid wood entry door made it impossible to view the interior. "You said that the food's better than the atmosphere, I believe?"

"Well, wait till you get inside." He climbed out of the truck and came round to open her door. Then they walked hand in hand to the entry.

A dimly but warmly lit interior and a sign that read "Seat Yourself" greeted them. Jim led her to a quiet spot—a highly varnished wooden booth, relieved by green plantings and green vinyl-covered cushions. The low-hanging table lamps were burnished copper. Jim was right, as usual—the overall effect was warm and intimate.

The menus were already on the table by the place settings. "I recommend the New York steak," Jim suggested. "It isn't too big. And the baked potatoes and house salad are great. How about it?"

"If you're sure the steak is small, sounds good—well done, please. No potato for me, but the salad sounds wonderful."

A smiling, redheaded, middle-aged waitress said, "Welcome. I'm Joyce and I'll be your server. Say, you look familiar," she added, looking at Jim appreciatively.

"I've been here a few times," he said.

"Yeah, I don't think I'd forget you," she said with a wink.

Jim smiled but otherwise ignored her remark, ordering their steaks and salads.

Somewhat rebuffed, the waitress asked, "Anything to drink?"

"Just water for me," Lesley answered.

"Me too."

"Okay, but save room for some pie. Want to order dessert now?"

"No, we'd better wait until after the steak," Jim said.

"Okay, then. It'll be about ten minutes. Anything I can get you while you're waiting? An appetizer? We have . . ."

"No thanks," they replied at the same time. Finally, she left for the kitchen.

"You were right about this place—except for the flirting waitress," Lesley said. "I guess I'll have to grow accustomed to fending off your female admirers."

"Aw, shucks, ma'am. What can Ah say?"

"Oh, you don't have to say anything apparently," she said, laughing. "Let's get back to some serious talk."

"No, let's not. Let's enjoy ourselves for a while. We haven't been together for a couple of days. I've missed you."

"I've missed you too."

They sat quietly for a while, holding hands across the table and listening to Ella Fitzgerald and Peggy Lee sing tunes from the jukebox.

"Good music," Lesley said.

"Yes, and you don't have to spend a quarter. The management keeps it playing all the time. The owner loves jazz and blues apparently."

"Another surprise."

The waitress interrupted their reflection, bringing their food, which smelled and looked good. Lesley almost forgot her problems in that delightful little hideaway, just as she'd hoped she would.

CHAPTER 28

After the brief respite from the troubles of the day, Jim and Lesley returned to his truck for the drive back to Park City. She hadn't really looked at the scenery on the way there, and now it was too late to see much more than black silhouettes of mountains against a clear, nighttime sky. But the moon shone on the open spaces covered with snow, creating a beauty unique to winter climes. Despite all of her problems, it had been a pleasant, romantic evening, and she thanked Jim for providing it.

"Ah've told ya before, ma'am, it pleasures me to please ya," he replied, in the style that had become their inside joke—possibly not humorous to someone else but shared, intimate humor for them.

"Well, we still have to decide what to do about the invasions into my house and about your discoveries concerning Silver Forks Mountain water—and the other things you've told me," she said.

"I know the sheriff," he said, and laughed. "Isn't that an old song lyric?"

"If it is, I don't know it," she said, smiling.

"Well, anyway, it's true. I've worked with the county sheriff's office on several animal retrieval jobs. I know Sheriff Hunt and his deputy, Colin Lee."

"Do you spell that C-O-L-O-N?" she asked facetiously.

"No, Co-*lin*—like Colin Powell. You know him, of course."

"I know *of* him."

"I'll call the sheriff's office tonight and see if someone can meet us at your house tomorrow afternoon. Then you can show the officer who comes what was done to your house. You're right, of course. It is an invasion of privacy—it's serious business—installing listening devices without legal cause and without a court order. Whoever's responsible will be in hot water. Oh, you started to tell me about what else you found."

"Yes, I—rather Grant—found some wiring imbedded in a crack under the banister. He said that it looked new."

"You're kidding."

"No, I'm not, but we didn't stop to find out where it led or what it's for. I had to get out of there. In fact, I'm not sure I want to go back," she admitted.

"You won't be alone. I have a job in the morning, but I'll meet you there at about two PM. I'll try to get someone from the sheriff's office there. If I can't arrange it, I'll call you. Otherwise, plan on it. Okay?"

"Okay, but please try to be on time. I really don't want to be up there alone."

"I'd pick you up, but I have another job in Midway, so I'll be coming from the opposite direction. There's a shortcut, a back road," he explained.

"Oh, all right. Just be there at two, please."

"Well, I guess we've done all that we can do for now. The water analysis is done, and I'll call in the morning and make sure the results are reported to the State. My attorney's still looking for those involved in Joe's business activities. And unless there's a hitch, we'll try tomorrow to find out who's been housebreaking and making modifications at your place. Now, do you think you can sleep tonight, knowing all this?"

"I'm tired enough, that's certain." With that she laid her head on his strong shoulder, looked at the moon and stars, and fell asleep.

Jim pulled up before the Silver Princess and stopped, waking her from what seemed a very short ride. "Are we here already?" she asked.

"Yes, you've been sleeping like a baby," he said, smiling at Lesley. He put his arm around her and kissed her.

"That's a pleasant wake up," she said. "Thanks, Jim, for everything. I don't know what I'd have done without you. When I left L.A. for a vacation here, I had no idea what I was really in for."

"I know everything hasn't turned out the way you wanted, but at least you can resolve some of the questions about your house."

"Yes, some of the questions—but I still have the problem of what to do with it. I can't sell it now because of the water problems. I guess I'll just have to close it up."

"Well, there is one other alternative. You could move it— have it moved."

"Can they move a house that large?" she asked, surprised at the suggestion.

"Yes, they can. The roads to and from your place are good enough and wide enough that they could move it. The total square footage is large, of course, but it's on two stories, so it wouldn't be prohibitive to move."

"But where would I move it?"

"You'd have to find a piece of land—maybe closer to Park City?" he suggested. "That would solve your problem about the house being too isolated. Also, you would have city utilities.

One other advantage is that it would be easier for me to keep an eye on it. Whaddaya think?"

"Oh, I don't know. It sounds like such a huge project. I'd have to find out how much it would cost. And what would I do with the vacant property?"

"Oh, you could turn it into a picnic area or a wilderness spot," he suggested. "That's what Robert Redford did with some of his high mountain property. But you don't have to decide tonight. Just think about it, and when we get this other mess behind us, we'll look into the specifics of the idea. Okay?"

"Yes, you've given me something to think about. Thanks again, Jim, for tonight and for everything."

"Do you want me to walk you to your room?" he asked.

"No, just watch me to the door. Then I feel relatively safe inside the hotel. But please be on time tomorrow. Okay?"

"Two o'clock sharp, I promise. Good night."

She threw him a kiss from the hotel doorway, waved, and went inside feeling better than she had earlier in the day but still wary about the goings-on at her house. Who really was responsible for the intrusions there?

Locked in her hotel room, she decided to take a hot bath and then to go right to bed.

After her bath she knelt by her bed, thanking the Lord for watching over her, for leading her to meet Jim and his family, and for guiding her in her decisions. She thanked Him that Jim had returned to the Savior's fold and for the promise that held for their future. She asked for His guidance and help in the investigation planned at her house the next day. She finished, praying for all the Lord's hurting children, and hoping that one in particular—Rachel—would finally be at peace.

She tossed and turned in her bed, thinking of the next day's challenges, but finally fell asleep.

CHAPTER 29

A blustery wind, gusting and howling around the hotel, awakened Lesley on Thursday morning. She looked out to see a very threatening sky and wondered if it was a portent of a bad day ahead.

She wasn't looking forward to going back to her house anyway. Her feelings about the place had changed much, and she began to understand why her parents and forefathers hadn't wanted to remain there for long.

She ordered breakfast from room service, deciding not to venture out before she had to. Maybe the weather would improve by afternoon. She sat down to read scriptures, having somewhat neglected that the previous day, but room service interrupted her before she read more than a few verses.

Barnaby didn't bring the food this time, so she asked the young, nervous, freckle-faced bellhop, "Barnaby's busy? He usually brings my tray up."

"Yes, ma'am. I think he was called away somewhere—earlier. Someone called and told him to change out of his uniform and go someplace. I don't know where. Sorry," he said.

"Oh, no. I wasn't particularly looking for him. It's just that he's been such a regular . . ." She'd almost said, "Regular *snoop*," but thought better of it. She tipped the boy and sat down to enjoy breakfast.

Then she showered, dressed warmly, fixed her hair and makeup, and decided to spend the rest of the morning rehearsing her lines. She became so totally involved in the make-believe world of the blind girl, visualizing her moving about her house, that she completely lost track of time. It was already twelve thirty before she realized it was time to start the trip to Silver Forks Mountain. She'd stop at a drive-thru and pick up some lunch on the way.

Chicken sandwich in hand, she drove to the freeway and started the climb toward Silver Forks. The weather hadn't improved. The skies were still dark and threatening, but it hadn't yet begun to rain or snow. *Guess we could use more snow for the Olympics,* she thought, trying to view the weather optimistically.

The remainder of the drive to Silver Forks Mountain was uneventful, except for the frequent wind gusts, which made it necessary to overcorrect the steering on occasion.

When she came to her gate it was locked, as she'd left it. After opening it, she said a quiet prayer before driving into her lane. Then she drove to the front entry, thinking seriously of waiting in her car until Jim arrived. She did wait for about twenty minutes, then decided to turn off the engine, which was heating up. The wind was blowing fiercely. There was still no snow, but she saw dry lightning flashes at the top of the mountains. It was too cold sitting in the car without the heater, so she finally locked the car and went into her house, locking the front door behind her.

She sat in the cold parlor, watching through the window the trees blown by the wind and the snow starting to fall heavily. The sky grew ominously dark, and she started worrying that Jim might get caught in a bad storm. She wished there were heat and electricity for lighting. She waited for almost half an hour, standing and pacing nervously to keep warm.

Frustrated at the wait and the cold, she decided to return to her car and was walking toward the front door when she heard it—humming from the upstairs attic room. Her first instinct was to run out the front door to the safety of her car. Then she thought, *Don't be foolish. Rachel hasn't harmed me—or anyone for that matter. She may have more to tell me.*

Cautiously, Lesley went to the foot of the stairway, looking up into the semidarkness for several moments. The humming continued—a tune she didn't recognize, and it was much louder and more distinct than in the early occurrences. She crept up the steps, stopping midway. Then she abruptly decided not to continue her climb. She turned and went slowly down the stairway. The humming stopped. Involuntarily she turned around to look up, and Rachel's image—again very clear—suddenly appeared in the mirror. Then the mirror went dark, and the mirror door swung slowly open, as if inviting Lesley to enter.

She saw a faint, moving light at the top of the attic stairs. She was frightened but also drawn toward it, wondering if Rachel's ghost was still present. Without conscious decision she again climbed to the top of the stairs, then stepped inside the attic stairway, and the mirror door slammed shut behind her.

She was disoriented in the darkness and turned to try to push the attic door open. But a big hand covered her mouth as a strong arm bent her elbow painfully behind her. She was forced upward into the attic, to the top of the stairs.

She tried to call out, but her voice was muffled by the smothering hand. Then she was released, but before she could turn round to see her attacker, a hood was slipped over her head, and her hands were roughly yanked behind her and taped together.

For a moment nothing more happened. She listened but could hear only heavy breathing. Her captor moved to stand behind her. She could smell his sweat. She was led a few steps and was pushed forcefully to a sitting position—on a trunk, she thought, from its height and the cold metal against her legs. She couldn't see but could now speak. "Who are you? And what are you doing in my house?" she asked in a shaky voice. For as much as five minutes there was no response while her captor seemed to be moving about, rearranging items in the attic.

But when the reply finally came, it sounded as if someone were whispering hoarsely or trying to disguise his voice. "Who I am isn't important right now, my dear. What is important is that you sign this document agreeing to sell your property—for one hundred thousand dollars—still a good offer, considering all the trouble you've caused us. Sign it," he demanded, thrusting a paper and pen into her hands.

She didn't respond immediately, dropping the paper and pen to the floor, her thoughts racing to identify the unknown voice. Her captor was tall. Was it Joe Spencer? She remembered how he had stood tall when he had threatened her, appearing stronger than she would have thought previously. But that didn't seem likely, since the voice was rather youthful—and because Joe surely wouldn't have had the strength of her attacker.

For a foolish moment she thought of Jim. Why hadn't he come? Where was he? Could he—no he couldn't have planned all this. Did he have some ulterior motive in winning her heart? Ashamed at her thoughts, she dismissed that foolish notion.

Next she thought of Barnaby, remembering that he had left the hotel for some unknown reason and destination. Was he holding her captive? He was tall enough and strong enough.

Could he have something against her, or would he be following orders again? She hadn't treated him unfairly—perhaps a bit firmly—but not so that he would want to hurt her, surely.

Finally she said, "I won't sign anything agreeing to sell my property to you—whoever you are."

"We may have to do something to encourage you," the voice said.

"What do you plan to do? Kill me? If that happens, my property goes to charity—it's in my will," she said, frantically trying to buy time.

"Oh, I don't think we'll need to do that—I don't even think we'll need to hurt you—physically."

"You've already hurt me—physically and emotionally," she yelled. "Take this sack off my head and untie me."

"Oh, can't do that—yet. But I do want you to hear something that may convince you to sign." He paused, breathed deeply, then threatened, "We have your boyfriend, Jim. He isn't really hurt—just a little bump on the head and a little blood—but he's unconscious and tied up in his truck. He could have a nasty accident, of course, like driving over a cliff on a mountain road."

"You've hurt Jim? But where is he? Where's his truck?"

"Well, you see, we overheard your conversation in his truck last night. We knew that you were coming here today at two and that Jim was using a back road."

"How did you hear our conversation . . . ?" She knew the answer as soon as she'd asked the question. "You bugged Jim's truck, too."

"Yes, and his other truck and your SUV," he said. "We've heard all your discussions—about this house, about the water problems, about Rachel, and about your personal life. We even heard your silly prayers. Where's your divine help now?" the voice asked with a sneering laugh.

She didn't give him the satisfaction of a reply; instead, she thought an earnest prayer for the Lord's help, believing that He wouldn't forsake her.

When she said nothing, her assailant continued his persuasion. "Well, your boyfriend can't help you, and we're watching for the arrival of the sheriff or his deputy. We'll find a way to delay him—at least before he comes up Silver Forks Mountain Road."

She still didn't respond but trembled at the realization that he also knew about the arrival of someone from the sheriff's office—and that he had planned for that arrival.

"You know, it all could have been so simple," he said. "You were made a very generous offer for your property. All you had to do was agree to sell it and none of this would have been necessary. But you had to be so stubborn—and so self-righteous—so superior. Guess that's to be expected, though—it's in your *genes!*" he said bitterly.

"What do you know about my genes?"

"Oh, you may be shocked to know that we go way back—your family and mine . . . or what was left of mine," he said angrily. She felt him standing menacingly over her and was actually afraid that he would hit her.

She tried to stall by placating his growing anger. "I really don't know what you mean. You suggest that our families had some past connection. Well, I hardly knew any of my forefathers; so why are you angry with *me?*"

"Well, I know you've been researching your family's history since you came back here . . ."

Just then, before he could reveal more, there was a muffled noise from downstairs. He commanded, "Stay right where you are and don't make a sound." She heard him run to the top of the stairs and hurry down. The attic door opened, and he was gone for the moment.

She wasn't about to follow his directions. She managed to stand and made her way to the stairs, hoping that the door at the bottom had been left open. With her hands still taped behind her, it was very difficult to descend without falling, but she moved slowly and deliberately and almost reached the bottom when she felt air rush toward her and heard the door slam, followed by the sound of a lock being turned.

"You don't do anything you're told, do you?" her captor said. He forced her to turn about and shoved her up the stairs, causing her to fall to her knees, scraping and bruising them. "Stand up and get back up those stairs," he said, forcing her by pushing his body against hers. He led her to the trunk. "Now, sit down and shut up, or I'll have to gag you," he threatened.

She wondered about the noise that had made him run downstairs. Was it the sheriff? Had Jim escaped from his truck? She thought of asking but knew he wouldn't explain.

Instead, he returned to his revelations about their family background. "Now, you're going to hear me out. You couldn't leave well enough alone. You had to snoop and learn about Rachel. You think you know about her *supposed* attacker. Well, that was all a bunch of lies, made up by Lewis Kern—by your great-grandfather—to give him an excuse to get rid of *my* great-grandfather. You see, my dear, your reputable and notable great-grandfather stole my great-grandfather's mining claim— *stole* it and then pretended he'd made the discovery. Everything that your family has enjoyed over the past century and more has rightfully belonged to us—to my family. Your property, your house, your money, your position—all were stolen from us. And your great-grandfather accused mine of attacking Rachel and then had him done away with."

"I don't believe it. From all accounts my great-grandfather was a good man," she said defensively.

"Not from *all* accounts. Oh, he built a great reputation as one of the Silver Kings. Money can buy anything, they say. But his beginnings weren't based on his own hard work and luck—he *stole* my great-grandfather's claim. The truth of that has been kept alive in my family ever since it happened. My great-grandmother had to flee to California—for her reputation and to try to find work to support her children. She told the story to them, and when they had families of their own, they retold the story too. My father told me the bitter tale of what had happened, of what your great-grandfather did to us, and how every generation of our family has lived in poverty since then—until I took action. I did something about it, and now I'm taking our property back—after all these years. I'm taking back what was rightfully ours—this whole mountainside."

"But why didn't someone—someone in your family—come forward a long time ago? Why is this just coming out now?" she asked, frantic to comprehend.

"Of course you wouldn't understand. You're the spoiled daughter of a spoiled father, whose father also spoiled him. You have no idea what grinding poverty can do to human dignity—to the human soul. We were beaten down and couldn't raise ourselves up—until I came along and fought to accumulate enough money to come back here and take back what is rightfully ours. Now I'll show *you* what *my* money and influence can do."

"You sound almost deranged. Even if all you say about my great-grandfather were true, how can you hold me responsible for that? And it seems very likely that Rachel was attacked. Was she to blame—am I to blame—for that?"

She could hear and sense him circling her where she sat. His venom growing as he spoke, he said, "No, but there was no proof that my great-grandfather attacked her. The great Lewis Kern just found it more than convenient to blame him—he found a way to get rid of him . . . a way that no one of that time would have questioned. The rule of the West was an eye for an eye, you know. Well, I'm applying that same rule now. I want your property, but unlike your ancestor, I was actually willing to pay for it. If that sounds deranged, so be it."

She tried another approach. "But you'd never get away with hurting Jim. In fact, you'll never get away with what you've done to me today. You'll never get away with what you've done to my house. Housebreaking and bugging are illegal, you know," she said weakly. Then she waited, but there was no response, so she tried still another tactic. "Just let me go—let Jim go—and we'll forget all of this ever happened. And you can have my property. I don't want it anymore, anyway. Somehow everything associated with it seems—dirty now."

"Oh, you're right—your great-grandfather's scheming was dirty—he played dirty in every way. He was a thief and a liar—and very likely—a murderer!"

He was becoming more agitated with every remark she made. She decided to sit quietly and try to think what to do. She prayed again that someone would find her—would find Jim.

Then in answer to her prayer, there was a loud banging downstairs and outside, followed by the sound of breaking glass and breaking wood.

"Sit right there and be very quiet. I have a gun," the voice warned, "and I'm not afraid to use it. There's too much at stake." He silently and stealthily moved down the attic stairway. She could barely hear his footsteps on the stairs, but she could hear his heavy breathing and pictured him waiting behind the closed mirror door.

She heard a scratching and wrenching from below, as if someone was trying to pry open the mirror door. Almost involuntarily she took a mighty chance. She yelled, "Help! I'm up here. He has a gun!"

There was a crashing sound from below, and Lesley sensed that someone had broken through the mirror door.

Then she heard a gunshot—and then a second one. Then someone hit the floor with a thudding finality. Was it Jim? Had he been shot? She panicked that he might be seriously hurt or even fatally wounded.

Then she heard Jim's yell. "Lesley, are you all right?"

She felt as if the breath had been knocked out of her, and she couldn't speak.

"Lesley, answer me. Are you okay?" There was another crashing sound from below, and she heard footsteps running up the attic stairs.

She said quietly, "I'm here, Jim. I thought you were hurt or even dead. Thank heaven you're okay." She began sobbing uncontrollably.

He yelled downstairs, "Colin, she's okay. Go ahead and take care of the mess down there." Jim came to her, removed the covering from her head and eyes, and bent to kiss her on the face. "Everything will be all right now. It's over." He moved behind her to gently remove the tape from her wrists.

She looked up at him then as he passed by her. "You have a terrible gash on the back of your head," she said, whimpering.

"I know, but I'll be okay. Did he hurt you?"

"I'm okay physically, but he hurt my spirit—in a real way. I thought he'd kill you or me or both of us if I didn't do as he said."

"I'm so sorry I didn't get here to protect you," he apologized, kneeling before her and taking her hands in his. "I drove up the back road—the road that's beyond those evergreen trees by the back of your house."

"I didn't know there was another road up here."

"Yes, I told you last night that I'd take a shortcut. I don't know how they knew, but somehow they were in wait for me there—out of sight of your house or the main road."

"I know how they knew. Your trucks were bugged—so was my Navigator."

He seemed to be repressing his anger. "That explains it." He paused for a moment, taking it all in. "They were waiting for me, as I said, and flagged me down. I stopped and got out to see what they wanted, and Barnaby crossed behind me and hit me on the back of my head with a tire iron."

"Barnaby! I thought it might be him, but he couldn't have the money and background that he talked about."

"Then you don't know?" He paused and took a deep breath. "I thought you knew who your attacker was, but obviously you haven't figured it out yet." He paused, suggesting that it was difficult for him to continue. Then he slowly revealed, "Barnaby—and Gareth Sanders—were waiting for me. After Barnaby hit me, they must have tied me up and put me on the floor of my truck."

He paused and caught his breath. "Luckily for me, the deputy, Colin Lee, decided to use the back road too so that the Silver Forks people wouldn't see him going up the main road. Colin saw my truck and stopped to see why I'd left it there, and Barnaby took off running as soon as he saw the deputy sheriff. Colin found me in the truck, untied me, and we both ran through the snow to your house. Seems we got here just in time. Gareth must have gone crazy!"

"Gareth!" Lesley was so shocked by Jim's revelation that she couldn't even think. She cried a little, realizing that Gareth, who had pretended interest in her, was only interested in revenge and in getting her property. She also realized that, ironically, he was a better actor than she was.

Jim waited patiently for her response, sitting beside her on the old trunk and holding her hands comfortingly.

Finally Lesley said, "Gareth was a Dr. Jekyll and Mr. Hyde. He's been so cool—so controlled. I didn't even recognize his voice. He seemed like a different person today. He sounded almost insane. He was totally obsessed with getting my property. He told me that my great-grandfather's silver mine rightfully belonged to his great-grandfather—that my great-grandfather stole the claim. He also said that Lewis Kern had unjustly blamed his great-grandfather for attacking Rachel and then had gotten rid of Gareth's great-grandfather somehow. He implied that my great-grandfather had killed his—to hide the real ownership of the mine. Apparently Gareth has been planning most of his life to come here and get back what he believed was rightfully his inheritance."

"Did he threaten you?"

"Yes—he threatened to hurt—or *kill* you," she said, and began crying again, "if I didn't agree to sell him my property— at a reduced price. I told him to take it—I didn't want this house or this property—and to leave us alone. But he was becoming more and more upset, and I don't know what he'd have done if you hadn't come." She began crying again, this time with a sense of relief at knowing all of this was almost over.

Colin called from downstairs. "I've contacted my office. They're sending an ambulance, but there's really no need. It's too late—Sanders is dead. They'll send some backup so that we can find that kid who hit you, Jim," he said, coming to the top of the stairway, dressed in his uniform. Colin saw Lesley, then asked, "You're okay, Miss Kern?"

"I—I'm okay, except for the fact that I'll never get over what happened today. Gareth Sanders seemed like such a steady person. I can't believe that he's been planning to get back at me—at my family—for so long. I can't believe that he's dead." She paused for a minute.

"You know, I just realized something," Lesley continued. "The first time I met Gareth on the plane, I knew I'd seen him before. He must have been on the set in downtown L.A. when I was making that movie—that's the only way I could have seen him. Then he must have arranged our meeting on the plane. He was actually stalking me, waiting for his chance to meet me and then gradually to persuade me that he had my best interests at heart. And I'm sure now that he's the one who followed me from the airport to Salt Lake City and then to Park City in that black Lincoln. So I wasn't being paranoid after all."

"Yes, you're right, Lesley. Jim's attorney found out that Gareth Sanders literally owned Joe Spencer. Sanders had blackmailed Joe for years about some of Joe's really shady business deals. Then apparently Sanders made a killing—sorry, that wasn't a very good choice of words—he made a *fortune* in real estate in Southern California and came here and bought Joe out at a fraction of what Joe's property was worth. Sanders owned the Silver Fork, the Silver Princess Hotel, the general store, and all of this land up here—except yours, Lesley. The only thing Joe had left was the bank and the health spa—oh, and Gareth's promise to him of a share in the profits from the condominium development up here on Silver Forks Mountain. Your discovery of the poisoned water put all Joe's hopes in jeopardy. He had to get you to sell your property too for that reason. Otherwise Sanders would have cut him out completely."

"Jim, why didn't you tell me what you'd learned?"

"Well, I wish I had now, but I'd said some pretty nasty things about Gareth before, and I'd resented him for so long because of his association with Jenny's death that I didn't want to accuse him until I had proof. I didn't want you to think that my change—my repentance—was so short-lived," Jim explained. "It was stupid not to tell you. I'm sorry."

She took his handsome face in her hands and kissed him. "No, it wasn't stupid. You were trying to do right by him, by me—and everybody. You always have, and I know you always will."

"Aw shucks, ma'am, ya make a feller blush."

"Well, looks like I better leave you two alone," Colin said, laughing nervously. "Jim, there'll be an investigation into the shooting. I may need you to attest that I fired in self-defense. For now, I'll go down and wait for the ambulance and the other officers."

Lesley looked up at the deputy's warm, brown eyes, wrinkled at the corners. He had come just in time. He had saved both her and Jim.

"I owe ya, Colin, for coming along when you did—and for saving Lesley," Jim said. "I'm so glad that you had your gun. Otherwise, you might be taking one or both of us back in that ambulance. Oh, and I'll be glad to testify if you need me."

"All in a day's work, I guess," Colin said, trying to make light of a very harrowing experience, even for a deputy sheriff. "Will you two be able to get back to Park City okay?"

"I'm not sure I can drive," Lesley said. "I'll leave my car here and ride back with Jim if you're okay to drive."

"Yeah, my head bled a lot, but I don't think it needs stitches," Jim said. "We'll go home and scare Mom to death. She's a great nurse, though. She'll fix me up."

"Going to your home sounds like the best of all possible destinations right now. I think I need some mothering too," she said.

They waited in the attic until the medics arrived and carried Gareth's body out to the ambulance. Jim said, "Hey, there's the missing photo album—on that little desk."

Lesley walked stiffly over to the desk and picked up the album. It fell open to the photograph that had included Rachel—but her likeness had been cut from the picture. "Someone's cut Rachel from the photograph," she said, showing the page to Jim.

"Hmmm. You don't suppose that they were using her picture to make us think she was still visiting your house, bringing the message that you should sell it?" He turned back to something he'd been examining while she was looking at the album. "Look over there at the top of the stairs—it's some kind of rear projector." He went closer to take a look. "I'll bet that they were projecting Rachel's image onto that mirror door. And here's a tape player with a speaker. If we were to run the tape, I'm pretty sure we'd hear humming—and an imitation of Rachel's voice telling you to sell your house."

"But where would they get the electricity to run the projector and the tape player?" she asked.

"That explains the wiring under the handrail. There's probably a generator under the stairs somewhere or hidden where I didn't see it down in the basement. Anyway, it's not important now, is it? The criminal that we could have used the evidence against has already met his—end."

They left the projector and the tape player behind as evidence to be found by the sheriff's department. Then they slowly helped each other downstairs, locked the front door, and went out the back door, trudging through the snow to Jim's truck. Fortunately the wind had died down.

There was no blood on the truck floor. If there had been, Lesley didn't think she could have ridden in it. The blessed heater started to work after only a few miles, making her realize just how cold she'd been held as a prisoner in that attic.

They raced down the mountain and out of Silver Forks, and at that point, Lesley didn't care if she ever saw the house on Silver Forks Mountain again. They went directly to Jim's place, and Carol was as upset as Jim had expected when she saw his wound and heard what had happened—to both of them. Julie hadn't come home from school yet, so she was spared the gruesome details of their experience and seeing Jim's injury. Carol gently tended to Jim's wound.

Then sitting back with cups of Carol's comforting hot chocolate, they were silent, trying to make sense of what they'd been through. Lesley didn't want to go back to the Silver Princess that night, knowing they'd have heard news of Gareth's death and, possibly, of Barnaby's involvement. Carol offered to let her stay in her room that night, and she would sleep with Julie. Carol didn't have to beg her. Lesley didn't want to be anywhere else.

CHAPTER 30

After a great night's sleep and a delicious breakfast prepared by Carol, Jim drove Lesley back to the Silver Princess and went with her to her room. She had decided that she couldn't stay there under the circumstances. She was proved right in this decision by the stone-faced stares of the front desk staff when they entered the lobby. The employees appeared to have heard of Gareth's death and seemed to be in shock.

They took the stairs to the second floor and hurried to her room, closing and locking the door behind them. "I'm going to call around to see if I can get a room somewhere else, until after the Olympics," Lesley said.

"Well, we've told you you're welcome at our house."

"I know, and I'm grateful, but I can't do that to you—to your family. If it were only for a day or so, it might be all right. I appreciate the thought."

"Okay, but if you change your mind, say so. I'm going to sit down over here while you call," he said, kicking back on the chaise.

"Does your head hurt?" she asked.

"No, not much. Anyway, I've had worse," he said stoically.

"Well, I'll look in the yellow pages for another hotel," she said, sitting on the bed and taking the phone book from the bedside table drawer.

Luckily she was able to book a room at the Holiday Inn—
no old-fashioned atmosphere, but somehow that didn't matter
anymore. "I'm in luck," she said. "The Holiday Inn had a
cancellation for a long-term stay just before I called." Now, all
she had to do was inform the front desk that she'd be leaving,
then pack, and check out.

"Can you get into the room at the Holiday Inn this early in
the morning?" he asked.

"No, I can't check in until after three PM" She thought for a
moment. "You know what I'd really like to do?"

"No, what?"

"I'd like to go back to the Family History Center and read
more in my great-grandmother's diary." She sat beside him on
the chaise.

"Are you sure? Maybe you ought to take a breather for a
while—distance yourself a little from the whole experience," he
said with real concern.

"Oh, I'll leave all the criminal investigation stuff to the
sheriff's office, and to whomever else they have to call in, but I
have a couple of things I have to find out for myself. I won't
rest till I do."

"What things?"

"Well, I have to see if there's any further reference in my
great-grandmother's diary to the stranger whom Lewis Kern
supposedly took in. I want to know if there's anything there
that would establish the truth of Gareth's charges."

"But why? What possible difference can it make now? Aren't
you just asking for more hurt?" he asked with a worried look.

"Maybe—and maybe I won't find anything in the diary. If I
don't, I promise I'll let it go. I can't do anything about what
may have happened, anyway. But there is something else that I
have to know."

"Yes, what?"

"I want to see if the diary makes any reference to Rachel's having been baptized before she died. If it doesn't, I want to make arrangements to have it done in the temple. Rachel's plea regarding water may have related only to directing us to find out why she died. Or it may be that she also came to ask for her baptism, her saving ordinance, to be done—baptism by water. Do you see what I'm thinking?"

"Then you still believe that Rachel really appeared?"

"Yes. Her appearance to Julie and me was quite different from the projected image on the back of that two-way mirror they'd installed. And her humming was different. She hummed an old Primary hymn—something that Gareth Sanders would never have known. Do you see why I still believe Rachel came?"

"Yes, yes—I do. And I'm sure you're right. That accounts for her repeated emphasis of that word *water*. Let's do it. Let's go to the Family History Center today," he said, and stood at the ready to go.

"Hold on. I still have to pack my things and check out," she said.

"Okay, let's do it. You call the front desk, and I'll start packing." He found her luggage and opened it on the bed.

She sat on the other side and dialed the front desk. "This is Lesley Kern. I've had a change of plans. I'm checking out today."

"Is there a problem with the room?" the desk clerk asked.

"No, there's nothing wrong with the room or with the hotel. Oh, I think you'll understand—I just can't stay here . . . after all that's happened."

"I do—understand," he said. "Our condolences upon the loss of your friend Mr. Sanders."

Obviously the hotel staff didn't know the whole story, so Lesley simply said, "Thank you," and hung up. She shrugged her shoulders to shake off bad memories.

They packed hurriedly, without worrying about organization or wrinkled clothes. Then Lesley double-checked to make certain she hadn't forgotten anything. Without calling for assistance, they hefted her luggage to the lobby and out to Jim's waiting truck. She went back to clear her bill at the desk, dropped off her keys, and left the Silver Princess with only one regret—that the promise of a joyful stay there had been marred by the knowledge that its owner—former owner—had intended her great harm.

CHAPTER 31

Jim sat beside her at a table in the Family History Center while she read her great-grandmother's diary. There was nothing more written about the stranger who had attacked Rachel, nor was there further mention of Rachel. Lesley was sure Rachel hadn't been forgotten, at least by her great-grandmother, but Lesley's great-grandmother had acquiesced to her husband's wishes and blotted out further reference to Rachel's existence.

"Well, I haven't found anything to substantiate Gareth's charges regarding my great-grandfather's harming his great-grandfather in stealing his claim or doing away with him."

"Can you let it go, like you said you would?" Jim urged gently.

"Yes—it all happened so long ago. And I can't do anything about it now. I'll leave it to heaven, I guess. But I do know that Rachel came to help me—and now I'm going to help her. I'm going to get her baptism done. I'll have to prepare the paperwork first, of course."

"Let's do it right here—on the computer," he said.

"Of course. Thanks, Jim."

They accessed her family's records and prepared and printed the information the temple would require for Rachel's baptism to take place. They returned the diary to the red special collections desk and thanked the missionaries who had helped them.

Then they stepped out into the crisp wintry air, feeling a tremendous sense of accomplishment, a sense of completion, and a sense of freedom. Lesley thanked the Lord in her heart for His protective care and for the promise of a future with the man she'd grown to love. Jim seemed to sense her optimistic thoughts, smiled that magnificent smile, and hugged her tightly.

The Olympics were ahead, and since Jim was a volunteer for the opening ceremony and the events hosted at Park City, Lesley would be attending with her newfound family—the Shepherds. And she had one more acting job—her role in *Touched by an Angel.* Then she would leave her house for the last time. She didn't know what she'd do about it in the future, but she did know that she'd never live in the house on Silver Forks Mountain.

EPILOGUE

Snow flurries were falling, but Lesley was bundled up against the cold in the Olympic Stadium, huddled with Julie and Carol and waiting for the opening ceremony to begin. Jim had just completed his duties as a volunteer greeter and was able to join them, sitting next to Lesley. He'd brought sacks of popcorn and drinks for each of them, passing them down the row. "Whoops, that one's not yours, Julie. It's Lesley's," he said. Julie winked at him and traded sacks with Lesley.

"But what's the difference?" Lesley asked, surprised.

Jim stumbled with his explanation. "Oh, I—uh—just thought you'd like that one better." He looked bewildered, then said, "Julie asked for extra butter on hers."

"Oh, okay," Lesley said, and Julie and Carol laughed, as if sharing some private joke.

Lesley shared her lap blanket with Jim, and they sat in great anticipation of this once-in-a-lifetime experience. Then she found a wad of paper napkin in her popcorn. "What is this?" she asked with distaste. "Somebody's left something in my popcorn sack. Ugh!"

Julie and Carol laughed, and Jim looked sheepish and nervous, but no one offered an explanation. Then Julie said, while laughing, "Look inside. Maybe it's someone's gum."

"Ugh, I hope not," Lesley responded, handing her popcorn sack to Jim and gingerly opening the napkin on her lap. "What in the world! What is this?" She held up a beautiful, sparkling, emerald-cut diamond ring and was literally dumfounded.

"Say, maybe this popcorn's like Cracker Jack—a prize in every bag," Jim said, smiling and looking at Lesley with anticipation.

"I don't have one in mine," Julie said, and Carol added, "Neither do I." They were all focused on Lesley.

"Jim, what is this?" Lesley asked.

"Honey, I know this is kind of a public way to ask you, but I had to do it this way." Then his words came tumbling out. "It's an engagement ring. Will you accept it? I know it's kind of early. We haven't known each other very long, but I couldn't wait. Well, how about it?" Jim asked, holding his breath.

Lesley looked up into those blue eyes that she'd fallen in love with the first time she saw him, and said, "Yes, yes. You've made me happier than I've ever been. I do love you." She leaned over to kiss him, and they realized that everyone seated around them was watching, and applause and cheers broke out just as the Olympic torch run climaxed at ground zero and the Olympic torch was lit. Fifty-two thousand people stood in awe, and Lesley felt almost as if the celebration were for her, too.

When the Tabernacle Choir began to sing John Williams's *Call of the Champions,* Lesley thought her heart would burst with happiness and pride. She reached out for Julie's hand, exchanged smiles with Carol, and stood at joyful attention on the happiest night of her life.

ABOUT THE AUTHOR

C. PAUL ANDERSEN received his Ph.D in theater production and dramatic literature from Brigham Young University. He taught in several Utah high schools, at BYU-Hawaii, and at Dixie State College, where he was Director of Theater and Dean of Fine and Performing Arts.

He founded Pioneer Courthouse Players Repertory Theatre Company and produced, directed, and wrote plays for the company for seventeen years. He also directed the Old Barn Theatre in Kanab, Utah, and consulted with other southern Utah communities in founding their summer theater programs. He also served the community as a member of the board of directors of the Dixie Center.

Upon his retirement from Dixie State College, C. Paul Andersen received a citation from Governor Michael Leavitt for his lifelong contributions to theater and the arts in Utah. Now he spends his days writing fiction and has three novels in the works. He and his wife, Kathleen, have four children and twelve grandchildren. They live in Roy, Utah, surrounded by their family and serving in various Church callings.